The Box

The Smoke & Fire Series

Book #3

By:

Keta Kendric

The Box: The Smoke & Fire Series

Second Edition

Cover art by Mayhem Cover Creations
Editor: A.L. Barron

ISBN: 978-1-956650-11-2

Table of Contents

Summary of the Smoke & Fire Series

The Smoke & Fire Series is a slow build into a paranormal world of lovable heroes and diabolical villains. The series' heroes and heroines are tragically flawed and some will straddle the line between good and evil. The characters are forced to learn themselves while discovering undeniable romances. They will embrace abilities that can help them navigate a developing supernatural world as they fight to survive forces intent on unleashing pure unnatural havoc on the *real* world.

Series Glossary

Some of the terms below will be mentioned in books throughout this series.

TOP (Top Secret Operations Program) - An above top-secret organization that recruits individuals on the supernatural spectrum to catch, capture, or kill supernatural criminals.

The Breeze – The Breeze is the birthplace of life. The Breeze is also known as The Passage and biggest gateway that leads to The Vault, the second dimension it birthed, and The Hollow, the third dimension it birthed.

The Vault – A place created or borne from the Breeze. Individuals from the Vault are called Mist Makers or Smokies, and no longer possess a physical body. Their energy signature registers as *life* because the essence of their soul is still intact. They can travel through certain gates and energy fields that other individuals cannot.

The Hollow – A place created or borne from the Breeze. Individuals from the Hollow are called Blazers and no longer possess a physical body. Their energy signature registers as *death* because a part of their soul has been sucked into The Hollow. The Hollow is said to be the gateway to hell.

Huntress – Supernatural female whose sole purpose is to hunt and kill vampires. A huntress' need to kill vampires is said to be three times stronger than a vampire's thirst for blood.

Hyphenated – Supernatural being with multiple abilities.

Toddler – Any supernatural being that is unknowledgeable or untrained in ways of the supernatural. Many believe that they are human.

Hindered – An underdeveloped supernatural being who, for reasons unknown, is delayed from reaching their supernatural maturity.

Vampires, Were animals, Shifters, Witches – All supernatural beings that are assumed myths by *normal* society but have escaped either the Vault or the Hollow and have made the Breeze their home.

Dedication

To the readers who remembered this series from my first self-publishing efforts back in 2014. Thank you for reaching out about The Smoke & Fire Series. I appreciate you keeping an interest in these stories as I'm having a great time revisiting the characters.

Synopsis:

When Agent Kris "Yala" Lawrence steps into the Medical Examiner's office, the last thing she expects to see is a human torso, encased in a glass box, that the Medical Examiner claims is alive. *Come Again?!*

Agent Kevin "K" Nazari requests to be partnered with Yala after a chance meeting leaves him yearning to see her again. They manage to find romance in the midst of tracking a psycho. Kevin learns the true meaning of The Box while helping to hunt a killer hell-bent on sending them victims—cut into pieces. Keeping a person alive when they are arriving in parts is as impossible as it sounds.

Note: This book is a Re-Release from the version originally published in 2014.

Warning: This book contains violence, explicit language, sexual content, and is intended for adults. If you don't enjoy paranormal, supernatural, or urban fantasy books, this may not be the book for you.

CHAPTER ONE

Yala

The January winds didn't offer Agent Kris 'Yala' Lawrence a good morning. Instead, they whispered with freezing nips at her ear, hinting at how the rest of her day would turn out. Cold. Wet. Frigid.

She stepped into the District of Columbia medical examiner's office, hoping to ward off the biting air, but the first few steps inside of this place presented a more gripping depth to the chill than outside. The ME's office sat, silently hidden, behind the larger, more bustling structure of D.C. General Hospital like it wanted to be kept a secret from the rest of the world.

A wrinkle lined her forehead when her new assignment crossed her mind. The preliminary notes she received on the case suggested she may be investigating the aftermath of a death which was not her usual type of case. Her normal assignments required her skills in combat or hunting down and taking out targets. Yala prided herself on being a shooter, not an investigator or puzzle solver.

However, the secret agency she worked for, Top, was apparently shaking things up by assigning agents cases that broadened their scope of knowledge and training. She'd passively heard other agents mention the changes recently. Since she wasn't affected until now, she hadn't considered how the changes might impact her career.

Goosebumps pricked her skin, making her rub up and down the rough jacket material covering her left arm. The air hummed with the silent cries of the dead the farther she stepped into the building. She shivered to shake off the piercing touch. It was like passing through a downpour of icy rain without the wetness.

Death was here, a voyeur within this space, peeking as she strolled down the dimly lit hall. It hovered above and below, silent and clinging from every corner. She followed the hall until she read the faded gold letters on the nameplate outside Dr. Hughes's office. Leaning in through his open door, she glimpsed inside and locked eyes with him standing behind his desk.

His disconcerted expression, searching eyes, and tight stance intensified the edgy feeling she couldn't shake. She stepped through the door cautiously before reaching out a hand across the desk to greet the doctor.

"Dr. Hughes, nice to meet you. Agent Kris Lawrence, but you may call me Yala."

The name was one of a few aliases she used, but he didn't need to know that. Unease sat restlessly in the doctor's eyes as he accepted her handshake. His hand swallowed her dainty one. She was sure her tight grip did nothing to change the doctor's perception of her. He was likely questioning if she was equipped to handle whatever situation he was about to introduce.

She had prejudged the doctor too, by entertaining the notion that the medical examiner would look creepy. Maybe even feel creepy. However, Dr. Hughes' stylishly decorated office and the fashionable button-up and jeans he wore shattered her presumptions.

Wisdom peeked through the unease she spotted and shone within the depths of his blue eyes. His tall, lean frame appeared well-kept and didn't reveal his age, which she knew was fifty-nine. His face and head of salt and pepper hair shone with glowing strength. His glasses sat atop his head like sunglasses and based on the lines of tension in his face and pinched smile, he was fighting to hide his stress.

"Agent Lawrence." He paused. "I mean Yala. Wasn't there supposed to be two agents?"

"There will be. The agency is short-staffed. Our recruiting quota is hard to maintain due to the nature of our work. My partner should be joining me within the week."

He nodded. "I asked for the agency's help on this case because it presents an air of hard-to-explain qualities. I didn't want to involve the local authorities until we can solve the complex situation surrounding what I've seen so far."

He gestured toward the door. "Follow me. It's best you see this for yourself before I attempt to force-feed you an explanation."

Yala followed the doctor hesitantly, although his statement made her curiosity spike. His tensely set shoulders and quick stride made her forehead tighten before she took off after him.

Dr. Hughes had undoubtedly seen more death and murder than her. He possessed many years of experience in hospital emergency and urgent care rooms before becoming a medical examiner. Death was his livelihood and as crucial to the doctor as guns were to her.

Is he nervous, or am I reading him wrong?

He was the one who had a knack for finding solutions to puzzling problems that couldn't otherwise be explained. Blood drenched crime scenes, bodies shredded like confetti, and whole rooms and buildings of items that defied gravity. His expertise in the emerging world of paranormal phenomena and supernatural individuals had caught the attention of TOP, making him one of the few doctors who knew about the top-secret government organization.

TOP pursued cases that delved beyond the delicate fabric that shielded normal society. Things that went bump in the night were starting to make more noise, and TOP was dedicated to fighting the worst of what was not supposed to exist.

Practitioner's like Dr. Hughes were open-minded about the transitioning world. He attempted to explain and interpret what others perceived as impossible. In other words, he explained bizarre murders and crime scenes that defied logic using science. When scientific explanations couldn't be reached, he figured out how the person or their powers worked so that agents could combat it. His scientific theories were especially useful when social media and television networks got involved.

However, instead of TOP calling Dr. Hughes on this specific case, the doctor called them this time. Upon entering his examination room, Yala expected to gasp or at least have her lips fall apart. Nothing caught her immediate attention.

The exam room introduced itself like a person who itched to tell their many untold stories. The stench of death, laced with cleaning products, jumped out first, traveled up Yala's nose, and rested at the back of her throat. The room was relatively empty, except for a large stainless steel table in the center that stood higher than her waist.

A large metal pole emerged from the floor and supported the table. Raised edges made up the circumference of the table with a hose at the head and a drain at the foot area. Straight ahead, a wall was dedicated to eight freezers, built to preserve and store the dead. Were there bodies in the freezers?

The remaining walls contained bookshelves and cabinets painted a dull white with a dingy finish. There were two tall-legged stools in case they needed to sit, and a smaller metal table displaying the doctor's tools and medical instruments.

Yala's gaze jetted around the room, searching for something gruesome. A badly mangled body or a horrific scene guaranteed to stick in her mind long after she moved on to the next horror. However, a glass box was all that sat atop the doctor's table. Inside was a human torso laid flat on its back.

The box reminded her of one that a magician claimed he could make things disappear from. She glanced in the doctor's direction for an explanation.

When he turned and locked them inside his exam room, Yala's chill returned and shimmied a two-step up her spine. She inched closer to the table, her inspection confirming a shirtless torso on display inside the box.

Although she wore a thick and long jacket, she swiped her hands up and down her arms attempting to chase away the sudden drop in temperature.

"Male, approximately twenty-four to thirty years old," Dr. Hughes said. She didn't miss the apprehension in his tone. "Agent, before I continue, I want you to look closely and tell me what you see."

She ambled around the table, eyes peeled and brain working hard to process what she saw. The torso was cut so the arms remained attached, but the head and lower body were missing. She spun in place, searching for the rest of the body. Maybe the upper and lower parts were in one of the freezers.

The musculature, hair, and chest confirmed the doctor's account that the victim was a male. The area where the head and lower extremities should have been, were now cleanly separated. There was no blood in sight, not a single drop.

The bottom of the box was wooden, like a hardwood floor, but the rest was glass. A small latch on the top of the box would open it.

Yala tapped on the ominous container, confirming it was glass, not plastic. The torso's neck and stomach areas were severed and oddly frozen in place, held there by something she couldn't see. The innards were as they should have been displayed if the body was whole. However, the veins, intestines, and other parts she couldn't name had been severed cleanly, making this display look more like artwork than an actual human torso.

Hues of red, black, and dark brown from the organs surrounded the spine. The backbone was revered as the pillar of strength for the body, but in this setting, it resembled a ghost peeking from the shadows.

Yala craned her neck and squinted. Maybe more focus would help her find answers. The peachy color of the skin should have been ghost-white which was what she expected on a dead body.

She shot a quick glance back at the doctor but didn't speak. He returned her stare and matched her silence. She refocused on what was before her, tilting her head. A side view showed the severed neck resting inches short of the glass encasement. The mystery of what kept the victim's insides from pouring out was something for the doctor to explain.

She scrutinized the display with her face pressed close enough to leave a fine sheen of mist on the glass. Sharp and jittery movements within the torso became noticeable. Had a modern-day Dr. Frankenstein created his masterpiece? She hoped Dr. Hughes would be able to explain what she was seeing.

"What do you see?" Dr. Hughes asked, his gaze volleying back and forth between her and the box.

Yala tucked a lock of her red hair that slipped from her ponytail behind her ear before inhaling a steadying breath.

"I'm not sure. Science says guts and blood should be spilled inside this box, yet this part is intact."

She glanced back, eyes squinted. Dr. Hughes was intentionally holding back.

"Where is the rest of the body? Is it being stored in the freezer?"

"This is it," he said, pointing at the torso.

Yala's brows tightened.

"It looks like," she paused, swallowing. "It looks like there's life in there. Were you able to determine a cause of death? What am I looking at, Doc?"

Dr. Hughes cupped his chin and eyed her for a silent moment.

"I called TOP because I can't explain this yet. This section of the body is intact and alive. There is life inside that torso."

She released a chuckle that didn't match her blank expression.

"Come again?"

She understood they worked unusual cases, but...*what?* Had zombies been added to the mix now? On second thought, she couldn't even call this a zombie because the doctor said it was *alive*.

Dr. Hughes used his fingers to accentuate his words. "I ran tests, took x-rays as best I could and observed and listened with multiple instruments. Not only did I found a heartbeat, but this torso is fully functional. There are no visible signs of decomposition, and if it weren't for the note attached to the box, I'd have mistakenly opened it."

She glared at the doctor, her body stiff with apprehension.

"Doc, you're telling me this torso is living without a head and lower extremities?"

She paused for effect, her head bouncing between the *living* torso and the doctor who may be losing it.

"Dr. Hughes, you are held in high regard among our community. I mean no disrespect, but have you been drinking the wrong kind of Kool-Aid?"

His lips twitched, fighting to keep from laughing at her question before his expression morphed back to a more serious one. Her brows pinched before she leaned closer and eyeballed the sight harder. She noticed what the doctor attempted to explain, but she didn't want to accept it.

She unbuttoned and peeled off her long jacket, revealing the leather jumpsuit she usually wore on her more active assignments. She supposed she should have dressed more conservatively, but she was here now.

Doctor Hughes wasn't quick enough to keep his eyes from widening in their sockets.

"This is what I usually wear on assignments. It's bulletproof, among a few other things. It looks like I may need to retire it for this case."

He nodded and swallowed hard. However, her outfit quickly took a back seat to what was on that table. The doctor dragged his fingers through his short salt-and-pepper beard.

"After I took x-rays from the outside of this box, I used my stethoscope and the ultrasound device to listen and attempt to see what was happening in there. I heard a heartbeat, and blood is flowing through the arteries and capillaries just as our blood normally courses through our veins. I didn't take a chance on piercing the glass, but after several tries, I managed to get a medium gauge needle through the wood bottom and retrieved a tiny piece of skin and a blood sample."

He lifted a brow and paused. "My findings so far prove what I suspected. The tissue is not decayed and is from living flesh."

He handed over a note. "This is what was attached to the box. I'm taking heed of this note because I believe its instructions and a warning. I get the sense that the note isn't meant to mislead us but to test us to see if we can follow through."

Yala inspected the note, eyeing, sniffing, and flipping it several times before reading it. She read it three times like the words would suddenly change. The context of this box was atrocious, but the note attached to it was simple.

1. This is box one: the torso.

2. Please do not open this box (it is one-third of a complete box set.)

3. Box two, the lower body, will arrive in 48 hours.

4. Connecting box one and box two will prove that this subject can be saved when the sections are rejoined.

5. Box three, the head, will arrive in 96 hours.

6. Failure to follow directions, more precisely opening any part of the box set before the three components are connected, will result in the subject's death.

Yala shook her head. Where the hell was the logic in all of this? Where the hell was the rest of the victim's body? Was the note implying that this man could somehow be reconnected into a whole person as long as the boxes containing the rest of him were put back together?

The suspect must have found a way to camouflage the rest of the body. There was no other explanation.

Yala's job was to find the rest of the victim, the person behind this act, and the answers to the mystery surrounding it. But, how?

If the torso was alive, like the doctor and the accompanying note claimed, she needed to do whatever was necessary to save this person from this nightmare he was currently stuck in. He was trapped in a body box. What else could she call this? Had she become a part of a sadistic magic show without knowing the secrets to the magician's trick?

She measured, snapped photos, and used instruments to tap on various parts of the box. She did everything except open the dang thing. Her findings only fueled more questions.

Aside from a few partial fingerprints, she found no other trace elements on the surface. It was wishful thinking, but she prayed the prints would lead to a culprit. Since she was not in her element with this case, she would have to send the prints to her TOP contact for further processing and pray that one of the partials would yield a match.

The note was simple, but her jarring reality was a glass-encased box with a living torso inside. The threat of death was imminent for the victim if they didn't follow directions and reconnect the missing parts when they received them.

The box's measurements and dimensions leaned toward a standard-size coffin. Yala leaned against the exam table and stared down the torso's neck.

"There's a heartbeat in there, and the tissue is alive?"

She eyed the doctor and pointed at the unbelievable. "He really is alive?"

Dr. Hughes nodded, eyeing the torso. "I'm sure of it. If you'd like, you can observe while I run more tests. I need to see if I've missed anything."

For about the hundredth time, Yala ran her hand through the empty space where the head should have been. When simply observing didn't produce answers, she climbed atop the table and laid her body perpendicular and parallel to the box.

She waited for something magical to ensue and checked to see if there was a way the inventor of this trick could have tucked away the rest of the body. There were no hidden mirrors or tiny lights that bent or distorted the view of the rest of the body.

While lying on her back atop the table, she glanced at Dr. Hughes.

"Doc, how did this box arrive? Whoever brought it here may have something to do with this or know who's responsible."

At her words, a tiny smile bent the corners of his lips, and his shoulders dropped about a half inch, losing tension. Yala finally hopped off the table.

Dr. Hughes sat on one of the stools while she dragged hers closer and sat beside him. The right side of the torso stared at them.

"I'm ready, Doc. Even if you don't think something has relevance, say it anyway."

He cleared his throat. "Last night, I conducted an autopsy, boxed the body, and cleaned as I normally would. I spent most of my night reading and studying."

He paused, swallowed and inhaled deeply before releasing it slowly.

"Whoever dropped this box off must have known my schedule and when the security team made their rounds. As I was heading for the parking lot, a little after 6:00 a.m., I stumbled into a large cardboard box in the entranceway. There was no mistaking who the box was intended for, as my name was written on the cardboard, in big black letters in permanent marker."

Dr. Hughes pointed to the large, neatly folded cardboard box near the freezers.

"This office is behind the hospital and hidden from the main traffic flow. The location makes getting away with something like this easier, but the box couldn't have been in the entrance all night, as security would have noticed it."

The doctor placed his fingers on his forehead and unconsciously massaged the area.

"I carted the box into this exam room and got it onto my table. Upon removing the cardboard and Styrofoam, I noticed the box inside was glass. I didn't know what to make of what was inside, thinking it may have been a prop, until I caught sight of the attached note."

He glanced up and stared at the wall in front of him, his eyes unfocused.

"I read the note several times before I checked the box more thoroughly. The note quenched my desire to open the box, and instincts made me follow the instructions."

Yala sat motionless, hanging on to every word.

"I locked myself in this room, and for three hours, I ran every test I could think of without opening the box. I called security, but they informed me that they hadn't seen anything. Before I called TOP, I made an urgent request to reroute all incoming dead to the county coroner's office, as I didn't believe we needed any additional traffic at this location."

The doctor's experience preceded him based on how he had handled things so far. TOP may not have recruited him as an agent, but he operated like one.

"When it became clear I wouldn't find answers right away, I called TOP, and here you are."

Yala inclined her head once, unsure what to make of the situation.

"While I chew on that, let's proceed with the examinations. I'd love for you to prove that what I think I see is true."

Eyes peeled and tracking his every move, the doctor lifted and slid the box slightly over the raised edge of his examination table. The action exposed a small portion of the wood bottom, which was nothing but a thin sheet of plywood. The doctor penetrated the wood with a needle she was sure would break, but it endured the pressure, and he was able to extract whatever fluids he needed.

The action proved they could get into the box to a certain degree, but like him, Yala wasn't willing to risk opening it fully. The note was straightforward about the victim dying if they did open it.

Yala shadowed Dr. Hughes. She stood on her tiptoes to glance over his shoulders as he took several X-rays, too blurred to reveal anything substantial but visible enough to confirm that the internal structure was intact inside the torso.

Where the hell is the blood flowing to if this section of the body is alive?

The steady beat of a heart thrummed through several of the doctor's listening devices. As a TOP agent, most of Yala's assignments were top secret or above, but this Box case definitely leaped to the top of the unusually unnatural list.

The doctor's voice drew her attention. "So, what do you want to do? I called TOP because I didn't want this to get out to the public."

She considered the question. "I think we should follow the note's instructions. If a box set somehow reconnects this victim and keeps him alive, we should at least follow the instructions, no matter how bizarre. I'll also pull surveillance and talk to possible witnesses who may have been in the area when the cardboard box showed up."

Dr. Hughes glanced up with a magnifying glass in front of his face, giving an enhanced snapshot of his blue eye.

"I agree wholeheartedly. I'll lock this room. No one else, except for my assistant, has access. I'll brief him that I'm working on a project that renders this room off-limits."

Yala stared at the box as if to receive answers through telepathy. She had her work cut out for her with this case. And as much as she valued going at it alone for most of her cases, on this, she wasn't too proud to admit she didn't mind a partner coming on to brainstorm ideas.

"I'll be back, Doc. I'll pull the surveillance footage and talk to security," she said after finally breaking the box's visual hold on her.

CHAPTER TWO

Yala

An hour of sleep and Yala was up and ready to go again. All she found the day prior were empty leads. After she studied the surveillance footage, she stopped at the hospital's Human Resources department to retrieve the personal information of the security team on duty at the time the box was dropped off.

An interview with the two guards produced a description of a black SUV, likely the same one in the grainy surveillance footage, but the quality of the footage was too dark to read the vehicle's license plate.

Yala's plan to interview the hospital's day and night crews was underway. She needed to tread lightly so as not to single out or spook any one person. The last thing she wanted to do was to alert the monster responsible for the Box and not receive the remaining two parts of the victim.

This is where her disguise skills would come in handy. Presenting herself as a new co-worker, a lost patient, or a cute girl looking to flirt—it didn't matter as long as it got her answers.

Dr. Hughes slept on the couch in his office to remain near the victim if anything medical or unusual happened. Although there were no requirements that they knew of in respect to medical care of the torso, the doctor was protective of it.

"Good morning, Doc," she greeted upon entering the office before they headed to the exam room. She approached the box with scanning eyes and a hesitant stride. The unseen complexities of it captured her intrigue as tightly as it had the day prior.

The doctor performed several tests before he left her posted up in the corner of the room to scan more surveillance footage. Her head jerked up as she thought she caught movement from the corner of her eye. Her gaze traveled over the box, but nothing appeared out of the ordinary. It pleased her to see the magician hadn't found a way to make the box or torso disappear.

She blew out a breath of relief before returning her attention to the video, sure that she was looking at a dark-colored Range Rover. But there it was again, movement in her peripheral vision. Her gaze shot up and roved the expanse of the room.

What the hell?

The air around her felt like it was closing her into a bubble, the sensation making her shiver. She should have taken the doctor's advice and worked from his assistant's office. Standing, she crept around the room, observing from every angle until finally, she spotted it. The hand on the torso twitched. It jerked like it had fallen asleep, and the man was fighting to rouse it.

She inched toward the box, noticing how the chest flexed with each twitch of the hand.

Is he lifting his hand?

The sight of the headless, legless torso attempting to move was freakish. The hairs on the back of her neck stood, mimicking the sensation of fingers marching up her back. She placed her hand atop her gun and took a few steps away from the box, the unknown making the hairs on her arm bristle too.

She needed Dr. Hughes and fast. They were the only two in the building so she stuck her head out the door and yelled for him. "Dr. Hughes! I think the torso is trying to move!"

Dr. Hughes ran into the room with the speed of an Olympic sprinter.

Usain Bolt, look out.

The doctor studied the box inquisitively, moving around the table with purpose. The hand strained to lift again, resembling a weird science project. The action made them stare at each other for confirmation that they were witnessing the same thing.

"Shit. Not good."

Hearing the doctor curse hyped up the seriousness of their situation. He ran toward the door, a flurry of words trailing his hasty exit. "I'll be right back. He may need a sedative. He could inadvertently open the box if he regains motor functions while contained inside."

Yala's eyes widened. "Shit! Not Good."

Dr. Hughes returned with his arms filled with medicines and equipment. Once his hands were free, he waved her over. "I need your help. I need to test his toxicity levels."

She didn't understand. "I thought you tested that yesterday."

The doctor had found low sedative levels in the torso's system but nothing life-threatening. "I did. However, he's been here for a day, and this is the first time he's attempted to move. I believe the sedative I found in his system yesterday has worn off."

Yala glared at the ceiling, attempting to process the doctor's words.

"If you sedate him like this, will the drug somehow find its way into the other parts of his body?"

"Exactly my thinking," he confirmed."

She twisted her lips and forced her brain to accept the concept. "No matter what part of his body receives physical contact, he may feel it the same as he would if he were whole?"

"Yes. It's what I believe," Dr. Hughes replied.

They worked under the assumption that the man's body could inexplicably be in two or three locations at once but function as a whole entity. The doctor was sure this man was a whole person physically, even if they couldn't grasp what was happening to him visually or mentally.

"Doc, if you're right, this means his head could be somewhere, viewing an area where his torso is supposed to be, and although he can't see it, he can feel it if touched by one of us?"

Doctor Hughes nodded, his lips tight and eyes fixed on the torso.

Goodness.

There wasn't a science class in the world that could make her put this into an acceptable, logical perspective. The doctor ushered his head toward the machine.

THE BOX · 19

"The test is almost done. What I don't want to do is accidentally overdose this man."

At the sound of the beep, he dashed over to the gas chromatography-mass spectrometer and retrieved a printout. He lowered his glasses over his eyes and read words and codes Yala was sure would give her migraines.

"The sedative in his system has worn off. It explains why he's starting to move." Concern rested in the creases of the doctor's face.

Yala was at a loss. She wasn't afraid to admit that this level of scientific logic was giving her brain cells a workout. The complexity of the situation made her head ache.

Her breath caught, and she lifted a shaky finger at the box.

"I think we should give him the drugs now. He's regaining full use of his arm, and the other arm is moving too."

Dr. Hughes prepared the needle and didn't waste time penetrating the bottom of the box. Once the needle hit home in the back of the shoulder region, the arms relaxed, like an addict getting their fix.

"Let's hope that someone smart enough to pull off something so complex would at least be smart enough to know the difference between sedation and cognitive awareness. They should be smart enough to anticipate, or at least figure out, that we've sedated this man."

"Doc, do you think we'll receive the next box like the note states?"

He nodded. "Yes. I believe we're being tested to see if we will follow directions. What I don't understand is, why? Why do this to someone? What motives does one have for doing this, other than to reveal to us that they are smart and psychotic? If we can't figure out how this is being done and who is doing it, the perpetrator will have proven he is smarter."

CHAPTER THREE

Yala

The next morning.

Yala waited in the shadows to catch the person or persons sent to drop off the next part of the box. Wide-eyed, she scanned the area, her stance stalkerish behind a patch of half-dead bushes.

Steam from her breath floated into the air as the cold folded her in a tight embrace. She'd been waiting for an hour so far. She rolled her eyes at the sun, whose rays did nothing to warm her numb fingers and toes. She flipped the collar of her coat over her ears and sank into her shoulders to seek warmth.

When she spotted a mail delivery truck speeding past the hospital and driving around into the medical examiner's small parking area, she ran to meet the driver. Dr. Hughes was hot on her heels as he shot through the entrance door to meet the delivery man.

Nothing was off as far as she could tell. This was a normal postal delivery, and other than her gawking at the man, he didn't display any emotion about what he was delivering. The box was large enough to be what they were expecting.

While the doctor signed for it, Yala eyeballed the mailman. Up and down, her predatory gaze ran over him, causing the man to shoot quick side-eye glances of caution in her direction.

The postal worker helped Dr. Hughes load the box onto the dolly he'd rolled out hours before the man's arrival. Once he wheeled the box into the building, Yala tossed questions at the delivery guy like they were cards from a deck.

When she was done, he hopped into his truck and sped away from her. She didn't believe he understood any of her questions about the origin of the box, who loaded it onto his truck, where it was originally received from, or how he'd come into possession of it. The man kept glancing back in his rearview mirror at her until he turned off at the end of the building and out of sight.

She didn't have to be an investigative expert to conclude that the man was clueless about what the box was or what it contained. However, she planned to visit his work location to figure out who'd shipped it.

Before venturing off to track leads, Yala joined Dr. Hughes to see if the second part of the box would do what the instructions suggested it would, which was to reattach the man's two parts.

Doctor Hughes cut away the cardboard outer shell of the box. He searched, but didn't find another note. Their eyes went to and remained glued to the sight of the man's lower body. His abdomen, right below his belly button, down to his toes, occupied this second box.

The doctor took the first set of measurements. Yala took the second set. The two boxes matched in area, but length was added to the second box to accommodate the man's legs. There was also a slight variation to the new box. It was shaved around the outer circumference to allow a small portion to slide into the first box.

Yala scratched her head, her eyes pinned on the object soaking up her attention. "Although box one is a Lego fit to box two, the problem of the glass separating the two parts remains."

Dr. Hughes scratched his beard while his eyes bounced back and forth between the two boxes. "I don't know. Let's do what the note says, slide the boxes together, and see what happens."

Yala set up a camera, while the doctor aligned the boxes, made of the same glass and wood bottom design. The man's legs in the second box were positioned as if he were lying face up.

Dr. Hughes slid the new box closer to the first, his movements meticulous, cautious. The boxes fit together perfectly, and as soon as the second box was edged far enough into the first, a distinct *click* echoed throughout the room. The sound itself was in question. How could a low tone like that produce an echo?

Yala and Dr. Hughes' wide mystified eyes were transfixed on the box, their lips falling apart and remaining open at the sudden connection. The boxes were now one, and so were the body parts.

They glanced at each other. She shrugged. The doctor's expression grew tighter. They hadn't seen any magic happen.

She, having a sprinkle of supernatural energy in her blood, didn't sense any unnatural currents, nor had they seen any sudden movements. She expected to see the flesh magically knitting itself back together, but that wasn't the case here. She released a hard breath of frustration. "I don't get it. What am I missing?"

The doctor stared at the box, not uttering a word. She fingered the small section that joined the two boxes and found the surface smooth. It was glass. There was nothing special hidden there and no detectable energy signatures. The glass panes that once separated the body were gone.

Where? Was it ever there? Was the wooden bottom the key? Had the extra glass slid into a secret compartment?

The man's torso and lower half were reconnected. This proved that the note from the first box hadn't been a trick. They were one step closer to saving this victim. All they needed to finish the puzzle was the victim's head.

A thought occurred to Yala. "If we pull this box apart, will it kill this man or simply make him two parts again?"

Dr. Hughes shrugged. "It's not a chance I'm willing to take. The bigger question is, will this man live if and when we receive the head? By live, I mean, will he be functional, brain dead, paralyzed?"

Over the years, she found ways to become useful and efficient in a multitude of unexpected situations, but Yala was at a loss in this one.

The fingerprints she found, hoping to identify who may be responsible for this phenomenon, hadn't turned up anything. The SUV on the surveillance footage was untraceable without a license plate. The suspect was in the wind and untouchable since he had the victim's head.

This case was a jigsaw puzzle missing many of its pieces. It wasn't every day she was presented with something that left no clues or trails to follow.

Although she didn't know who her partner would be yet, she prayed it would be her agent friend Sori, also known as Smoke. Sori was one of the few people she looked up to. She was also knowledgeable about these types of cases. Since their initial meeting a few years ago, they have been as close to friends as possible in their world.

Despite this case giving her a mental headache, she would do what TOP agents did best: save this man and track down the person or thing responsible.

CHAPER FOUR

Yala

A day and a half later.

Finally taking a break, Doctor Hughes stepped out for a bite to eat, visiting the closest diner open at three in the morning. Time unfolded and released a rainstorm on his drive back.

He hardly acknowledged the thump of raindrops pelting his car or the screech of the wiper blades because the anticipation of receiving the third part of *the Box* dominated his every waking thought.

As he pulled into the dark parking lot, it was hard to miss his assistant's white Honda Accord, parked and running with the headlights illuminating the path to the entrance. Doctor Hughes squinted, focusing on seeing through sheets of rain to view a person sitting in the passenger's seat of the running car.

There was no telling what James Bryant had forgotten in the office. He was currently completing his probationary period, which would lead to him becoming the assistant medical examiner, and whatever he'd left must have been important to pay a visit at this unholy hour.

Dr. Hughes had heard many of James' detailed stories of his exploits with men and often warned him about his propensity to overshare. But, unbeknownst to James, Dr. Hughes enjoyed his energetic personality, and his stories always drew a laugh from him.

James quickly jumped at the chance at the week of paid administrative time off he was offered, unaware that it was meant to keep him away from the office and the mystery locked inside the main exam room.

The doctor moved swiftly in his attempt to dodge the heavy downpour while balancing his chicken-fried steak breakfast. Once inside, he shook off the raindrops and blew out a sigh of relief. His intention was to stop at James's office, but the cracked exam room door drew a loud gasp from him. He'd locked that door, and James wasn't supposed to have a key.

Deciding that breakfast wasn't as important as what was hidden inside the room, he dropped the Styrofoam plate of food along with the umbrella. His stopped heart followed the items to the floor.

In a mad dash, he took off toward the room, screaming loud enough to make his lungs burn, "DON'T OPEN *THE BOX!* DON'T OPEN *THE BOX!* DON'T OPEN *THE BOX!*"

Dr. Hughes tore through the door, breathless and still yelling. The thud of his heartbeat and his shrieking yell could have been a hook for a heavy metal song.

He stood at the door, stopped cold when his eyes landed on James's hand holding the box open. Horror seized the doctor, its stronghold strangling his ability to speak and stalling his motor functions.

The top of the box slammed shut as James jerked his trembling hand away from the latch. James joined the doctor, frozen and staring as the headless man began to convulse. His legs and arms thrashed about, threatening to break the glass. The stub of his neck rose and fell with sharp jerking motions like he was being electrocuted.

Dr. Hughes slammed his eyes shut at the realization that he could do nothing to save this man. He reached out a hand and took a few gut-wrenching steps. His legs jellied and stalled, moving him sporadically. The doctor possessed the makings of a cheesy actor, acting out a badly written melodrama in a B-movie.

He gathered his composure by taking a few deep breaths before walking the rest of the way to the box.

James remained unmoved, his face ghost white. He snapped out of his trance with a jerk, his eyes growing wide and alert. One hand thrashed against his chest, and his other covered his mouth as he stared at the convulsing, headless body.

James had stopped in to pick up the box of sex toys he'd left there a week ago. His reaction to what was playing out on the table made him unaware that he'd dropped his own black box and spilled its explicit contents all over the floor.

Dr. Hughes' foot swiped a dildo out of his path as he melodramatically, still in character, made his way toward the convulsing body in the box. The doctor's laser focus on the box made him unaware or he didn't care about what decorated the floor. He kicked a set of ass beads, sending them under the exam table as he tried to get to a victim he knew he couldn't save.

By the time the doctor cleared a path through the impressive sex toy collection, the section where the victim's head should have been had exploded. Blood squirted against the glass, and a pool made its way around the victim's shoulders, covering the bottom of the box.

James's head swiveled back and forth between the box and his boss as his hand continued to flap against his chest.

The victim's body ceased all movement except the legs jerking every other second from the man fighting to hang on to the last strands of life. Each pump of the heart sent squirts of blood from the arteries in his neck and shot it against the glass like squirts of thick dark ketchup.

The events taking place and Doctor Hughes' reaction kept James from being embarrassed about his toys displayed all over the floor. He may have been inclined to faint where he stood if he didn't work with bodies regularly. The idea of a headless body inside a glass box fighting to stay alive would have put abject fear in anyone.

"Dr. Hughes, I...I...I'm so sorry. I stopped in to get my stuff," he said, his voice shaky. He lifted and aimed a finger at the body part. "What's going on? What have I done?"

Words escaped Doctor Hughes. For the first time in his long career, he didn't know what to say. James needed an explanation, a word of encouragement that he wasn't in trouble, but the words were lost in the abyss of the doctor's despair over what was happening in front of him. He took out his phone and dialed Yala.

***

Yala was climbing into bed when Dr. Hughes called. She spent the evening and night harassing the team of mail carriers after conducting a thorough search of their facility. All she found were dead-ends.

"Hello," she answered, sensing trouble since he was calling at four in the morning.

"There's been an incident. How soon can you get here?" he asked, his words rushed, hard.

"About fifteen minutes. See you soon," she replied before hanging up.

She knew not to ask him to explain. Speaking on a sensitive matter like the man in the box wasn't something they could discuss over the phone. Yala threw on a pair of jeans and a turtleneck and tugged on her shoes before stumbling out the door of the hotel.

She raced back to the medical examiner's office, pushing her rental car over the speed limit. The black Nissan Sentra shot around to the side of the hospital like a bat straight from hell. The doctor's call had one of Yala's legs tapping while she fought to keep the other from ramming the gas pedal through the floor.

When Yala entered the exam room, her foot swiped a purple ring-like object with spikes that was oddly out of place. The stench of death coated the air, and she did the last thing she needed to do—and that was to take a deep breath.

The rest of the scene came into focus in full force like a hard blow to the face: the grief-stricken man who must have been Dr. Hughes' assistant, the pained expression on the doctor's face, the black velvet box at the man's feet, and the bloody headless body inside the bigger glass box atop the table.

Yala took the long way around the room and stood between Dr. Hughes and James. There wasn't much to say. They'd screwed up, and the victim had lost his life. Her heart sank at the thought of how close they'd been to receiving the victim's head to see if he could be saved.

She'd chased ghosts since the day she walked into Dr. Hughes's office and, for the first time in a long time, felt like a failure. She maintained as calm a voice as she could muster.

"James, none of this is your fault. You didn't mean to do anything wrong. This situation is out of our control. We are at the mercy of a demented killer, and all we have left is to examine the evidence. We were studying this body to determine what was done to it."

Were her words enough to calm James while hiding the unbelievable truth about the headless body in the box?

James wrinkled his brow, and she could almost see his thoughts playing out on his face. The hint of fear within the depth of his gaze conveyed that he may not have wanted the truth. James placed a shaky hand on Dr. Hughes's shoulder.

"I'm sorry. I didn't mean to mess up anything."

After he gathered his toys, James stood with hunched shoulders and a lowered head.

"What should I do? I didn't know I wasn't supposed to open the box. I had a spare key and thought it would be okay to run in and get my things. I usually keep this stuff in my car, but when I let my sister borrow it a few weeks back...oh, God. I feel horrible. I don't know what I just did. I don't know what this is all about."

"Your date is waiting for you," Yala reminded him. "Go home and enjoy your time off. Doctor Hughes and I will take care of this."

Dr. Hughes nodded and forced a placating smile. "It's okay, James. Agent Lawrence is right. I'll call you when you can return to work. And James, maybe I should hang onto that key until you return."

James handed Dr. Hughes the spare key and ran from the room, clutching his box of toys.

Dr. Hughes dropped his head, kept it down, and shook it.

Yala understood the doctor's position. He shouldered a mountain of responsibility. He was the person others ran to when they didn't know how to explain situations like this. He was as desperate as she was to save this man.

This loss added pressure to an already crushing situation for her and the doctor. They needed to save the person who could have provided answers to a mystery of which they had barely scratched the surface. Instead, she failed to track any suspects or secure any promising leads.

She stared at the victim's bloody body and swallowed the thick knot of grief and regret that clogged her throat.

"Identifying him is what's most important at this point. If we can figure out what his life was like, we may be able to piece this puzzle together and find some answers," she said, glancing over her shoulder at the doctor.

"Do you think the lunatic doing this will send the head? If your theory is correct, Doc, our Dr. Frankenstein is still in possession of this victim's head and has now become a murderer."

Breaking from his trance, Dr. Hughes placed his hand against the side of his neck to stretch it. The cracks and pops of tension sounded off.

"Let's hope we receive the head, as it may be all that identifies this man since the fingerprints didn't give us an identity."

Yala took out her phone, preparing to text a coded update to her TOP contact.

CHAPTER FIVE

Yala

The last four-and-a-half days were spent fighting to figure out the impossible. Now, damn D-words, like disheartened and disappointed, wreaked havoc on them. The little shred of hope they clung to had died with the victim.

Before removing the body from the box, Dr. Hughes wanted to test to make sure the man was dead. The large amount of blood spilled into the cavity of the box was a clear indication. But this wasn't a typical murder.

A few hours had passed since James opened the box, but the body had already gone ghost-white and dispelled the odor that marked the beginning of decay.

Yala assisted Doctor Hughes, taking his direction on how to properly remove the body from the box. They photographed an impressive collage of tattoos on the man's back, and after running numerous tests, the victim was pronounced dead. Yala dug deep into her mental reels to find the logic that tied the victim's life and death to the box.

She made futile attempts to take the box apart, but it wouldn't budge. It was fully connected like it had never been in two parts. She and Dr. Hughes scanned every corner of the inside and outside and found it was glass and wood. Whatever made the box special was gone. Or, had it ever been there?

Yala studied the doctor's movements as he positioned his hands and prepared to make the Y incision on their headless John Doe. He'd performed this task on many occasions. However, this time, it would be on a headless man who'd been alive in his examination room for four-and-a-half days.

She squinted. "Doc, what if we're looking at this all wrong?"

He cut through the dead skin like he was creating art.

"How so? This man was alive and didn't die until that despicable box was opened, just like the note stated."

She probed the area where the box was reconnected.

"What if the magic was never in the box? What if the magic came from the person or thing that made the box? What if this box was all an illusion to keep our suspicions amiss?"

Doctor Hughes peeled back and pinned a large flap of skin from the man's chest.

"If that theory is true, it means the perpetrator has an extraordinary ability that could suspend a person and leave them hanging in the middle of life and death."

He pinned the second flap of skin open, exposing most of the man's tissue and chest plate.

"I haven't figured out how to connect this to science yet, but that doesn't mean I'm giving up. If this isn't science, I'll continue to do my best to figure out how this works."

"I understand and so will I."

She pointed at the box, shaking her finger at it. "The person doing this is a monster. They want us to know what they can do and would probably like to be found out. They are hiding behind those boxes. What can they accomplish by doing this though?"

She talked and paced. "Would the victim have lived if we could have put him back together? I don't know, but I don't believe the magic or science that kept him together and alive is in that box." Yala stilled, allowing her mind to go adrift.

"Agent Lawrence?"

She jerked her head up and answered the doctor after realizing he'd been calling her name.

"Yes."

"Are you okay?"

She nodded, but her gaze remained fixed on the box.

"This has been one of the most bizarre cases of my career. It's also the first time I've been an investigator." She tapped her fingers against her hip. "I think I have been sending my energy in the wrong direction. Instead of chasing who dropped off the box, I need to look into the kind of person who can pull this off."

She resumed pacing. "I believe it may be someone in the medical field who knows the ins and outs of human anatomy as well as how much trauma they can put a body through before they go into shock."

Dr. Hughes continued his examination, observing the man's lungs and other parts. He paused, scalpel ready to slice through more tissue.

"You're thinking a doctor did this?" he asked her.

The doctor performing the autopsy was better at enduring the repugnant scent filling the room. Yala cleared her throat and swallowed a heavy coat of nausea. The mask Dr. Hughes gave her to wear wasn't working to keep the stench away.

"Yes. Identifying this unfortunate soul and researching his ties to any doctors or medical personnel could lead us to the one who did this to him," Yala said.

Dr. Hughes's lips tilted into a smile that didn't reach his eyes. "I agree. It makes sense that someone with a medical background is more likely to have the necessary skills to try something like this ."

The victim's official cause of death was decapitation. A sharp blade had passed through the meaty parts of the man's neck. The scrapings on his bones indicated that someone may have taken the time to repeatedly drag a sharp blade through them. The sick person doing this took the time to cut through every bone, tendon, and artery.

This man had lived for four-and-a-half days in that traumatic state. It was a mystery the doctor couldn't explain. As long as the man was inside the box and it stayed closed, he remained alive. Opening the box was the kill switch and had somehow severed the connection to what was keeping him alive.

***

While Yala made her rounds interviewing the hospital staff, Dr. Hughes called, informing her that he'd received the victim's head. This time it was a guard who knocked on the morgue's door to inform Dr. Hughes of the box sitting outside it.

Yala observed her current interviewee, a doctor so old he probably wrote his prescriptions on parchment paper. Dr. Cox may have been one hundred and fifty years old, but his eyes worked and remained locked on Yala's chest. She wore a conservative top and jeans, but it didn't stop him from gawking.

She called him away from his targets. "Dr. Cox?"

His gaze raked over her body.

"Can we continue the interview later?" she asked.

His voice rasped low but husky. "Sure thing, young lady. Pleasure looking at you."

She stifled a grin. Did he notice or even care about his tongue slip?

Yala made a swift exit and headed to the front of the hospital. Since Doctor Hughes had just received the head, she hoped to catch a glimpse of the person who'd dropped it off or any other suspicious activity. Anything out of the ordinary would motivate her at this point.

She wasted an hour asking questions and not receiving answers. A quick check of the surveillance footage didn't turn anything up either. Not one vehicle appeared entering near the ME's office in three hours, and none had dropped off any packages.

It must have come from someone within the hospital. This unexpected lead could give her something to work with.

By the time she made it back to Dr. Hughes, he'd removed the head from a cardboard box. The deranged psychopath hadn't bothered to put the head in one of his fancy glass boxes.

Yala snapped photos of the man's face while the doctor took X-rays. Hopefully, facial recognition and his dental work would provide an identity where other means had failed.

CHAPTER SIX

Yala

Two days later.

The victim, Juan Carlos De La Cruz, was identified as a twenty-eight-year-old Hispanic man. Based on his criminal record and gang affiliation, the streets had educated him. Juan's records listed a wife and one son—his parents deceased.

Yala paid a visit to Juan's last known address and discovered he no longer lived there. The new tenants, friends of Juan's, claimed he and his family had come into some cash and moved to Oakwood. Juan hadn't shared where he'd gotten the money, but the friends provided Yala directions to De La Cruz's new residence.

Sitting in the parking lot of the Oakwood Apartments, she noticed that this new neighborhood was a drastic upgrade for Juan and his family. Unlike his old area, this one didn't have crowds of people hanging out on the streets, no profanity being shouted from every direction, and no arguing couples putting on a free public show.

The front office gave Yala the apartment number after she flashed a badge. The woman she assumed was Wanda De La Cruz answered the door. A petite Hispanic woman, conservatively dressed, Wanda projected a naïve innocence Yala didn't expect from the wife of an ex-gang member like Juan.

The taut lines over her forehead, hunched shoulders, and the concern peeking through her wide gaze revealed her stress level. Although Yala flashed one of several badges she owned, Mrs. De La Cruz barely glimpsed at her fake credentials.

As soon as she stepped inside the apartment, Wanda went on and on nonstop.

"He's been gone for a week. Juan would never stay away that long without contacting me," she said. "I went to the police station twice, but no one cared much about assisting me, not for a reformed gangbanger. They pretended to jot down notes, but I could tell by the way they assessed me when I said his name that they didn't care."

This was the first time Yala faced notifying an individual of a deceased family member. She sat a hand on Wanda's forearm to stop her.

"Ma'am, I have bad news." She inhaled deeply before blurting, "Juan passed away. He was in the hospital and died from his injuries. Unfortunately, he was found without identification, so we couldn't identify him until today. Otherwise, we'd have contacted you sooner."

The story wasn't entirely false, but it was the best Yala could come up with on the spot.

Wanda sobbed, choking on the cries she released. Sorrow played out in the creases of her face and her glazed eyes as tears dripped like raindrops.

She stared at Yala, her head shaking to combat the impact of the news. This was new territory for Yala. How were you supposed to help someone carrying this much sorrow? She reached out a hand, and Wanda gripped it like her life depended on it.

The strength of emotions played out like a film in her eyes and acted out its role in subtle, uncontrolled movements of her body. The sight drew Yala closer. She rubbed the woman's arm and shoulder with hesitant but caring strokes.

Yala took in the woman's face, the way it was balled into a tight knot and the continuous movement of her hands like she wasn't sure what to do with them. Droplets continued to leak down her cheeks like she'd lost control of her tear ducts.

Uncertainty plagued Yala, but she prepared to sit with Mrs. De La Cruz for as long as she needed and seeing this added fuel to her determination to find justice for Juan. She waited until Wanda's tears stopped falling before she asked a few questions.

"Ma'am, will you tell me about Juan's job? Was there anyone he worked for or with who could have intended him harm?"

Wanda wiped at fresh tears. "No. Not that I know of. How did he die? Was he shot?"

"His neck was broken. The doctors did everything they could to save him but lost the battle. If it is okay with you, we'd like to keep Juan with us for a while longer. We may be able to find evidence on his person that can help us find the person who hurt him."

Yala was used to talking, uncensored, about death with other agents. Still, she couldn't tell Wanda that her husband was decapitated, was cut into three parts, and put into three separate boxes like a science experiment. Civilians didn't take the messiness of death well.

Wanda's body shook when she sucked in a sob. "He worked as a janitor at the Mayflower Nursing Home. He said he'd found a way to make extra money." She paused, staring into the space right in front of her.

One of those hiccup sobs escaped her before she continued.

"He said he was working with a scientist at a small lab. He didn't give me many details, but I believe it was one where they tested animals. They paid him in cash for samples of his blood. I told him it wasn't a good idea but he said with the money they gave him, we could move to a nicer neighborhood and have a better life.

"I didn't care. I didn't want him getting involved with anything like that, but he did it anyway. I don't know what this scientist was doing to him when he would come home late, but I never saw a difference in his appearance or how he acted. After a few weeks, he had already made enough to move us here. When it appeared everything would be all right with the scientist, I stopped pestering Juan about it—and now, this."

Yala didn't offer a reply. She believed the woman needed an ear more than she needed placating words that wouldn't make her feel any better.

"He left home one morning and didn't return. I couldn't get through to his cell or anything."

Wanda broke down again; her shoulders quaked as she struggled to speak.

"Will you give me his number? Maybe we can locate his phone."

"I used the Find a Friend App. I even asked the cops if they could track his phone another way. They took his number, but I know they didn't do anything."

The woman's words mixed into her sobs, but Yala understood enough to know what she said. She tightened her hand around the woman's while she brushed light strokes up and down her back.

"I believe the scientist also recruited one of Juan's friends. I only know him by his first name. Lennie," she said.

After nearly an hour of questions, Yala finally left Wanda to grieve. Her next step would be to probe Juan's old neighborhood for answers before visiting the nursing home where he'd worked as well as track down any information on a scientist paying people cash to conduct shady experiments on them.

Thankfully, Yala possessed the perfect remedy that would allow her to fit into each environment she would be investigating. One of her well-kept secrets was her ability to pull off disguises. The world in which she worked was built on secrets, and her ability to disguise or 'shift' as some called it, wasn't something she went around advertising.

She checked in briefly with Dr. Hughes. He heeded her advice to take a break and went home to rest. There wasn't much more he could do with Juan's body except keep it secure and preserved.

CHAPTER SEVEN

Kevin

A sharp pang of loneliness pricked Kevin in the heart, making him brush his fingers over the area. He sensed things differently than the average person and often caged his abilities or eased into them with guarded focus.

Like a steady downpour, the nagging emotion he currently struggled with always washed away his positive thoughts. Maintaining a normal relationship had never worked. Hanging out with friends didn't either.

He was different. It ruined his personal life, but gave meaning to his professional life. Therefore, work became the medicine that kept most of his unwanted emotions at bay.

Dusk began to blanket the day and darken his view of the tightly compacted project buildings and littered streets teeming with people and fast-moving cars. They cursed, sped along, and flashed each other middle fingers with no sensible reasoning behind their actions. Rudeness was an acceptable norm in this neck of the woods.

Small business owners dragged security bars down to safeguard their property and locked multiple deadbolts on their front doors. Kevin observed the ongoing activities through a scope from his third-floor hotel room window.

His plan was to infiltrate a small band of drug dealers he was keeping tabs on. The group may be the key to getting into a much larger group he was gathering intel on— the Truleta Cartel.

Over the years, Kevin earned a reputation for his ability to infiltrate organizations deemed untouchable. The agency to which he belonged, TOP, labeled him one of their best trackers.

He continued to observe the multiple levels of activity unfolding below. However, it was the group of thugs closest to his location that currently came across his sights. This was a new bunch. The group's posture, body language, and menacing gestures made a sinister vibe snake its way up Kevin's spine.

Something shady was about to go down in that alley, and since it was located a few blocks away from his cheap motel, his instincts urged him to check it out.

The lighting wasn't illuminating enough to get an accurate look into any individual's face, specifically their eyes. His specialty was getting into people's heads using their senses. The downside to his ability was that he needed a way in, and the eyes always allowed him easy access.

Another peek through the scope showed the group of four circling a smaller guy like hungry vultures preparing to pounce. Kevin knew, from experience, the man was about to get robbed, murdered or beaten to a pulp.

He rarely interfered in the norms of street life unless someone's life was at stake. This situation drew him in, making his senses go berserk.

Out of nowhere, the first blow was delivered, a wildly thrown punch that connected with the smaller man's temple. The force of the impact sent the man to his knees, and the rest of the group closed in on him.

Kevin flung on his black jumpsuit and jetted from his third-floor balcony like a superhero. He'd been an agent with TOP for nearly five years. If there was one thing he learned, it was to have an alternate escape route in any situation. In less than a minute, he emerged in the alley.

He placed his thumb and middle finger between his lips and released a shrill whistle that drew the group's attention. All heads turned in his direction, including the little guy being beaten.

Layers of light sparsely illuminated the alley, shining in patches from the moon and streetlights. The January winds pressed against Kevin's clothes like tiny frozen fingers as alley-stench tweaked his nose hairs.

A lone dumpster and mounds of trash decorated the dark alley and the valley between the back of low-income apartment buildings. A lonely pole spotlighted the gang, and the light attached to it buzzed like an energetic strobe light.

The darkness became Kevin's camouflage, the shadows, his weightless cloak. In all black, the group snapped to attention at his initial whistle but didn't see him until he stepped from the shadows.

Their frowns, sharp-eyed glares, stiff postures, and defensive stances spoke for them. Not appreciating him disturbing their party, the group drew weapons. One aimed a gun, while the others wielded knives and a bat spiked with nails. With this selection of weapons, Kevin questioned if he'd been transported back to the eighties.

Kevin hadn't holstered a gun before leaving his room. His confidence led him to believe he could challenge this group without one. His first objective, disarm the man with the gun. The darkness prevented him from getting into their heads to use their senses against them, so he would have to rely on his training.

With only a metal baton in his possession, the odds were stacked against him, but Kevin possessed another weapon that couldn't be seen—his agent's mentality.

His head rocked side to side before he flexed his arms and leg muscles, preparing for battle. He hadn't practiced his hand-to-hand combat in months. This situation was the perfect opportunity to keep his skills fresh without loss of life.

He waited and allowed the man with the gun to approach first. The man didn't stop until the cold metal of the weapon kissed Kevin's temple. The gunman stepped close enough for his rancid breath to reach Kevin's nose.

Kevin returned the cold, metal kiss he received from the man by letting his baton loose against the back of the man's gun hand before he delivered two hard whacks to the side of his head. The licks echoed into the night and mingled with the street noises, and the gun clanked against the pavement and skidded into the darkness. The man's toe-curling scream sounded and made his friends freeze their predatory approach.

Ducking in time, an electrical charge whizzed by Kevin's head. Someone had discharged a Taser. The gang had exhibited the viciousness of warriors at a distance, but their primitive weapons represented their low-level bad-guy mentalities.

Kevin continued to hammer the baton against his opponent's hand, striking the man hard enough the metal vibrated in his hand before the crunch of bone registered. The remaining men jumped Kevin, finally closing the circle around him.

One went stumbling back, gasping for breath and holding his busted nose after a swift uppercut connected with it. The other took a boot to the stomach that folded him enough for the baton to sound off against the back of his head.

One-on-one with the last guy, Kevin's spinning elbow connected with the man's jaw while baton strikes rained down on his head for good measure.

The man who shot the Taser didn't have enough remaining brain cells to stay put. Bending over into a runner's stance, his muscles and jaw tensed as he ran toward Kevin, full force and yelling his agitation.

Kevin saw an opportunity to use the man's own momentum against him, so he spun and delivered a swift roundhouse kick to the man's face.

Sweet dreams.

Kevin paused when he noticed the little guy, the victim, climb the wall like a human spider before he executed an acrobatic jump over to the knife wielder. He sent a swift kick to the man's face while flipping into the air before he faded into the darkness like a puff of smoke.

He reappeared. Had he morphed from another dimension before taking out the gunman who managed to limp

back to his feet? Again, the guy took out his bigger opponent and disappeared like a spray of dark mist.

The search for the casualty in this situation was point-
less. However, Kevin was no longer concerned about the
would-be bad guys.

How had the victim in all this gotten to the knife
wielder and gunman so swiftly without them even knowing which direction he came from or that he was even
coming at them?

It wasn't lost on Kevin that the prey possessed skills
he should have used against the gang earlier in their attack. Had he been suppressing his ability to fight back for
a reason Kevin was unaware of?

Now that he no longer had a visual of the person he'd
come to help, Kevin marched away from the alley without
a backward glance. The chorus of groans that followed
him brought a proud smile to his face. The sound of assholes in agony was music to his ears.

His smile grew at an idea that popped into his head.
*Assholes in Agony. Wouldn't that be a good title for a
song?*

Like something from an eighties Sci-fi flick, the
speedy little wall climber who was being attacked earlier
appeared from thin air and trotted alongside Kevin as
though he'd been there the whole time. No sound or warn-
ings alerted Kevin to his abrupt approach, and the trick
had Kevin glancing around to see where this guy could
have been hiding to make such a dramatic appearance.

Was that it? Did this guy have a gift? One that allowed
him to do what normal society deemed impossible? In the
world in which Kevin operated, nothing was impossible

anymore. He gave his surroundings another once over before he dropped his intrigued gaze on the one walking next to him.

The streetlights gave Kevin a better look at the guy. Bruises and scrapes decorated his face revealing clear evidence of his encounter with the would-be bad guys: Assholes in Agony. The guy was young. He couldn't have been more than sixteen or seventeen, a kid.

Kevin stared at him. "What did you do to make them want to kick your ass? And please, don't tell me you wanted into that piece of shit gang of theirs."

He glimpsed more bruises and lacerations about his head and neck. He was Hispanic and wore his dark hair in cornrows, braided straight back.

"I didn't need your help. I could have taken care of myself," he replied, his tone dry and nonchalant.

Not one to hold his tongue, Kevin shot a sharp glare at him.

"From the looks of things, you were having your ass handed to you. Excuse the hell out of me for not standing by while you got your ass kicked or worse."

The kid didn't reply this time, and the sound of their footfalls echoed off the pavement, the steps in harmony with the sound of the city blaring around them.

The guy leaned in, edging closer to glance at Kevin's face before he swiftly backed away.

Kevin sat a hand on his baton while keeping an eye on this weird guy, unsure of what to make of him.

"I apologize if I sound ungrateful, but believe it or not, I was working," he said, his tone low and smooth.

Kevin's brow lifted while his head tilted in doubt. "I don't understand how getting your ass kicked constitutes working."

"I'm undercover. I do the same kind of work you do," he replied.

His statement made Kevin cagey, twitchy. He glanced around to make sure no one walking past them had heard his claims.

"I don't know who the hell you are or what you think you know, but I don't know you, and you definitely don't know me or anything about what I do."

The guy glanced around this time before speaking.

"I'm on assignment. Tango Bravo six-two-one-eight, which means you're on the Tango Charlie assignment. They mentioned in the briefing that there would be another agent nearby, but I didn't know we'd be working damn near on top of each other."

Kevin understood now. The series of phonetic letters and numbers was like an assignment fingerprint as far as TOP was concerned.

They stared at each other while trekking further away from the alley, where the gang were likely scraping themselves up to make their way to the street.

"You stepped on my assignment. I was getting initiated on purpose. Although those guys aren't that bright, they don't trust easily. I was hoping I could use my charm to gain intel on my case from that gang before taking an ass-kicking, but it didn't work out," he admitted.

"Look, man, I apologize. I'll do whatever you need to get you back on track with your assignment. I was made aware of another agent, but it never occurred to me that it was you. No offense, but you look…young."

He chuckled. "Looking young plays a major part in most of my disguises. Creating realistic disguises is one of my specialties."

Kevin knew now how the guy had pulled off those amazing moves in the alley. In the agent world, they all possessed a set of skills; and this guy had moves hidden up his sleeves as well as his claim on disguises.

He shoved his hands in his pockets and continued to walk along in silence.

"You don't have to do anything special concerning my assignment. I already have a backup plan," he finally replied to Kevin's offer.

His nonchalant tone made Kevin do a double take at him.

"You aren't mad that I screwed up your job? How long have you been working on those guys? What do you go by anyway? I'm Kevin, but most people call me K."

"I go by Kris. This is day five, and I've spent about a half day with those guys. Believe me, this case is a bit of a puzzle. Lost a victim yesterday, and the last thing I want is to see another round of the boxes they arrive in."

Boxes?

Kevin's brows tightened, but he didn't reply.

"So far, the only lead I had from the victim's background led me back to this place, his old neighborhood and gang. With no solid leads, I'll do whatever it is I need to do to find answers. I'm usually doing wet work or breaking into and out of places, you know, a shooter, even a lock picker, not an investigator. As much as I hate to admit it, I do need the experience. I just made two years, so I presume TOP expects more from me now."

In their world, two years was a lifetime. If you survive that long as a TOP agent, you were deemed capable of surviving anything. TOP didn't hold back, either. They threw you into the lion's den and expected you to come out with the lion's head.

Kevin reduced his pace, wary of leading Kris to his room.

"Well, Kris. I'll be honest with you. If you'd messed up my job, I'd be mad as hell, and you would be helping me find a solution."

He shrugged. "I should have come up with a better plan in the first place. I'm glad you stopped it, but if you want to help me out, I could use a little patching up. I may need a few stitches in my back."

Kevin stared at the battered man, contemplating his decision despite believing his claim of being an agent.

"Sure, man," he decided. "It's the least I can do."

Kevin led Kris into his motel room, allowing him to walk into the room first, still skeptical about him. Kris shrugged off his jacket and walked to the mirror in the little entranceway leading into the bathroom. He rubbed his shoulder and winced.

"How good are you at stitching?"

In their line of work, it wasn't unusual to patch yourself up, continue the assignment, and seek medical attention later, if you needed it.

Kevin shrugged. "I'm not an expert, but I have gotten some practice. If you're worried about the cosmetics of it, I'm not your guy."

Kris shook his head and turned his lip up, his attempt at being macho, Kevin supposed. The T-shirt he wore was dirty, torn, and bloody.

Kevin fumbled around in his bag and took out a clean, white wife-beater that he handed to Kris.

"Put that on. I'll get the needle and thread ready."

Kris accepted the shirt. "Can I use your bathroom?"

Kevin pointed. "Yeah, man, no problem."

Staring oddly at the shirt in his hand, Kris headed into the bathroom.

CHAPTER EIGHT

Kevin

Kevin was hard at work on his laptop when Kris exited the bathroom.

"Are you ready to sew me up?"

Thrown off by the change in Kris's voice, Kevin automatically reached for his weapon before he spun.

The voice came from a pecan-brown-skinned, model-slim woman. She raised one hand since the other gripped the waistband of the pair of oversized jeans that threatened to slide down her small frame if she let go.

Kevin peeked around the woman for Kris. There wasn't a window in the small bathroom. Had this woman been in his room the entire time?

"Who the hell are you? How the hell did you get in here?"

He wanted answers and didn't care about the order in which they were given. The woman pursed her lips like she was suppressing a smile despite him aiming his gun in her direction.

"Kevin, it's me, Kris. It occurred to me when I headed into the bathroom that I should have informed you that my ability to disguise myself can be extensive. It's my specialty and one of the reasons Top recruited me."

Kevin wasn't convinced, so Kris used the male voice he was familiar with, which freaked him out, and made him continue to brandish his weapon. After a minute of staring, Kevin lowered his gun but didn't put it away. He slinked toward the woman who claimed she was Kris.

She stood motionless, allowing him to determine whether he would trust what she claimed was true. He gawked while taking her in, his lips parted. Periodically, he would glance into the bathroom, expecting the real Kris to exit.

A moment ago, he was sure Kris was a young man. Everything about him read male. Now, he, she, or whatever the hell they were, was gone and long, wavy red hair hung over her shoulders. Her skin even appeared darker than it was before. The light caramel complexion was now a smooth brown.

Kevin sensed a woman now, which had him questioning his ability. His senses were his strength. They allowed him to see, hear, taste, smell, and feel what others couldn't. There was no mistaking that this version of Kris was now a woman. How had she hidden that from him earlier?

Three times Kevin circled her, his gaze sweeping her from head to toe. His shuffling feet and the hum of the heating unit in the background beat back the eerie silence that filled the room.

"I have questions."

Kris smiled.

"Shoot," she said. "Well, maybe that's not the right word, considering you drew your gun on me. Ask your questions, and I'll answer as best I can."

"Are you a woman or a boy? How the hell did you change your skin? Your face? I've seen disguises but nothing like that—this. You had the face of a teen boy. You were a different person. My senses rarely fail me. I am sure you were a different person."

"I'm a woman. This is truly me. As I mentioned before, I'm sort of what others consider a master at disguises. It's easier to pretend to be a male since I've done so for many years in about seventy percent of my assignments."

Kevin tilted his head and let his gaze sweep her from a different angle. He gripped her shoulders and squeezed. Kris stood still and let him inspect her.

She was slender but definitely all woman. Her features were elegant and delicate enough that he understood her need to disguise herself as a man.

She couldn't have been taller than five-two, but she stood on a sturdy frame that radiated strength. Her adorable brown eyes never stopped smiling despite the pensive facial expression he knew he flashed her. He found it difficult to understand how such a beautiful woman had transformed into a man.

"Is this your natural skin? Face? Body? The *you* who was born and grew up?"

She nodded.

"I can tell that you aren't one to be fooled easily, but this is me, all naturally me. There aren't many people who have seen me without one of my disguises. Since you're a fellow agent, I'm hoping to get stitched up without making a trip to the hospital. As I'm sure you know, the agency and the civilian hospitals ask too many questions and need too much paperwork. Plus, I couldn't get stitches while in disguise as it would pose a major problem."

Kevin's gaze roamed over her body while attempting to figure her out. She had to be a shifter, a supernatural being that he learned in his training that no longer existed.

Kris kept calling it a disguise, but there was only one thing that he knew of that could become a whole other person. And was it just him or was she avoiding saying what she was?

"I apologize for staring, but you made such a convincing guy. It's hard to believe that...he was—is—you."

She bit her lip to hide a smile before she stepped away and headed to the sink to stand in front of the mirror.

"I have worked with other agents numerous times, and each time, they believe it is the first," she said, sounding proud of her ability to trick people into thinking she was someone else.

"Now, I understand why you weren't worried that I messed up your assignment. You can regroup and transform yourself into another guy?"

It was more of a question than a statement. In other words, could she wear any face and body she wanted?

She checked out the coffeemaker he used to heat water and glanced back.

"Believe it or not, I've screwed up a few of my assignments and was fortunate to have recovered them. Can't make the same mistake twice, right?"

He nodded, continuing to track her every move as she sterilized the needle and thread. It should have been his task since he would be sewing her up, but he continued to reel over her ability to become another person. He dropped his eyes when she glanced up in the mirror and caught him staring.

Her face twisted in amusement. "I don't blame you for staring. As I said, only you and a few others know my true identity."

Kevin inclined his head before he dragged a chair to the vanity so she could sit. Agent or not, what did she see in him to make her want to trust him with her identity?

The more he stared, the more he appreciated her as a woman. Kris was gorgeous. The lighter-brown flecks sparkling in her big brown eyes complimented her soft and delicate features, and her wearing his wife-beater didn't help his admiring eyes. She was slender with enough curves to get major attention, and her beauty was undeniable.

He washed his hands before he eased into her personal space to get a better look at the wound. She slid her hand inside the shoulder of the sleeve and slipped it down, revealing a large gash on the back of her shoulder.

She was right about needing stitches. The deep and jagged cut had blood glistening at the surface and waiting to spill over.

The shirt fit loose on her, allowing him to see a large portion of her back.

"I don't see any other scars. Is this your first injury?" His hand automatically skimmed across her skin, making her jump.

"I've had many scars, been stabbed and shot, but my scars heal clean."

His forehead creased. He'd never known gunshots or stab wounds to heal *this* cleanly, human or other. He carried wounds he'd take to his grave. His hand hovered over the lightning-strike-shaped gash that opened her shoulder.

"This one will definitely leave a scar."

When she lifted the shirt to fully expose her back, the loose fit, combined with the mirror, gave him a glimpse of her perfect round tits. She adjusted the shirt quickly and settled it over her chest before she dropped her head. Her cheeks had flashed a reddish tint indicating that her little peep show wasn't intentional.

Kevin cleared his throat. "How's your pain tolerance?"

The mirror revealed her smile and he couldn't tell if it was real or forced.

"I was about to take a beating to gain headway on my assignment. Need I say more?"

"No," he answered.

He reached into the first-aid kit for the peroxide before placing a towel under the wound and pouring the liquid. The peroxide hissed and sizzled, eating away what didn't belong. Kevin glanced in the mirror at Kris, impressed that she didn't move. Instead, she closed one eye, gritted her teeth, and endured the sting.

Once satisfied that the wound was clean, he picked up the needle and prepared to sew it shut.

With her hand out in front of her on the counter, Kris leaned over it to give him more exposure to her back. Their eyes met and locked each time he glanced at her. When he shoved the needle's point through her skin, a small frown twisted her face, but she didn't cry out. It was like she was testing to see how much pain she could endure.

Since the needle wasn't curved, Kevin used his fingers to pinch her skin together and hold it in place before pushing the needle through each stitch. After his third pass, their gazes met again.

"You do have a high pain tolerance," he pointed out.

Her smile made his gaze linger on her lips. "Can you tell this isn't my first rodeo?" she asked.

He looped the thread through her skin once more and tied off the end.

"I can tell," he replied while tying the thread twice more to ensure it kept the wound closed.

"I'm nearly finished," he announced.

He didn't have a pair of scissors to cut the thread, so he used the next best thing—his teeth, which landed his lips on her warm, bare skin in the process. The sensation the touch gave him made him pause. Her skin was soft, supple, and inviting. It wasn't until she inched her shoulder up that he jerked his head back.

"Sorry."

What the hell is wrong with me?

***
Kris

Usually turned off by any form of intimacy, Kris found that she enjoyed Kevin's lips on her.

Hmmm?

The sensation was odd but enjoyable and soothing in a way that it made her close her eyes until wisps of his breath on her skin made a chill run up her back.

She didn't speak about their connection, but she'd noticed it the moment she'd glanced into his face, perfectly tanned, the glow from the lights had reflected off his skin earlier. She had never contemplated a man like this, but her gaze swept the expanse of Kevin's tall, medium-built frame while he dug around in the first aid kit.

Dismissing ideas of his splendid features, she picked up the hand mirror and glanced at his handiwork.

"Ever considered becoming a doctor?" she asked.

He flashed perfect white teeth and a smile that could melt female hearts from miles around. What was his superpower, charming the opposite sex into doing whatever he wanted? She was never like this, especially with someone she didn't know, fellow agent or not.

"No. But I may consider it if my current career doesn't work out," he said.

When she reached to pull his shirt back over her head, he stopped her.

"Wait. I have to cover your wound."

He applied a touch of the outdated antibiotic ointment before covering the wound with gauze and taping it in place. Kris sensed he liked touching her due to how often his hand brushed lingeringly over her back like he wanted everything he did to be perfect.

He had a gentle touch, the delicate strokes leaving the surface of her skin tingling. Although she'd endured worse injuries, most of which she patched up in half the time, she wasn't afraid to admit that she enjoyed the extra attention.

Once he was done with his task, he backed away and turned around to allow her privacy. He turned back when she was finished.

"Let me check your face and those lacerations on your neck," he volunteered.

Her mind said no, but her mouth said, "Okay."

The few lacerations and scratches on her face and neck weren't a concern until he mentioned them. He let his fingers flutter over her cheek before palming her jaw and tilting her head to get a better look at her neck.

"It may sting a bit, but I need to clean these wounds."

She'd gotten caught in the maze of his gorgeous greenish-brown eyes and missed whatever he'd said.

"Hah? Okay."

What was that?

She was never like this with any man but this one: he distracted her. Instant trust had blossomed from the moment she glanced into his eyes on the street. He'd risked his life to save her, a stranger. The act revealed a part of his character.

He cleaned her superficial scrapes with alcohol-soaked swabs. The sting his fingers left on her skin dominated the bite of the alcohol. She closed her eyes to the newest sensation, his fingers sliding along her cheek.

This wasn't anything like her usual wound-cleaning sessions. The pulse point in her neck caught fire and attempted to keep pace with her thundering heartbeat.

Even with her eyes closed, she sensed him staring. When her eyes did flicker open, she found his face inches away from hers, his gaze on her lips and his thumb stroking the tender skin under her bruised eye. She blinked and swallowed the insane impulse to kiss him.

"Are you using some kind of glimmer magic on me or something? I've never seen one, but I do know that other agents hunt vampires."

He chuckled before he lifted his gaze to meet hers. His smile disappeared when their eyes met and locked, and a seriousness akin to burning flames danced in his eyes. The connection flaring between them rocked her to her core. She was helpless to do anything but sit there and stare back into his eyes.

The buzzing flow of energy being exchanged between them made it feel like she was plugged into him. It was a straight shot of living perfection traveling through her body and sparking in her blood.

Her world rocked on its axis. Why were there emotions stirring between them? She didn't know this man, yet this single moment, this distinct event she shared with him, had changed everything she assumed she knew about men.

Her eyes roved left to right, probing his possessive gaze. Whatever this force of nature occurring between them was, it sizzled in her body before it started seeping into her mind.

Kevin's eyes were devastating all on their own, but when he licked his sexy lips, she needed to take a breath or risk suffocating.

Instincts that were new to her insisted she lean in and kiss him, but her mind kept her from making such an insane move. His actions, however innocent, had her leg bouncing against the chair and her fists clenched tight enough for her nails to dig into the palms of her hands. She couldn't turn away, nor could she speak.

"Doesn't look so bad. You're still beautiful."

His words released her from the mesmerizing hold he'd placed on her. Was he flirting? Was that smile on his face his way of letting her know that he knew how much he'd unhinged her? This encounter was weirdly intense and required her to put the brakes on this strange attraction that had risen like a magical storm.

CHAPTER NINE

Kevin

After their magnetic connection was severed, Kevin turned away from Kris and busied himself. He put away the medical supplies and discarded the used gauze. A woman had never affected him like this, making his hands shake and his insides feel like he was stuffed from head to toe with silly putty.

Did Kris know how badly she made him want to kiss her? This was a first, especially this soon. He didn't know anything about this woman. A moments ago she looked like a teen boy.

He glanced back over his shoulder and smiled at her. She'd accused him of being a vampire, but he had questions about her abilities. Was she using her gifts to hypnotize him?

In the few seconds he'd gazed into her eyes, he found more there than he bargained for and experienced emotions foreign to him. Staring into her eyes was like staring into his forever. Like he'd known her way before they'd met tonight, and it had taken everything in him not to kiss her lush, rosy lips. Even now, he couldn't stop imagining her lips sliding against his.

How could this be?

Was she using her ability? If their connection was natural, it was powerful and demanded attention. He turned back to her, more at ease now that they weren't so close.

"Where are you staying?" he asked.

"I have a room about thirty minutes from here in downtown DC."

They were more at ease now, her smile shining through her eyes.

"I know we aren't supposed to talk about our cases, but this one has me at a loss, and I'm at a crossroads of what I need to do to find a suspect," she admitted. Kevin could tell that the admission on her part wasn't easy, but she wasn't too proud to admit that she'd hit a roadblock in her case.

Standing, she began pacing, and he recognized the action as one he practiced when thinking up his next move where it concerned work. His gaze followed her as she trekked toward his bed, thumbing through the menus she'd found.

"Looking at these menu pictures has my stomach roaring. I haven't eaten a decent meal since I started this case."

This being a roach motel, room service wasn't an option. Mobile and many of the other delivery services didn't frequent this area of the city either. Instead, a stack of takeout menus of the few businesses that were brave enough to provide food service was sitting on the cigarette-burned bedside table.

She glanced up from the stack of menus in her hand. "If you don't mind, I'd like to place an order."

He shook his head. "Be my guest."

"Would you like anything?" she asked.

He liked her easy-going spirit. It kept a smile on his face. "I'll take whatever you're having."

She eyed him, and he didn't miss the twinkling smile in her gaze.

"I may not have much by way of body mass, but I have a big appetite," she admitted.

"Are you planning to order an entire menu? How about I take a little of whatever you're having? I'm not that hungry, but the delivery guys don't come out to this area after eight, so I'll take it while I can get it."

Thankfully, she dragged her long-sleeved shirt over his wife-beater. Without a bra, she wasn't helping his blood pressure.

The motel phone had a short in the cord, so she fished around in her jeans and withdrew her cell. He lifted an inquisitive brow while listening to her order two club sandwiches, a fried shrimp platter, fish and chips, a slice of pecan pie, a piece of cheesecake, and two large lemonades.

Where was she going to put all that food?

She swiped her phone off and smiled at his raised brow and questioning glint. She shrugged.

"I have a big appetite, and I don't cook, so when I have a chance to eat, I overindulge."

He nodded. Her ordering food meant she was sticking around longer. Not that he intended to put her out now that they were getting to know each other. So far, her company has been enjoyable. Moreover, she was a fellow agent he could share things with that he couldn't tell others.

They weren't supposed to engage each other as they were on assignment. They were breaking a significant rule in the agent handbook, but it wasn't the first time, nor would it be the last time he ignored the rules. He turned back to her.

"You don't have to leave if you don't want to. Not that you can't handle yourself, but it gets wild out there at night, even for people like us. This room is huge, and I don't mind sleeping on the couch."

The room wasn't huge at all. The couch he mentioned sat on rickety legs with thread bare upholstery and sunken seat pillows. It wasn't long enough for him to stretch out his six-foot-two frame. Kris stared around the space, likely thinking the obvious.

"I don't want to invade your space, especially not while you're on an active case. So, I'll get out of your hair after I eat."

He shrugged. "The offer is open if you'd like to stay."

In the back of his mind, the chant grew louder.

Stay. Stay. Stay.

***

After the food arrived, they sat at the wobbly table, ate, and shared a few agent war stories. Kris had worked in some of the same agent circles as him.

She lifted her pecan pie, offering him a bite. "You want some?"

He accepted her offer by reaching across the table and sticking his fork into her pie. His interactions with her were natural, almost an automatic reflex, like they've always known each other.

He couldn't recall how they broached the current subject, but he'd never laughed so hard as Kris expressed, in exaggerated movements, the ways of men. The lazy slouch, the hand shoved into the top of the pants, the way they fingered their facial hair, even if there wasn't any.

"I learned from studying you all on television," she said.

"You learned how to be a man from television? "

She shrugged. "Not only television. I study you guys in passing and during everyday interactions. It's not hard to copy your mannerisms and, often, men, not all of you, but most have one-track minds."

She'd captured his interest now. "Give me an example."

She stood. "Gladly."

Getting into character, she stuck out her chest and somehow managed to slouch at the same time.

"Whenever a pretty woman walks by, men's eyes always stray. Heck, the woman doesn't even have to be pretty as long as she's got two lumps on her chest and a curve to her backside. I've seen guys pretend like they're stretching to get a peek."

She demonstrated the exaggerated stretch move, her arms over her head, as her eyes followed the invisible butt she eyeballed.

A telling laugh tugged at the corners of his lips and he dropped his gaze, guilty of doing what she described.

"I have even seen men knock things over, shift their eyes to extreme positions, and even grip their foreheads and peek through their fingers."

Kris whipped her head, stretched her neck, and widened her eyes to show how men reacted to women. He admitted that some of it, but Kris exaggerated on purpose, to make her monologue comical.

"Seriously, a man could be talking to the president about a terrorist invading the White House, and his attention could still be pulled away in a flash if tits and a nice ass catch his eye."

She twisted her top while talking, which outlined her tits, and proved her point. Kevin's eyes went directly to her chest. He laughed while covering his face and shaking his head.

She released her top and sent him a teasing smirk.

"Now, do you understand why I can pull it off so easily? All I have to do is lose focus, adjust my balls, and grab my package every once in a while."

She stood, adjusted her non-existent balls, and allowed her eyes to chase an invisible ass. Kevin could tell at a glance that Kris enjoyed making him laugh. The rapport they were building induced good vibes that stirred around them like something touchable. He already hoped he could see her again.

"Seriously, it's like guys aren't even aware that they're touching their junk. It's like your hand hovers there, gravitates there like it's going to—all of a sudden—get up and walk away."

Kevin couldn't recall the last time he just laughed.

Kris continued. "Trust me. You don't want me to tell you some of the pickup lines I've learned."

Kevin threw up his hands. "No, I don't think I want you to do that."

The teasing session died down when Kris stretched and stifled a yawn.

"I think I may take you up on your offer to stay. I'm more tired than I thought."

He liked that idea. "Of course. Stay and get some rest."

She flashed him an unreadable expression, her eyes zeroing in on him and squinting slightly.

"I'll stay if you sleep with me."

Lips drifting apart, Kevin was unsure how to reply. She'd come off more conservative than her words suggested.

His slack-jawed expression must have made her aware of her unintentional suggestion.

"What kind of a girl do you think I am?" she proclaimed, failing to keep a straight face. "I'm not talking about *that*. Didn't we just have a discussion about guys and their one-track minds?"

Kevin laughed.

She pointed at the bed. "We can share that huge bed."

Now, she talked of things being huge when they weren't. The bed was ordinary, not big or small.

"I don't want to put you out of your bed. Besides, we're agents. We've slept in way more compromising and bizarre places than with each other. I have spent nights in male lockups with my face in the dirty armpits of drunks. I've had to sleep with addicts who were desperate enough to steal my kidney to sell it if I weren't a light sleeper."

"Good point," he agreed. He pointed at his laptop. "I have a few things I need to finish up. Make yourself comfortable and relax."

***
Kris

Kris wished Kevin a good night before she dropped her jeans and climbed into his bed. Had she truly climbed into his bed? A man she hardly knew. The idea of how long they had known each other kept popping up in her head despite how comfortable she was with him.

The connection was a first time experience, one that had her mind twisting and twirling constantly. The instant trust surpassed her comprehension. She should have left, but the longer she stuck around, the more she wanted to stay.

She was using being tired as an excuse, but her training and conditioning taught her to push through fatigue like it was no more than an irritating side effect that could easily be suppressed.

Kevin put meaning to the words tall, dark, and handsome. His bright green-brown eyes were the icing on the cake.

She twisted and turned on the lumpy mattress until she found the perfect position on her side. She sensed his eyes on her every move. After a horrific sexual assault as a teen, it had taken her years to figure out how to be near a man, let alone closed off alone in a room with one. Some issues remained, but her training and confidence had reconditioned her mentality.

Her past fears were one of the main reasons she learned the art of disguising as a man so perfectly. Taking on the identity of a man alleviated her from having to deal with men on a personal level, and a man's physical features didn't usually linger on her mind like they were doing now.

She couldn't help acknowledging her secret attraction to the wickedly handsome Kevin. He was different. In the way he felt and interacted with her. If a woman didn't take the time to admire him, it would be her loss. He reminded her of a handsome Arabian prince. His five o'clock shadow added to his rugged handsomeness.

She imagined raking her fingers through his head of dark, silky hair and getting lost in his deep-set, hazel eyes that looked brown one moment and green the next.

His penetrating gaze, if she let him, could hold her hostage and plant lustful thoughts into her mind. His mouth could make a girl swoon if she caught him licking those sexy full lips of his. All of those splendid features were set on a handsome face with a well-defined jaw.

She was ready to fight him in the alley for interrupting her until she saw his face. As if his features weren't enough to stop a woman in her tracks, he exuded a charm and calmness that made her want to linger in his presence.

Before she drew the covers up, she glanced down at herself. Maybe the lemonade had been spiked, or perhaps the cheesecake had been laced with drugs. She was obviously high and drunk at the same time. She'd never done anything this reckless and unpredictable and was virtually naked, in nothing but his wife-beater and her boxers.

Had she been hit upside the head harder than she assumed?

She barely admitted the weakness to herself let alone to anyone else, but men usually made her nervous, especially if they expressed an interest in anything other than casual conversation. It was an unpleasant emotion she had learned to hide well.

She was naturally more at ease with other agents, male or female, but this thing with Kevin was unsettling and comfortable at the same time. An exhilarating spark of chemistry constantly teased her senses. Although a new experience, the impacting hold it had on her roared blatantly enough that it couldn't be ignored.

Kevin had instantly sparked an understanding between them that she couldn't explain, and every action he projected said she could trust him.

***

Kevin

Kevin stole glances at the mysterious agent in his bed. The moment she revealed her identity and he truly took her in, he never stopped admiring her. He wanted to know everything about her: her name, interests, her loves and hates. Everything.

The day proved to be a long grueling one. Sleep beckoned, but nothing called as loudly as the woman that made his heart pound fast and overloaded the circuits of his brain. He crept quietly to the bed and stood, admiring her. Surprisingly, he found no signs of the agent he now knew her to be, just this beautiful delicate woman who didn't appear capable of doing the things required of a TOP agent.

Her chest rose and fell in a measured cadence, chasing her breaths. The relaxed expression on her face reflected peace.

Kevin walked around to her side of the bed to turn off her lamp before returning to his side and climbing in. Although being careful, the cheap and rickety mattress jiggled, and the springs popped and cried until he settled.

***

Kris

"Are you asleep?" Kris whispered.

She sensed his smile shining through the dark.

"No. Why?"

The mattress springs groaned and dug into her side as she turned to see him better.

"I don't know. I'm awake, and, as much as I shouldn't admit this, it's good to be around someone who understands me. That knows who I am and what I do."

She caught a glimpse of the smile that creased the corners of his mouth before he turned and closed more of the space between them.

"Is that your way of saying you like me?"

She avoided his question with a burst of laughter.

"I'm saying you're easy to talk to and enjoyable to be around."

"I enjoy you as well," he replied. "Most people are so irritating, but you, I like."

She went silent. The way he said he *liked* her. More was hidden within the depth of those words. Was she reading too much into this?

Their conversation carried on until well past midnight. No subject was off limits. The more they talked, the more their bodies gravitated toward each other.

As Kevin talked, Kris stole glances at him and vice versa. She finally revealed a short snippet of the Box case in which she currently worked. His face bunched, his eyes going up in thought.

"Even after two years, it's highly unusual for TOP to place an agent on a case outside their element without a partner. However, with the big rise in unexplained crimes, I could understand putting a TOP agent on the case versus the locals. I'm intrigued. I wish I could help you with it," he said.

She wished the same but didn't comment. As TOP agents, their jobs entailed learning and adapting to new and dangerous situations, not creating them.

Kris remained silent to allow Kevin to sleep. She noticed the weariness in his eyes earlier and would no longer be selfish with his time. A glance at his bedside clock displayed 2:06 a.m.

While Kevin slept, Kris rose at the first sign of the sun peeking through the dingy lopsided curtains. After she sneaked into her clothes, she stood in place and stared at him. She wanted to remember every detail of the first man she'd voluntarily spent the night with.

She decided to keep his wife-beater on to have something tangible to remember him by. After one last glance, she strolled away from his sleeping form and drifted away from him as quickly as he'd entered her life.

CHAPTER TEN

Yala

How did investigative agents solve any of their cases? A substantial number of questions lingered in Yala's mind as she brainstormed ways to approach the case.

Blessedly, she finally received the update she was waiting for. The one informing her that her partner would arrive soon. She prayed for someone like Kevin. If not, at least someone willing to give actionable insights that could help track down a suspect and prevent another innocent victim from ending up in one of those boxes.

"Hello," she answered her phone, noticing it was Dr. Hughes.

"We have another box. This time it's the head first. Same instructions."

She released a deep sigh, shaking her head.

"I'm on my way," she replied before hanging up. While she drove toward the medical examiner's office, she prepared her mind to scrutinize a head in a glass death box.

Twenty minutes later, she was sure she was walking into the beginning of the apocalypse when she saw a living head inside a glass box. Dr. Hughes had also thought it best to pull in another doctor for assistance.

Dr. William Pendergast, like Dr. Hughes, had connections to TOP and possessed experience, specifically in hard-to-explain cases.

***

Kevin

Kevin couldn't let go. Every stray thought involved Kris. Therefore, he called the one person he knew who could find answers when he couldn't.

Sori, his friend and fellow agent, answered on the first ring. "Hi, K. What's up?"

Sori had worked with him on several occasions and preferred to call him by one of the code names he went by—K. Beautiful and unpredictable, she was one of the deadliest and most dangerous agents he'd partnered with.

While most people feared her penchant for death and destruction, Kevin managed to see through the electrified fence she threw around herself and earned her friendship.

He relayed the story of accidentally crossing paths with Kris. He also told her the bizarre details about the Box case. However, he left out the part about Kris spending the night with him.

Sori's exceedingly long pause filled the silence after the story.

"Why are you telling me this? Are you requesting to be partnered with her?" she finally answered with a question of her own.

He stifled a smile, although she couldn't see it.

"I was thinking maybe I could work with her since I interrupted her case. I'll be finished with my current case by tonight or tomorrow."

Sori remained silent for so long that he removed the phone from his ear and glanced at it to make sure the call hadn't dropped. He'd work with many partners, but had never asked for one and therefore didn't doubt his request had thrown her off guard.

Her voice returned, easing his mind.

"Since you're one of the few people I like in this world, I'll see what I can do. I know Kris. If you think she needs help, and she admitted as much, I'll definitely do what I can."

His smile couldn't be helped. "I'll appreciate anything you can do."

"Yep," was the last word she uttered.

Sori was gone.

One thing he loved about Sori, she didn't waste unnecessary words or actions.

***

A day later.

Kevin retrieved his keycard from the front desk and headed to the suite that would serve as his home for an unspecified amount of time. A light traveler, he only had one large bag slung across his back.

His inspection of the suite hadn't turned up his new partner, so he would be in suspense until she arrived. Assigned the downstairs bedroom, he unpacked, showered, and retreated to the living room to await her arrival.

As soon as he began a gradual descent into a nap, a keycard stroked the lock. He snapped up, staring in anticipation, and waited until the door sprang open.

Kevin's heart dropped into the pit of his stomach when a tall Caucasian man entered the suite. He stretched his neck for a better view, unsure if this was one of Kris's elaborate disguises or one of the hotel employees. He fought the tight grip of disappointment long enough to remember his manners.

He stood to greet the man but not before taking a moment to scan him inquisitively. He bore no resemblance to Kris. Kevin forced a smile while introducing himself. The man took his outstretched hand with a firm grip.

"Damien, here for assignment Tango Bravo six-two-one-eight."

At a loss, Kevin peered at the door, hoping Kris would walk through it. The agent who briefed him hadn't mentioned Kris having a replacement. As a matter of fact, the briefing agent assured him that Kris would fill in on the specific details of the case to get him up to speed.

Fingers to his lips, eyes focused on nothing, Kevin's inner dialogue came alive, arguing over whether it was Kris or truly another agent. "I'd like to take a quick shower before discussing the case," Damien said.

"Of course," Kevin replied before he fell back onto the couch. His body slumped in defeat. He desperately wanted to reunite with the beautiful Agent Kris. Surely she would have already revealed herself if she had been fooling him with one of her disguises. He released a heavy sigh, relaxed on the couch, and flipped the television to a sports channel.

***

Kevin drifted in and out of sleep until the sound of Damien's footsteps descending the stairs alerted his approach. His eyes didn't stir away from the television until Damien stepped in front of his view.

When he glanced up and found Kris smiling at him, he froze, struggling to sit upright as the soft couch cushions kept pulling him back. Kris hovered above him with a smile plastered across her beautiful face. She wore a comfortable long-sleeved, flannel-blue pajama set and a sneaky grin.

"Close your mouth before it gets stuck like that. You look like you've seen a ghost," she teased.

Kevin asked the obvious. "How the hell did you do that? I was convinced you weren't him." He stood and peered at Kris. His gaze locked on her while awaiting an answer.

She may as well have been a big-screen television on a sales display. He got up close and personal, this time checking for an Adam's apple and any other telltale signs of a man. His inspection had Kris laughing out loud.

"I hoped I'd get to see you again," he admitted, not hiding his desire.

He paused to take her in fully. His smile started at his eyes and inched down his face to his mouth. "You embody the male persona better than most men, to the point that I can't tell the difference. You were at least six feet and muscular, your hair short, and you even had a five o'clock shadow. There is more to your disguises than meets the eye. I am sure of it now."

Kris maintained her smile. "Like I mentioned before, I have spent most of my career posing as a man. I know how to imitate you guys well.

"I've noticed, but there is something else you're not telling me," Kevin insisted.

He wagged his finger at her and continued to eye her suspiciously. He refused to fall for her flimsy explanation this time. Imitating a man was one thing, but being one involved something entirely different.

"Are you going to tell me your secret or leave me in suspense? You can't leave me hanging like this."

Kris flopped onto the couch, avoiding his question. He joined her, sitting close enough that the warmth of her body radiated into his. He refused to give up until she revealed something.

"Will you share your disguise secret with me? Please," he begged with his lip poked out.

She flashed a cheeky smile. "Maybe. If you share your secret with me. I'm sure that I'm not the only one who thinks that all TOP agents are touched; by what? I have no idea. But I'm not blind."

Kris' 'wow factor' captivated him more fiercely than Kevin remembered. She didn't have to do anything special to attract his attention. Her presence alone took possession of it. Despite voicing his opinion on the matter, he did agree with her statement about TOP agents. The agency guarded an agent's secrets like they were their own and only released information on a need-to-know basis, especially where it concerned the unique abilities of its agents.

Kris's beautiful red hair was pulled into a messy ponytail, opening the doorway to her big, adorable eyes.

"I'm sorry for staring, but it's difficult not to. It's not every day I see a six-foot Caucasian man transform into someone as beautiful as you."

He didn't miss the tint of color that flooded her brown cheeks from his compliment. She cleared her throat. "Thank you."

Under her breath, she said, "One track mind," before she smiled and asked, "Do you promise to show me yours if I show you mine?"

His eyes widened.

"Show you my what?" He dragged the words out like he didn't know what she was talking about because he wanted to be sure.

"You want to know the secret to my disguises. I want to know why I've been so at ease with you from the moment we met. I sense that there is something different about you, but I can't imagine what it may be. Are you willing to share?"

He nodded, his smile growing wider.

"Definitely."

CHAPTER ELEVEN

Kevin

Kevin placed his hands atop his knees and concentrated on calming his revved-up anticipation. The idea of finding out what he believed would be a fascinating secret about Kris had him fidgety and cracking his knuckles while his leg bounced.

Kris sat immobile, contemplating what she wanted to reveal. Finally, she sucked in a deep breath and released it slowly. "I thought I was ready, but I've never done this in front of anyone. I don't know if I can do this right now," she said.

Kevin sat a gentle hand atop hers and found it shaking.

"Whatever you share will always remain with me. I'll never push you into doing anything that you don't want to. If you're not ready, I respect your decision," he said, keeping his eyes trained on hers until she acknowledged his words with a nod.

"Maybe, you should go first," she suggested.

He took her hand, enjoying the warm softness.

"You don't look like a screamer, but I'll say this anyway. Don't scream and keep an open mind about what I'm about to show you."

"Okay," she answered. A high level of uncertainty reflected in that one word.

Silence filled the room for a heart-snatching moment before he instructed, "Close your eyes, please."

She closed them, but the trembling in her body increased, revealing her level of anticipation.

Time dragged by. The air and all that surrounded them were frozen in time.

"Now, open your eyes, Kris," Kevin said, breaking the tension apart.

***

Kris

When Kris opened her eyes, she was staring into a mirror.

Wait!

Her gaze darted around the room and back at herself. She slammed her eyes shut and peeled them back open.

"Kevin, what's happening? I'm sitting on the couch, looking at myself. Where are you? I know you said not to scream, but is having a heart attack out of the question? I just saw myself rub my eyes."

"Look down," Kevin instructed.

He talked, but she couldn't see him, yet she sat and watched as her own mouth moved in the reflection from the mirror.

She held her hands up for balance but couldn't see them. The sensation gave her a strange sense of vertigo. "I need a moment."

The mouth under her eyes in the reflection wasn't hers. A glance down showed Kevin's body. Her eyes viewed things, not from within her body but from inside his head. At least, that's what she could gather from her disorientated state. Seeing herself react as her face expressed the fright she harbored had her closing her eyes repeatedly.

"Kevin. Please tell me what's happening. Am I inside your body? I'm freaking out right now."

"I traded sight with you." He calmly voiced. "You can see through my eyes, and I can see through yours."

She screwed her face up, and her forehead tightened.

"But. I feel myself. When I lift my hand, I know I'm lifting it. I know that my leg is bouncing because I feel it. "

His voice remained calm and relaxing as he squeezed her hand.

"Kris, whatever you do, don't stand; stay in place."

Her muscles clenched, and her mind trembled in anticipation of what might happen if she did move.

When Kevin stood and began walking, she stilled on the couch; but her sight didn't remain on the couch with her. She stared back at herself before swiveling around to scan the bathroom, the kitchen, and finally, outside into the hall. It was one of the freakiest moments she'd experienced.

Kevin had anchored her vision to his body. Wherever he walked, she saw it like her eyes were traveling around the room without her body. She clung to her unraveling sanity as she forced her body to stay put and not chase her sight. Hands, she couldn't see, clinched her knees so tightly that her fingers raked her kneecaps.

The sensation of walking inside a dream overtook her mind, and her body swayed. Kevin glanced in her direction, and she saw herself sitting on the couch from the doorway. She fidgeted, a ball of raging energy on the verge of overload.

Kevin approached the window and called back to her. "I'm going to turn on double vision. Again, don't get up because you'll have vertigo until you're used to it."

"Don't worry. I'm too afraid to even lean in either direction."

Double vision must have meant getting her eyes back because she could see from her own body again. Panic took a quick U-turn, and her heart skipped several beats when she could also see the view outside the window. "Oh, my God! It's not possible."

Her hand waved absently in front of her, thinking she was within reach of the window.

"You can make me see from two different bodies at the same time? It's almost like I'm hallucinating."

Closing one eye, she saw everything in the living room, and from the other, she peered at the view outside the window. Kevin had taken her eyes on the journey of a lifetime. When he returned to the couch and returned her sight to normal, Kris took a much-needed deep breath.

Kevin explained, "It's like I have an extra sense. I don't know what it is or where it came from, but it allows me to manipulate my other five senses in unique ways. For example, I can trade and share sight with people or sneak a peek from behind their eyes without them noticing. Comes in handy when I need to catch a killer or see the keypad code to a secure location or vault."

Kris gawked. "You can do this sort of sensory manipulation with all of your senses?"

"More or less," he replied.

If he could do this much with sight, she couldn't imagine what he could do with his other senses.

"I can also magnify my vision and hearing. I can sense depth and distance from touch. And my eyes aren't all I can swap with others. I can sense what others feel and actually manipulate their moods. It's not as easy as it sounds. I can't take over whenever I want. I have to be touching the person or at least be in close proximity to look into their eyes."

His last statement put a little spark on her nerve endings. Kris leaned closer to gaze into his eyes.

"Have you done that to me? Do you make me feel things I wouldn't on my own?"

He shook his head, and the tenderness behind his gaze calmed her. "I'd never do that to you. You know that, right?"

She nodded, and her eyes fluttered closed when his hand slid tenderly against the side of her neck. Many questions she needed to ask Kevin remained, but they would have to wait. She was too busy getting lost in his gaze.

His voice lured her back to reality. "I can sense a buzz in you and in some others with abilities. It's like your energy signature has an extra weight to it," he said.

That was a clever way of labeling what they sensed in each other. Despite the insightful information, Kris continued to fight to control the tremble in her hand. The idea of revealing her secret to Kevin fueled the raging energy flooding her system.

She drew in a deep breath, her shoulders dropping a few notches as she blew it out. Kris sat taller and concentrated on the wall straight ahead. A tingling sensation climbed up her spine and spread over her body.

The moment her skin rippled, and her bones began to shift, there was no turning back. Kevin gasped, but she couldn't stop mid-shift. While her body twisted uncontrollably, she caught a glimpse of Kevin, inching back on the couch with a hand covering his mouth.

"Oh shit. Oh my God," slipped through his fingers.

He blew out quick breaths to ease his mind because of what he was witnessing. When he regained his ability to speak, he stated the obvious. "You changed into another person right in front of my eyes. You're Damien again."

Kevin stood and sat back down twice, keeping his assessing eyes pinned on her. She reached out to him, and he jumped back. The arm of the couch stopped him.

"You're a shapeshifter! No. It's not real. You can make me see things. There are no such things as shapeshifters. Other than were-animals, aren't human shifters extinct? Wait? Are you a were-animal?

He rubbed his eyes like it would erase what he witnessed.

"How? I mean, it can't be."

Kris cleared her throat. "I'm not sure what I'm called technically or if I'm something that should be extinct. I'm human as far as I'm concerned, no were-animal genetics. But you have to think about both sides of the coin. You took my sight, gave me yours, and walked around this apartment with it. You made me see two different views at the same time. The fact that I can change the way I look is no more amazing. The most mind-blowing thing is that we possess abilities that allow us to do extraordinary things. Besides, it's not like we didn't sense it before now."

She could see the tension leaving his body as his breathing slowed.

"You're right, but to see it happen, to see you change shapes, it's unfathomable, incredible. It's unlike anything I've ever seen up close or experienced. And it wasn't like they portray it in the movies either. You didn't burst out of your clothes. Arms, legs, face, it all slid and maneuvered to where you wanted it."

He stood, but his gaze remained pinned on her as he lowered his voice and leaned in close enough for his breath to whisper across her face. "That's why you're so good with disguises. You can shift. No one else knows that you can do this?"

Worry etched both of their faces.

"Many of those I've worked with sensed I had an ability, but you're the only one whose seen it while it's happening. And based on the way you're looking right now, I'm not sure I should have shown you."

He blew out a quick breath before he scooted closer and took her hand, despite her being disguised as Damien.

"Look, Kris. I'm in shock right now, but please know that I accept you for the many people you are."

He fought the smile teasing his lips, and his attempt at humor had her fighting a smile of her own.

"You know one of my deepest secrets. What now?" she asked.

He lowered his head in contemplation before he answered.

"This stays between me and you always unless you say otherwise," he said, giving her hand a little squeeze.

"Now, we have the freedom to use our gifts to our advantage and solve this case. I appreciate you showing me this more than you could possibly know."

She shifted back to herself, more relaxed now under Kevin's penetrating gaze. She was relieved to know he trusted her enough to share his secret and that she wasn't alone in this emerging world of supernatural powers.

Agents like her and Kevin were hired to stop others like them from releasing their evil intentions on the rest of the world.

Supernatural abilities aside, she could have stared at Kevin all night.

Hours and many conversations later about superpowers and agent war stories, they remained amped up, although they needed to sleep to have refreshed minds for the Box case.

"You have the perfect cover, you know. Do you disguise yourself every day whether you're working or not?"

She brushed her palms over her pajama pants. "This is my first assignment as an investigator. I figured I'd be myself with the doctor and shift when needed. But, to answer your question, no, I don't shift every day."

The way his gaze dashed over her body when he talked made her insides quiver. Kris crossed her arms over her chest when the heat of Kevin's penetrating gaze hit her full force. His lips twitched as he eyed her. Did he sense her shift in mood?

She lost pieces of her calm with each pass of his eyes. Why was she so aware of him all of a sudden?

She couldn't trust her fascination with this man so she simply chalked her reaction up to their heightened adrenaline due to the revelations they exchanged tonight. She cut their personal conversation short by switching the subject to the Box case. The detailed synopsis of the case she furnished to Kevin had his forehead pinch with what appeared to be a mix of intrigue and confusion.

"The doctors, Hughes and Pendergast, received the head of another victim today. I didn't mention it earlier since there isn't much we can do except look at it and wait for the next part of the box."

Kevin nodded, but the V between his brows hinted at his uncertainty.

"Since there are two doctors on the case now, they will call us if they need us before tomorrow. Your fresh insight may uncover details the doctors and I haven't seen or noticed. I also have hours of surveillance footage we can scan. So far, I've had a few shaky leads, but no suspects."

He nodded and kept his expectant gaze pinned on her lips.

"We aren't expecting the second part of the body for roughly another day."

This case had legs and arms and would grow into a whole body with each paragraph she added. Living parts of a whole person at some point in three different places simultaneously. He stared at the ceiling like it would allow the information to soak in faster. Having time to absorb the enormity of this case beforehand was a gift he wasn't taking for granted.

At eleven o'clock, Kris stood.

"It's time for me to call it a night." Her smile met his gaze before her eyes did. "Sleep well, Kevin. I'm looking forward to working with you."

"Night. See you in the morning," he called after her, his gaze lingering until she disappeared from view. He glanced at the cracked door to his bedroom and decided he was fine on the couch.

CHAPTER TWELVE

Kevin

Sleep didn't ease its strong hold on him despite reality seeping into his consciousness. Kevin took in the beautiful face hovering above him while coming fully awake.

"Good morning. Are you hungry?" Kris asked.

He sat up on his elbows. "Good morning, and yes."

"I'm going downstairs to the little café for breakfast. Would you like to join me?"

"Yes. If you don't mind waiting until I freshen up and use the restroom?" he asked.

"No problem. I have to comb my hair and throw on something anyway," She shrugged.

She was still in her pajamas. Kevin reflexively threw back the throw he used for a cover and glanced up at Kris to see if she noticed the bulge in his sweats.

Thankfully, she was already turning away and heading back to her bedroom. He jumped up and sped toward his own bedroom. Glancing back, he flashed a fake smile at Kris, who squinted at his abrupt departure.

Moments later, Kevin returned to the living room with his jacket thrown over his shoulder and dressed in his usual jeans and a fitted T-shirt. Occasionally, he dressed to suit the climate of his assignment but preferred to keep it simple.

When Kris stepped back into the living room, he glanced up, and his eyes got stuck. He swallowed hard. Was she trying to give him a hard-on? She didn't comment on his reaction but drew on a long jacket over the outfit. He'd seen the black leather jumpsuit on other agents due to its built-in protective properties but seeing it on Kris took it to another level of hot. He noticed curves he hadn't gotten a chance to see the first time.

Her hair was brushed back into a neat ponytail. She smiled at him, assessing her. He snapped his fingers, grateful a subject had popped into his head.

"I don't know why I didn't ask you this earlier, but what should I address you as? First, you were Kris, next Damien, and now you're…"

"I'm Agent Kris Lawrence, but you can call me Yala."

He tilted his head, smiled. "Yala. I like it."

He repeated her name several times as they exited their suite.

"So, is Yala your real name or another of your clever disguises?"

Her eyes flashed a mischievous glint and she gave a cheeky grin. "I've told you enough of my business. I ain't telling you, no mo," she said playfully.

He chuckled. Her playful personality was a quality about her that he appreciated. He dropped his eyes when she caught him eyeballing her with interest. When had he turned into a nerdy teen with a crush? Surely she knew he didn't request to be her partner *just* because of the case.

Although the case was an intriguing one, she motivated him to volunteer.

"I see you thinking, Kevin. You can say what's on your mind. I prefer straightforwardness," she said.

He picked his words carefully. "I have never met such a beautiful woman who, based on what you've told me, prefers to portray yourself as a man. As TOP agents, our work schedules are relentless, meaning you're in disguise more often than not."

She lifted a brow but didn't comment right away.

He contemplated asking the following question but went for it anyway.

"Does it mean you prefer the soft peaks and valleys of a woman over the hard rocks and torrents of a man romantically?"

Her cute giggle tickled his eardrum and deepened his smile. She glanced in his direction and motioned her hand in a wavey gesture that portrayed the female form. "I can glide along peaks and valleys if it's necessary to maintain my cover. However, valley liquids are an acquired taste I haven't developed an appetite for."

His brows lifted before his lips slid into an easy smile that deepened as her comments sunk in. Intrigue crept into Kevin's mind. Her smile hadn't disappeared yet. Was she joking, or had she admitted to being with women if it had to be done?

"I prefer men," she stated, dragging his mind back from the gutter in which it was headed.

"I choose to admire most of you from a distance because I've had some unpardonable difficulties with men that make me a bit standoffish."

Kevin wasn't sure how deep down the well her last statement sank, but her cryptic honesty unveiled what could be translated into her wearing man-repellent armor. A man had hurt her, and she wasn't receptive to them much anymore.

"I can respect that," he said. A question was supposed to follow his statement, but he kept it to himself.

"I believe I know what you want to ask me and the answer is no. I don't date. And to answer the other question, which I know you would like to ask but won't because you're a good guy, the answer is also no. Sex is overrated."

Kevin didn't know how to respond to her candor. Her words had also set fire to the notion of his chances of getting to know her better personally.

They entered the café silently, but her last comments remained alive in his head. Despite what she said, his new partner had a depth to her that he craved to explore.

***

An hour later.

They met with the doctors in the exam room, who were already poring over medical and statistical printouts concerning the box and the head inside.

Kevin kept swallowing air in an attempt to digest what he was seeing. The pre-briefing he'd received from Yala last night hadn't fully prepared him for what he saw now.

He'd seen torn-apart bodies, gruesome gunshots, and stabbings, but this was different. There was life here. He sensed it. Seeing a head, not attached to a body, exhibiting normal functions sent a chill racing up his back.

The lips twitched randomly. The eyelids shuddered. The rapid eye movement made the man appear to have fallen into REM sleep, unaware that the rest of his body was missing.

Unconsciousness made it challenging to pinpoint what the man may or may not have felt. Yala and the doctors allowed Kevin as much time as he needed to examine the box, explore, and make his own assumptions and notes.

Yala eyeballed him when he began to sniff. He caught a whiff of something but couldn't discern the spicy and sweet scent.

Upon further scrutiny, he found a fingerprint. Although too faint to pull by conventional means, Kevin sprayed it with a solution he mixed with supplies found around the exam room.

The solution plumped up the lines and grooves of the print, making it visible. After several photos of the fingerprint were taken, he began the process of running them through several databases for a match.

Oddly, the head drew Kevin's attention the most. He inspected it from every angle before pausing to stare with his arms folded over his chest. The sound of Yala clearing her throat caught his attention.

"I believe only someone with a medical background can pull something like this off. The mystery of whatever it is that's keeping him alive is a science I don't yet understand," he said, eyeing the doctor and Yala.

"I think we should backtrack, start with the surveillance footage and conduct a few more interviews.

Sometimes witnesses don't know they're witnesses to anything criminal until you can get them to think deeper and harder."

Yala nodded along with the doctors. For now, he would hang on to his assumption that the scent he detected from the box may have been body oil or cologne.

***

Yala

After the first few interviews, Yala noticed Kevin got much more from the interviewees than she had previously. She'd been in disguise, but apparently, she hadn't chosen a handsome enough man to mimic.

Kevin's empathic ability helped him steer the conversation in his favor, giving him a unique way of manipulating information from people without them even realizing it.

One of the security guards she'd previously spoken to changed his statement, suggesting that the SUV was a smoky gray in color instead of black and that he believed the driver might have been lost. Was he guilty of anything? She prayed they found an answer to the question.

Kevin took advantage of the nurses at the nurse's station. The women took every opportunity to snatch his attention and gawk at him. It didn't take much convincing on his part to get them to share their speculations and volunteer information that had nothing to do with the case.

Vying for his attention, one went as far as to shove another out of the way so she could get her turn to be questioned by him. At the sight of this, Yala excused herself to the bathroom with an eye roll.

When she reappeared on the scene, the hungry eyes of the nurses crept in *Damien's* direction. She fought not to laugh at the sight of Kevin fighting to keep a straight face while asking serious questions and taking in her in male form. He stumbled over what he was saying a few times when she, as Damien, began flirting with the nurses.

By the time they left, they discovered that Dr. Charles Nolan, the hospital's chief of staff, had a mistress who was bold enough to frequent the hospital. Ironically, the mistress drove a dark-colored Range Rover and had visited the hospital the day the first box showed up. Clues were falling into place, and for the first time, Yala felt optimistic that the mystery behind the box was a step closer to being solved.

Kevin's tech skills allowed him to triangulate Doctor Nolan's current cell location as well as his whereabouts on the day the box was dropped off. The doctor was away attending a medical convention in New York, just as his staff told them.

However, his phone was currently pinging from a location in southern Virginia, about four hours away. The doctor was apparently hiding something.

Yala and Kevin considered that the doctor being away didn't necessarily mean he wasn't the one calling the shots. Therefore, they planned to question him extensively as soon as they tracked him down.

"I would have never considered the doctor's side chick might have anything to do with this case, but she could be doing his dirty work while he's away."

Kevin nodded, agreeing. They approached and climbed into her rental. Once strapped inside, she drove away.

"When I checked out the first and new boxes earlier, I picked up a scent like body oil or perfume. It was the reason I wanted to visit the nurse's station, to see if I could pick up the scent there."

Yala flashed a smile, impressed at how easily he could connect dots she would never have found.

"That's why you kept sniffing in the exam room," she said. "Your heightened senses were at work?"

He nodded before turning and reaching into the backseat. He unzipped his laptop from its carrier and flipped it open.

"I should be able to use traffic footage to see if we can follow the SUV from the hospital that day. The nurse squad also put the mistress's vehicle at the hospital the day the second box arrived. She claimed she had been looking for Doctor Nolan no less than twenty-four hours ago. It could all be a coincidence, or it could be connected."

Yala's brows pinched.

Hacking and IT was a side of the spy world in which Yala had training but not on the level that Kevin was currently engaged. She never believed she needed to be equipped with that sort of knowledge. However, she was learning that she shouldn't limit herself, and working with seasoned vets in her world was a privilege and a necessity if she were to become a more well-rounded agent.

Normally, when she needed tech support, she'd put in a call, and TOP would assign what they called a tech assassin. They were agents who could shoot as well as destroy a firewall.

She kept an eye on the road and sneaked peeks at Kevin's rapid keystrokes and at the snapshots of what popped up on the screen.

"I'm in," he announced. She lifted a brow. Apparently, his nose for finding clues and leads wasn't specific to just scents.

He'd tapped into the first traffic camera so quickly, she'd missed the lesson. He rubbed her arm playfully.

"Don't worry. I'll teach you everything I know."

"Are you a Tech Assassin, too?" she asked.

"No, but I was partnered with one for about six months, and you'd be surprised at how much I picked up in such a short span of time."

The traffic cams gave him multiple views before he stopped the rapid flow of images at the exact spot that revealed a clear picture of the SUV's license plate. In minutes, he was using different camera feeds to track the SUV across the city.

"So how is it that you can track that specific vehicle from a week ago? I assumed all of that type of information was erased after a certain amount of time."

"TOP doesn't let anything get erased, no matter what the owners of the footage decide to do with it. We swoop in without anyone noticing and collect it all. You know that saying, 'One person's trash is another person's treasure?'" He aimed a finger at his laptop. "This is treasure to TOP."

While she drove, Kevin hacked into the DMV database. He used the plate number to locate the vehicle's registered owner.

"Elizabeth Paul," he announced as they pulled into a gas station to fill up her rental.

"I'm impressed," Yala stated. "If TOP wants me to keep doing these types of assignments, I'll have to put in more training. It saves time without involving a third party."

"I heard through the TOP grapevine that they plan to start incorporating this type of training in the new recruit curriculum."

She nodded, and memories of her rigorous training brought a smile to her face. Though one of the hardest tasks she ever faced, training to get into TOP had instilled a level of confidence in her that she never believed she'd have despite her ability to look like whoever she wanted.

"What now?" Yala asked.

Kevin shot her a mischievous glance.

"I'm getting her home address."

Less than five minutes later, Yala steered the vehicle toward Elizabeth's residence, and Kevin continued his cyber-spying expedition.

"Ms. Paul is in med school, so she is definitely a suspect now."

Moments later, the unanswered chime of her doorbell and her SUV not being in the driveway of her condo was a good invitation for them to snoop.

The small townhouse-style condo had an unlocked gated yard area that led to the back of the building. Yala made quick work of picking the lock to the back door. She couldn't hack into the DMV, but she knew how to breeze through locks and safes of all kinds.

The scent of freshly squeezed lemons and cinnamon permeated the air once they stepped inside. Looking at the blueprints before they arrived allowed them to navigate the property swiftly. The back of the townhouse led into a small dining room where you could view the kitchen, large living room area, and the stairs leading to the two bedrooms and bath upstairs.

The design scheme throughout appeared to have been professionally decorated with a traditional theme. Gray and beige colors for the large furniture and pops of reds and yellows of vases and knick-knacks were strategically placed over the large living room.

"I'll check upstairs," Yala volunteered. Kevin nodded, and based on the way he tilted his head and wrinkled his nose, he was already picking up on a possible clue.

Closet, drawer, under the bed, Yala conducted a thorough search while being careful not to leave anything out of place.

Ding Dong. The doorbell chimed.

Yala slipped down the stairs and found Kevin at the window, attempting to get a look at who was at the door. When keys began to jingle in the doorknob, she scrambled to find cover, but she was caught when a woman suddenly stepped inside. Yala didn't recognize the woman.

Kevin glanced at Yala and went wide-eyed before he fixed his face and returned his attention to the woman.

"Bethy, why are you looking at me like you just saw a ghost? And who is this?" she asked, barely casting a glance at Yala, who was posing as Elizabeth. She'd had seconds to shift and wasn't sure she'd gotten the size of the original woman correct.

"This is my friend, Brett," Yala introduced. The woman stared Kevin up and down hungrily, licking her lips.

"Are you the kind of friend that doesn't mind being shared among good friends?" she asked, taking a few steps closer.

"Sorry, I'm all hers," Kevin replied, aiming a finger in Yala's direction.

"That's too bad," she said, her eyes practically undressing Kevin. The vibe he gave off to the opposite sex was masculine and invigorating in the way it drew you in. Reluctantly, the woman focused on Yala.

"You forgot about our interview, didn't you?" the woman asked, looking her up and down, believing she was seeing her friend. "Wasn't that dress ruined by that asshole who thought it was okay to give you a golden shower?"

Yala nodded. "I managed to salvage it."

The woman's face creased.

"What's been wrong with you lately? Should we reschedule?"

"Yes. Please."

"Maybe you shouldn't take on anymore new clients. Ever since your favorite doctor left without telling you where he was going, you've been acting...off," she said, running an inquisitive eye over Yala.

"Dr. Nolan," Yala stated for confirmation purposes.

"Who else would I be talking about? Are you seeing any other doctor besides him?"

She squinted, eyeing Yala more closely now, likely sensing something off but not putting her finger on it. "Is he still not answering your calls? You don't think something happened to him, do you?"

"I don't know. He's usually responsive, especially to me. And now…"

"He's ghosting you," the friend finished. "You think the wife knows he's been seeing you."

Yala shrugged. "I don't think so."

The friend put her eyes back on Kevin, and the smile in her gaze sparkled. She reached down and began rummaging around in her purse.

"Let's set up a new interview time."

Yala aimed a finger at the door. "We were actually heading out," she said, glancing in Kevin's direction.

"Oh. I'll call you later then," she said but didn't make a move to leave. Her gaze kept bouncing from Kevin to Yala. Finally, she walked up to Yala and slung her arms around her neck.

"Be careful of that one. He's the kind that could make you fall in love," she whispered before placing a quick peck on Yala's cheek. She backed off, her smile wide and teasing.

"I'll call you later or tomorrow. You two have fun, and please don't hesitate to call if you would like a plus one."

Kevin and Yala nodded while looking at the woman as she walked out the door. As soon as it closed, they ambled over to the front window, acting the part of a nosey neighbor until they saw her pull off in a white Nissan Maxima.

"How did you pull that off, making yourself look like Elizabeth? Don't you need to see the person in order to copy them?" Kevin asked.

"I've been building a database in my head of people that I've copied or may want to copy. It comes in handy when I need to become someone else in order to gain new leads or information. In Elizabeth's case, I got lucky. I was just looking through her pictures and reading through some of her personal information lying around upstairs. Most of her profile, height, and weight, I guessed at, but I was close enough to fool the friend. It's too bad I can't become Doctor Nolan. The few snapshots of his face I saw at the hospital weren't enough for me to work with."

"Let's straighten up here, and I'll trace his phone and see if we can ping him to a location."

CHAPTER THIRTEEN

Kevin

Kevin's senses tingled the whole time he was inside Elizabeth Paul's house. Not finding a clue to match the sensation vexed him. They backtracked, went out the back door, and crept through the side fence. If nosey neighbors peeked, they would assume they were visiting someone or passing through.

Once he hopped in the passenger seat and Yala behind the steering wheel, they glanced at each other.

"Is it just me, or is someone watching us?"

"I feel it too," he said, scanning the area without appearing obvious.

"That black Honda Accord. It wasn't sitting there when we arrived. Someone's inside."

Through the car's dark tint, he sensed eyes on them. Yala drove off at a leisurely pace, but the car didn't follow.

"Let's make a long loop around and drive back to see if the car is still there. They didn't have front plates, so I didn't get a number," Kevin stated.

"Kevin," Yala called, eyeing the rearview mirror.

"I see it," he replied. "Dark gray Nissan SUV."

They picked up a tail in the few blocks they'd driven to make their trek back to the black Honda, which remained parked on the street nearest Elizabeth's house. It couldn't have been a coincidence that they picked up a tail while Elizabeth's house was being watched.

"Someone is staking out her house," Yala said absently, one eye on the road and one on the black Accord.

"Bethy is quickly taking up the number one spot in our suspect pool. However, right now, we have a dilemma. Do we confront the house watchers or see if we can get this tail to chase us?" Yala asked.

"I say we pass by like we are unconcerned and make the SUV chase us. The watchers will be there when we return, or they'll be back later if they're that concerned about Elizabeth."

"I agree. As soon as we are out of sight of the Honda and on a safe stretch of highway, gun it."

Three sharp turns dragged on forever, with the SUV mirroring each move she made. They didn't hang back far, only three car lengths . They either didn't know how to tail properly or assumed they hadn't been made since Yala hadn't done anything to draw their attention.

She slammed her foot on the gas at McCloud Boulevard, sending Kevin back into the seat. The SUV picked up speed, accepting the invitation to chase them, despite no logical reasoning.

"How're your driving skills?" Kevin asked Yala while pulling out a gun and cocking it.

"I've been in a car chase or two," she replied.

"They took the bait. Do you think you can find a way to get rid of them without damaging us in the process?"

"One vehicle crash coming right up," Yala said. She swerved into a hard right turn before pulling off a smooth drift around a sharp left turn. The car's tail end missed the front of an oncoming truck with an inch to spare."

"Holy shit," Kevin said, eyes wide and neck on a swivel to see if the pursuing car would make the turn.

"I can't believe you made that turn." He cast a glance at Yala. "How did you do that in *this* car?"

"Lots and lots of practice," she said before glancing at the gun in his hand.

"What if bullets don't work?" she asked.

In their line of work, they didn't know if they would be dealing with humans or something else. And lately, they needed to be prepared to combat supernatural abilities they hadn't anticipated.

"I'm hoping we don't need them, and if we do, I'm hoping they work."

Tap. Tap. Tap.

The loud strikes against the outside of the car answered at least one of their questions. Who the hell was chasing them, shooting at them, and why?

"We have to find out who the hell this is more than ever now. If they were hanging around Elizabeth's house, she must be directly involved or has become a target in this case."

"I agree," Yala said before making the tires squeal so loud under the car that Kevin was waiting to see if one would fly off. This car wasn't built for sharp turns at deadly speeds, but she forced it to do her bidding.

Bam!

The jolt to the car's rear end shook his insides, and instead of his first instinct being to protect himself, his arm shot out in front of Yala. The seat belt snatched her, but the hard jolt didn't affect her ability to keep the car on the road.

Another hard lick and Yala turned sharply into the spin, letting the car fly free. What Kevin assumed was them spinning out of control was her positioning the car in such a way that the driver's side front bumper came around and swiped the tail end of the SUV.

The tap, combined with the vehicle's speed, caused it to swerve hard, and the SUV endured a sharp twist in the opposite direction. They narrowly missed a metal sign pointing them the interstate two miles ahead.

The vehicle kept swerving, the driver fighting to get it back on the road and off the median. They took the interstate and picked up speed. Running now, they likely didn't expect the aggression Yala returned.

She chased them down and gave them a dose of their own medicine. She rammed them, sending them speeding towards a telephone pole in a grassy field off the side of the interstate. Trees lined the hilly area behind the formation of telephone poles propping up thick cords of power lines.

The sound of metal twisting around the hard, unflinching wood sounded like a violent storm was at work outside. Yala came to a screeching stop, with the front of her car facing the wrecked vehicle. Her side bore more exposure to the SUV, the criminal inside lowering the driver's side window.

Kevin and Yala leaped from the car with their guns out and aimed at the SUV. They used their doors for shields as bullets pinged off the surface of the car's hood.

Tap. Tap. Tap.

They dove for cover when bullets began flying from the back and front driver's side windows. Either three people were inside the SUV, or the front passenger had hopped in the back to increase their chances of taking them out.

The criminals ducked low inside the SUV, shooting blindly from what Kevin could tell. Although under attack, he was thankful that they were dealing with humans versus others. When he lifted to get a better shot, he only had a split second to dive onto the ground to avoid more incoming fire from behind them.

He lifted and fired off a couple of rounds at another dark gray Nissan SUV, a replica of the first. He and Yala had fallen for the trick, distracted by the first SUV when another was lurking in the background and targeting them too.

Despite him crawling on his elbows and sliding along the ground on his stomach, he could hear Yala on the other side of the car continuing to fire off rounds at the first SUV.

"Are you good?" he called out.

"Yes. You get them. I got this," she replied, her voice jerking since she was on the move. He rolled out of the path of a bullet that missed his head by inches and let off three rounds, one striking the passenger who hung out of the window of the second SUV. The man slumped over the open window, his gun falling to the ground as blood dripped from a place in his head.

The passenger side taillight of Yala's rental shattered just as he ducked beside the back tire and attempted to get a fix on the driver. Despite his own battle, his attention was also drawn to what sounded like a fight taking place on Yala's side of the car.

She left the safety of the vehicles' door shielding her to advance on the SUV. One of the criminals must have been bold enough to do the same.

Shots continued to pelt the back of Yala's rental, and other motorists slowed to get a peek at what was taking place, some even bold enough to stop. Kevin crawled to the back fender and slid under the tail end of the car just enough that the other shooter in the second SUV would have to exit the vehicle and risk exposure to get off a good shot.

He laid the side of his face against the ground and stretched his body enough to see Yala fighting with one of the guys from her SUV. She threw a punch that landed square in his jaw, backing him up before a quick knee crushed his balls.

The second shooter inside was aiming at Yala and the fighting man. They were setting her up for a kill shot as the one who remained inside the vehicle had his gun aimed and ready to take her out when he got a clean shot.

The one whose balls she rearranged got a grip around the top of her body, bear-hugging her. "Got you now, bitch!" he yelled out. He was set to accomplish his goal of giving his friend in the SUV a target.

Panicked at what he was witnessing, Kevin crawled out to help but immediately rolled back under the vehicle's tail end to keep bullets out of his body. The driver of the second SUV still had him pinned down.

His partner was in trouble and Kevin desperately needed to do something, anything. Another peek showed him his worst nightmare. The man swung Yala around and shoved her away from him and into his partner's line of fire.

"No!" Kevin yelled, rolling out from under the car and firing off a barrage of bullets at the driver of the second SUV while narrowly dodging multiple shots coming at him. One of his shots hit home, making the shooter cry out.

Although injured, he and the guy continued to exchange shots. His greatest fear was watching Yala die. If he didn't get to her in time, today just might be the day. Bullets flew toward her, and his heightened senses slowed the scene down like he was watching a movie.

The sight had him gasping while he ducked periodically to avoid the bullets meant for his face. Distracted, he almost missed the guy exiting the SUV and attempting to sneak up on him.

Right before the first bullet slammed into Yala's body, she transformed into what he believed to be a brick column. The bullet's impact had chunks of the wall flying into the air. Kevin didn't know she could transform into inanimate objects. *What the hell?*

Yala's dramatic transformation ended up distracting his attacker long enough for Kevin to aim, shattering the man's left ankle, and then his face when he fell to the ground.

Up and on the move now, Kevin shot a quick glance at the SUV to make sure the passenger and driver were out of commission. He ran to the other side of Yala's rental in time to see her already back to normal and turning the tables on her two attackers.

She circled the wide-eyed and stiff-bodied man behind her, using his body as a shield before she let off rounds at the one inside the SUV. The stupid man released several shots, a few hitting the man Yala used as her shield.

While the injured man screamed his head off, blood seeped from his neck and lower stomach area, wetting his tan T-shirt. Kevin crept around the vehicle with caution so as not to spook anyone and make the scene any worse for Yala. Thankfully, none of the onlookers who stopped were foolish enough to come near an active shootout.

"Open the door and come out with your hands up," Yala called to the man inside the SUV.

Tap. Tap. Tap.

Kevin ducked but took up a position to get a more precise aim at the man trying to kill his partner. He didn't have a good shot at his angle, but he could at least fire off a few shots to keep the man distracted.

More cars slowed, phones were more than likely recording whatever they could capture at a distance. Yala dropped the dying man in front of her, his slumping body not worth the weight she held up.

Pop! Pop!

She fired two shots before the one inside the SUV got any more shots off at her.

"I missed you on purpose. The next one goes in your head," she told the man.

"You can toss your gun and climb out, or I can come over there and extricate your soul from your body and let the devil decide what he wants to do with you."

Damn!

Kevin stood upright at those words but maintained his steady aim, just in case there were more bad guys ducking inside the SUV.

The last man alive lifted his hands before the gun dropped out of the window and clattered to the ground. The next thing he saw was a leg dangling out the door before Yala rushed over, grabbed the man, and slung him against the side of the SUV.

She may have looked like she weighed a hundred pounds soaking wet, but she could handle her own in a car chase and a gunfight. This was the type of work she was used to doing. To say that he was impressed was an understatement, especially when seeing her roughing up the man who had at least a hundred pounds on her.

"Aww!" He yelled out in pain from the way she twisted his arms around before she slapped cuffs on him. Where the cuffs had magically appeared from was beyond him. Had she manifested them like she had that wall that kept her from being shot?

Kevin sensed the crowd behind them before he turned his head to take a look. They had eyes on them from every direction now, and of course, phones aimed at them and recording their every move.

It was too bad that TOP's R&D team hadn't devised a magic wand to make people forget they'd seen anything. However, TOP had their ways of cleaning up messes.

Kevin lifted his phone to his ear while marching back to the car when Yala snatched up the man to get him moving.

"Clear K, 47-6262 North, 122.3359 West, and we need a digital wipe of a half-square-mile radius," he said, glancing at the people and forcing a fake smile. They were going to be pissed when they discovered that all of their electronics had been wiped clean.

Yala shoved the squirming guy along while Kevin dashed ahead to open the back door. "We need to take him to the nearest black site for questioning," Yala suggested.

Kevin nodded, glad to see they were on the same page concerning handling their suspect. Yala hopped in the backseat after shoving the man inside.

***

Kevin rolled into the underground garage, and the dark silence filling the space swallowed the car. At least the darkness had shut up the suspect, who claimed his name was Randy.

Yala glanced around, taking in the gray concrete walls the headlights bounced off. They rolled into spot 125. Kevin put the car in park and left it running while they waited.

A faint flash of light came alive and died so quickly she'd have thought she'd imagined it if she didn't know they were being scanned.

The rumble of rolling metal sounded before the car lowered, descending slowly underground while the parking spot closed above them. The car stopped on a long stretch of hallway, wide enough to be lined with a row of parking spots on one side, two lanes of traffic, and a walking lane.

Yala shoved the man from the back of the car before she climbed out behind him. Kevin didn't fight his smile. He enjoyed the way she manhandled the man who towered over her by at least a foot.

"Where the hell are you taking me? I'm a two-bit criminal. I didn't ask for all of this crazy shit. This has to be a secret government facility. I've heard about places like this where they experiment on people and shit."

They ignored the man. Their footsteps echoed off the wall as they approached the wide, blacked-out glass doors. The pristine shine on the glass resembled sunlight reflecting off a mirror.

"You're going to get me killed. I keep telling you that I didn't have a choice."

She and Kevin ignored the man. During the trip, they had repeatedly asked him to elaborate on why he believed he didn't have a choice and who he worked for, but he was too dumb or too afraid to give up his boss.

The large black doors slid apart at their approach, and the three marched through them as a group with the suspect in the middle, continuing to ask questions that weren't getting answered. He finally stopped talking when the stark contrast of the air quality made them suck in a quick breath. It was thinner like breathing two-percent air versus whole air.

The bright sterileness inside the building had them blinking against the strong beams shining down like they walked under multiple spotlights. Yala had visited this site twice before, and based on the way Kevin regarded it with familiarity, this wasn't his first time inside the facility either.

They marched the man down a long hall of white on white floors, walls, and ceilings. No windows, no decorative items. It was like the space was meant to cleanse you before you went any deeper inside. They pushed past another set of doors and entered the first room on the left opting to remain on the first level of the facility to conduct their initial interrogation.

A table and three chairs were the only pieces of furniture in the room. Two chairs on one side of the table, and a single chair for the suspect sat on the other. His view was of them as well as the large television mounted to the wall behind Kevin and Yala.

Screensaver photos of landscapes flashed over the large monitor periodically. On the other side of what the suspect saw as a television was a viewing room. Although there weren't any other agents on the opposite side of the monitor, the suspect was being recorded to see if they could detect anything Yala and Kevin may have missed.

They sat across from each other, not saying a thing. The suspect huffed and puffed and eyeballed them.

He lifted a hand. "Aren't either of you going to say anything?"

One of his arms was cuffed to the table, similar to what would happen in a real interrogation room. However, the man had no idea those specific cuffs suppressed supernatural abilities.

This man, however, was human. His erratic movement and assuredness that the person he worked for would kill him were all the information he was willing to give up. Whoever his boss was, they had something big hanging over this man's head.

"Who do you work for? Why were you in that neighborhood? And why did you do something as foolish as chase us?" Kevin asked.

"If I answer your questions, will you let me go?"

Yala and Kevin glanced at each other before locking their gaze on the man.

"Yes."

"Yeah." They answered him.

"Bullshit. You must think I'm dumb as hell to believe that."

"You said if we don't let you go, your boss is going to kill you. What does the person look like?"

"Aww!" The man yelled out before he doubled over the table.

"They must have found out that I've been caught. He's going to kill me!" The man yelled in horror. The screaming from deep within his gut couldn't be faked, nor could the intense pain radiating from his wide eyes. Yala sensed the man's distress.

"What's happening to you?"

He gripped his stomach and panted so hard that Kevin stood—his own breathing now matched that of the man's.

Kevin took a step and staggered against the table, his palm pressing into the top of it to remain steady.

"Kevin?" Yala stood, but he lifted a hand for her to stay in place.

The man's scream intensified, his eyes shut tight and his mouth gaped open as he rocked his now bent body from side to side. He clawed at his stomach like it was being ripped out by something they couldn't see.

"Tell us who's doing this to you so we can make them stop," Kevin gritted out.

"It's too late," the man murmured between cries.

Kevin stood over him now, attempting to assist him to stand upright. Yala stared wide-eyed, lips parted.

It took effort, but Kevin finally got the man standing. The man groaned now, but the pain playing out on his face and pouring off his body wasn't as intense.

Kevin lifted the man's shirt, and Yala froze, along with the blood racing through her body. Kevin stared wide-eyed at the man's missing mid-section.

Where there should have been a torso, chest, and stomach there was nothing but empty space under the shirt.

"Who did that to you? You have to tell us something so we can find this person and stop them before they…."

"Aww!" The man yelled out before tumbling to the floor, still grabbing at where his stomach should have been. Kevin took a knee beside him, looking over him as if figuring out how to help him.

Yala ran over and took a knee before grabbing a hold of one of the man's hands. Her eyes caught movement before widening at the sight of it spreading rapidly over the area below the neckline of his T-shirt as well as the area at the top portion of his pants where he was dissected.

"Who did this to you? You have to tell us to avoid this happening to anyone else."

"Do…Doc," the man attempted to spit out, but thick globs of blood spilled over his quivering lips.

"Please tell us who did this to you?"

Yala leaned closer to his trembling lips.

"No," the man said. "Doc…tor No…no…lan."

"Doctor Nolan," Kevin mouthed, piecing together the man's broken words.

"Was he making you watch Elizabeth's house? Was she helping him? Is she his victim too?"

A guttural sound bubbled up his throat, accompanied by the loud gasps that replaced his words. A cold tremble began in his body, his skin already paling. He jerked against Yala's hold and Kevin's touch—one, two, three hard jerks before he went still.

"Fuck," Kevin muttered. Yala stared at the dead man, his eyes half-mast, his mouth still open.

The sick fuck doing this had taken his game up a notch. He was blackmailing people into doing his dirty work while lurking silently in the background with their body parts as his leverage.

CHAPTER FOURTEEN

Yala

After the day and night they had, Yala could hardly wait to get back to their suite. Where most people would have been concerned about what they just witnessed, Yala had met her quota on how much more she could process that didn't make sense about this case.

However, there was one thing that never stopped lingering in the back of her mind. As soon as her feet crossed the threshold into her bedroom, her fingers swiped over the shiny surface of her phone.

Sori was an insomniac, so Yala didn't think twice about calling her after 3:00 a.m.

She answered on the first ring, her voice a breath of fresh air.

"Hey, Yala. What's up?"

It was beyond Yala's understanding how someone with such a deadly reputation and a nickname like Smoke could sound so friendly and carefree. Sori had one of the most menacing stares Yala had ever seen, one that could put the fear of God in the most hardened person. But, in the same breath, she could look sweet and project innocence.

She also cursed like a shit-faced drunk, and most of her assignments ended with a stack of dead bodies. Half of Yala's body count as an agent came from assignments she'd worked on while partnered with Sori.

"How are you doing?" she asked to avoid jumping right into the subject she'd called about in the first place.

"Are you okay? You don't need me to kill anybody, do you?" she asked. Although Yala knew that she was joking, there remained a touch of concern in her tone.

"I'm fine. I don't need you to kill anyone, but I do have a personal problem I could use your advice on."

She'd just been in a car chase, been shot at, and watched a man running around with his mid-section missing. However, none of those were the reasons she'd wanted to speak with Sori.

"Oh, really? I hope it has something to do with a man who has you all whipped up at this late hour of the night."

The woman was a step away from being a fortune-teller. Did she have any idea she'd hit the nail on the head?

Sori had recently discovered she had two older brothers who quickly made a habit of setting her up with blind dates. Although she considered herself a lost cause where men were concerned, she endured the dates anyway.

Yala, however, wasn't sure she wanted to test the waters where men were concerned. Her past demons spewed such vicious intent that she hadn't been interested.

Until Kevin came along, the voice in her head shouted.

She filled Sori in on everything about Kevin, even disclosed that she spent the night with him the first time they met in that alley.

"Unfortunately, I fear my curiosity about him is starting to get the better of me. A few days ago, I walked into my suite and found that he was my partner. He must have asked for a big favor to get transferred so quickly. If I hadn't been in one of my disguises, he would have seen right through all the shock and awe I was hiding." She pushed out a long breath. "Although this is ultimately about the case, his reassignment also solidified that I didn't imagine our connection that first night."

"Trust me on this. K knows his shit," Sori said "You couldn't have asked for a better partner. There are a total of three people I like to work with, and you and he are two of them."

The rare compliment made Yala smile as Sori wasn't one to give out praise.

"Thank you. But I didn't know that you two had worked together before."

"Yes. He's one of the few not afraid to work with me. He can easily deal with my strong personality despite his penchant for sensing shit I never knew was there in the first place." Sori chuckled.

"I'm attracted to him, and I think it's beyond friendly. I like him, which alone can be a big problem in our work. And the way he looks at me makes me nervous, and not in a bad or defensive way." Yala spat out her dilemma to Sori to get it all off her chest. She lowered her voice like someone was listening. "I need you to tell me how to turn this attraction off before it gets out of control."

Sori howled with laughter loud enough for Yala to jerk the phone away from her ear. The statement was a joke, but some truth remained hidden within the words. She didn't know whether to be offended or embarrassed as the cackling continued to light up the phone lines.

Sori finally settled down enough to talk, but laughter remained in her tone.

"There is no off switch. And if he's looking at you the way you described, he undoubtedly has the same attraction to you as you have to him. So at least you're not on a one-way street."

Yala rolled her eyes at the ceiling when Sori, on the other end, failed to conceal more laughter. "Have either of you discussed the situation?"

Still ticked off at Sori's laughter, a prominent frown remained on Yala's face as she talked. "No, we haven't talked about anything. I pretend there's nothing happening. I don't want him to know that I'm into him. We have a serious job to do and neither of us is here to create a bad romance. I want this to be about the job and not my own personal...I don't even know what to call this. We just met. It's too fast."

This time, Sori's voice softened. "I understand what you're going through better than you might think. When you're facing a case or a scenario that looks like it may be impossible to solve, what do you do? You don't say screw it. You do your best to rectify the situation and solve the problem. You do what you have to do to catch the killer or eliminate the monster. You deal with it. You need to do the same about your situation with Kevin."

Yala hadn't considered it in that aspect. Sori sounded like a midnight DJ giving out love advice over the airways.

"I can't say I fully understand what you're going through. All I can tell you is...if you feel strongly for him and the feelings are mutual, see where it goes. As long as you don't let it interfere with your job or endanger your lives, trust your instincts," she urged.

"You're a TOP agent. If you didn't have some of the best instincts in this country, you wouldn't have been chosen. That being said, this world has more to offer than this job. Knowing that someone cares about your day, your mood, and your well-being is an incredible sentiment that can ease the most stubborn mind. If you're lucky enough to stumble upon someone like that, you shouldn't let them slip through the cracks, especially someone like K."

Yala took heed to Sori's words. The respect in her tone toward Kevin put her concerns about him at ease.

"I appreciate your advice. But, just to confirm what I heard, you're saying I'm stuck like this, and there are no shortcuts? I can either embrace this or let it go?"

Sori released a chuckle. "You're not stuck. In my honest opinion, I think you should give it a shot with him and see where it goes. If it's not something you want, you have a job that can remove you from the situation easily."

Sori's words went from soft to serious. "It took a couple of recent near-death experiences and traumatic childhood memories to resurface for me to acknowledge what I should have in the first place. I needed to embrace living and enjoy life more, and although it's difficult to be social and open to relationships, I'm trying anyway. You should do the same. Instead of skimming through life, live it a little."

Yala's smile deepened. Did she just say she was *trying* as in, she was currently dating someone? She wanted to be nosey but decided that Sori would tell her whatever was going on with her in her own time.

"I understand what you're saying and appreciate it. Thanks for the talk."

She hung up and sat in place staring at the phone. The questions on her mind were piling up, but she felt better. After a long shower, she prepared for the nap that she would convince herself was eight hours of sleep when she woke up in a few hours to start another day.

***

Kevin

Laptop in hand, Kevin's mind drifted to pleasant but distracting memories. He'd never wanted anyone as badly as he wanted Yala, but his desire to respect her boundaries kept him from pursuing her further.

The undeniable chemistry between them couldn't be ignored, but he sensed early on that Yala wasn't the type of woman who made impulsive decisions regarding the opposite sex. His good sense reminded him—*case before romance,* but his passion for her was a relentless monster.

They were partners who shared the same suite, which didn't help. He'd underestimated his ability to handle their attraction. After he showered, he attempted to relax, but sleep remained elusive. Yala invaded his dreams and imagination, renovating his mind to include a special place for her.

He would have called his cousin, Devin, to talk through his dilemma, but he was a newlywed, and Kevin knew better than bothering him and his new wife. The one other person Kevin could call was Sori.

She answered on the first ring.

"K. What's up?"

Her cheerful tone at such an ungodly hour made him smile. He wasted no time telling her of his and Yala's encounter in the alley and was comfortable enough with her to disclose that she'd spent the night with him. He'd easily admitted to his attraction, which pointed to the truth and depth of it.

"Everything is happening so fast. We hardly know each other, but it feels like we already do."

"I'm glad you're not afraid to own your feelings," Sori said, her tone smooth and reassuring.

The people who knew them would have thought him crazy to ask Sori, of all people, for advice, but he could count on her for discretion and to give him solid advice that he needed to hear. She wouldn't sugarcoat anything.

"It's difficult to foster a relationship doing the type of work we do. But if you care for Yala, it doesn't matter. You'll find a way to make her an important part of your life. You'll find a way to convey to her that you're willing to tackle tough obstacles to prove her importance to you. You two won't have a traditional relationship in any sense of the word. However, if you play your cards right, you could end up with something special."

He allowed her words to soak in before he replied. "Can I ask you something?"

"Yes."

He'd known Sori for four years. In one breath, she could be lovable, and in the next breath, she could turn into an unyielding deadly force. But she always knew more than she would have you believe.

"Her name is not Kris, or Damien is it?"

A long pause followed his question. When he'd asked her about her name that last time, he'd sensed her guard up.

"No. And I know why you're asking. I'm not telling you her real name. I'll tell you this, though. If she tells you her name, her full name, it means she is willing to invest in you as much as you would invest in her. It took me over a year to get her name."

Damn.

"Thank you," he said before hanging up.

CHAPTER FIFTEEN

Yala

The following day brought the second Box victim's second part: his torso. A severed head lying in the center of the exam table, next to a detached boxed torso, was a difficult display to comprehend. Two separate body parts belonging to the same man and unexplainably alive and functioning.

How were they supposed to wrap such a scene into logical understanding? How was anyone supposed to comprehend the reasoning behind these boxes?

The doctors slid the torso box into the box containing the head, and the magical reattachment followed. All that signified that anything substantial had taken place was the low *click-pop* that sounded when the parts came together.

The instantaneous connection wasn't something that could be explained by eyesight alone. Magic at play here, the type of paranormal activity that leaves you scratching your head to find logic when there wasn't any. The body looked like he'd never been taken apart.

Yala glanced at Kevin.

Had he seen the reconnection differently than her and the doctors? Was he putting together scenarios no one else had?

He shook his head like he sensed what she might have been thinking. It would take time for her to gain understanding of his abilities.

They called up the video recording of the reconnection and studied it frame by frame. Unfortunately, the slow process didn't reveal anything substantial.

Kevin submerged the original box in water in an attempt to find anything that would yield clues. He also checked to see if the murderer used any special tools to give the appearance that the rest of the man's body was missing when it was actually right in front of them.

As the doctors checked and rechecked the victim's vital signs, Yala and Kevin studied the video of the man's reattachment. They weren't certain if the split-second blur that flashed across the screen came from the camera angle or a hidden pocket of energy within the box.

Kevin had witnessed many extraordinary sightings that couldn't be explained doing this job. This box was one of the most baffling. Yala and her capacity to reel him into her world and make him want to live there proved just as remarkable. Add to that her ability to shape-shift into other people, and it all left his mind in jigsaw pieces.

This case was proving to be a treasure trove of hidden abilities and inexplicable anomalies. Was he in the middle of a science fiction movie versus a case? The inventor of these boxes possessed a special gift. There was no doubt about that. However, were these abilities a blessing or a curse?

The doctors couldn't explain the logic behind the boxes, and although the first patient hadn't survived, they were optimistic that their current victim would. There was also the man from the black site that the doctors spent time studying. So far, they hadn't found an explanation for how he could function with his middle section missing.

Enough of the second boxed victim was missing that he wouldn't survive if they opened the box before receiving the third box containing the lower half of his body. In his present state, the victim couldn't eat or drink. There was no accurate time frame of how long this man had been in this state prior to arriving at the medical examiner's office.

The questions kept stacking up. How long could a person live suspended in this condition without suffering the effects of hunger or dehydration? How would their heart, lungs, or even their brain be affected in the long run? Were they in pain? Did they comprehend that parts of them were in different locations?

The realization left the doctors and agents thinking that a mad magician scientist was pushing his victims to the edge of death because it correlated with the timeline he was using to deliver the boxes and keep the victims apart.

**

After they spent hours studying the victim, Yala and Kevin set out to investigate once again. They staked out Elizabeth's home and used the phone number they found to ping her phone for her location. The phone trace didn't work and neither had staking out her place as she or the Honda she drove hadn't returned to her house.

They checked in with the doctors who performed an autopsy on the man from the black site. Like the original, the man's body, what was left of it, wasn't telling any stories that would produce a lead.

They canvassed the hospital grounds, Yala in disguise and Kevin using all six of his senses. However, the loose lips weren't loose enough and tired was as good as an emotion based on what Kevin sensed. His ability to detect the slightest hints of criminal intentions, malice, and deception led them back to the security guards.

Kevin didn't pick up on anything unusual until the energy signature of the guard Yala currently questioned, Mark Jenkins, shifted from warm tension to boiling pressure. The guard emitted a kind of stress that made a criminal run before the police got the chance to ask them a question.

Several questions and mean side eyes from Kevin later, it turns out Mark happened to be working the day both boxes were dropped off. Kevin's eyes narrowed at the way the man shifted, his body twisting in a dance like he needed to scratch but was forcing himself to ignore it. The faint scent of alcohol he'd drank in his coffee or guzzled before he left his house tickled Kevin's nose.

His eyes kept straying away from Yala and landing on Kevin, whether she spoke or not. Heightened senses weren't necessary to know this man was lying.

They returned to the office, and Yala watched over Kevin's shoulder, learning and picking up knowledge while he called up Mark Jenkins' background. His criminal record listed two B&E's and an aggravated assault charge.

"Is it safe to assume that Mark has become a suspect?" Yala asked while they walked back to the small workspace they had carved out in the break room of the medical examiner's office. Kevin preferred speaking face-to-face with suspects, but this case was unique in that they needed to keep their suspects in the dark.

There was no way to know if the individual behind the box was pulling other victims' strings to do the dirty work they needed done. They faced the most important aspect of this complex case. Until they received the last part of their current victim, they didn't want to risk the chance of spooking the spook and the victim ended up dying.

A delicate thread was holding this case in place, and the murderous mastermind had pulled it from a book of tricks that left them chasing their tails. Now, they would need to recruit extra staff to keep an eye on Mark since they weren't sure if he was involved, as a victim, or a suspect.

They were not willing to risk the box victim for the glory of catching the culprit. However, as soon as they received what they needed to save this individual, all bets were off, and they would pursue the suspect with relentless force.

***

Later that evening.
"Hello," Yala answered the phone on the first ring.
"Something is wrong with the body," Doctor Hughes said.

"We'll be right over," she called into the phone, her gaze locked with Kevin's.

Fifteen minutes later, they walked into the side door of the hospital. They zipped down the cold hall of the ME's office and entered the exam room.

The doctors were draped over the box in an attempt to keep it in place. At least, that's what Yala assumed she was seeing.

"He keeps having seizures," Doctor Hughes announced. If we open the box, he dies. If we leave it closed, he still may die."

Yala was at a loss for words, and Kevin had gone unnervingly still. She sprang into action, placing a firm hand on the box to keep it in place. The man's hands repeatedly bumped the glass, each thump driving more tension into the room.

From the corner of her eyes, Yala spotted Kevin searching for something. His head jerked around while he shoved tools aside on one of the doctor's instrument tables. He ran over, secured the latch, and locked it in place with zip ties.

"We gave him a sedative," Doctor Pendergast stated. "But it's not working."

The repetitive movement of the man's body, and the constant pelting on the box, caused a crack in the glass to form above the section of his torso. Things took a turn for the worse when the six-inch fissure in the glass began to run.

When the man struck the cracked glass, blood trickled down the back of his hand. The display provided more indisputable evidence that the man was alive.

The doctors stood helplessly by when the man, missing his bottom half, ceased movement with a sudden jolt. Yala stood powerlessly on the sideline. The scene tore at her heart because there wasn't a thing she could do to ease his suffering.

"Come on, guy, one more day," she urged. She prayed her voice would help calm him or at least reassure him that others were there rooting for him and wanted to help save him.

"One more box, and you will be as good as new," she said, her tone low, soothing.

They needed the man to survive so he could at least tell them who did this to him and resume his life.

A few minutes passed before another set of seizures shot through the man, sending his hand straight through the cracked glass. The group froze, their eyes stuck on the area where the glass was broken. Blood leaked down his hand, running in rivulets like it was being called from his body.

Air was vacuumed from the room, giving Yala's lungs a good workout. It appeared the man needed the extra oxygen in the room to prolong his fight for his life.

"Technically, the box isn't open, so he should be okay, right?" Yala asked. The question was meant for anyone in the room with an answer, although her gaze was locked on the man.

He stopped seizing, and everyone instinctively sucked in a breath. Yala eased the man's bleeding hand back into the box and covered the hole in the glass with one of the doctor's thick medical books. She couldn't recall where she snatched the book from, but it made a good patch for the hole.

Kevin glanced over his shoulder at the door. "I'm going to find reinforcements to keep him inside that thing."

When he turned around and took the first step, an ominous *splat* sounded and stopped him in his tracks. His boots made a grunting sound against the floor before he froze. Yala gasped, eyes wide and searching. The doctors glanced at each other before they put their wide gazes back on the body.

A muffled *squish* sounded next and sent rippling chills up Yala's spine. The man's innards began to spill out and into the box.

This death was messier than the first. Instead of blood leaking and squirting out in spurts, this victim's insides popped out like they had been under pressure.

It looked like he was dropped, and his body burst open from the impact. His entrails crept out like scared rats whose hiding place had been discovered. Chunks and bits of tissue slid down the glass, resembling overcooked lumps of spaghetti with meat sauce.

The victim's eyes popped open and frantically searched for understanding. Had he become aware of what was happening to him?

No one mentioned the odor, but the scent made Yala's knees go weak, and she swallowed hard to keep her breakfast down. Death tortured their nasal passages.

Yala's eyes began to water. The pungent stench gripped her by the throat and wouldn't let go. She took sips of air as she struggled to breathe normally and fought to keep her stomach from doing somersaults.

The air and space surrounding them became bricked in by death's aroma. She swallowed saliva with every breath she took. Her eyes darted toward Kevin. With his sensitive nose, the scent was likely wreaking havoc on him.

Dr. Pendergast spoke first.

"The scent is strong because he is dissected across the intestines. He was cut at an angle, so he would be missing too many vital organs to survive without his lower extremities. The killer knew exactly what to cut."

Kevin's watery gaze remained pinned on the victim. "Who would do something so cruel to someone?"

The man's eyes popped open, wide and wildly searching. Yala leaned over the box and stared into the victim's distressed gaze. His body shook as his heart continued to pump blood into areas that could no longer circulate it.

Was he suffering? She leaned closer to the glass, enough that her own breath bounced back to brush her face. She pinned her gaze on his wide, frightened one, eyes that reflected the hollows of someone's worst fear.

Her voice cracked. "Can you say your name, sir?"

Staring into the man's eyes, seeing that he was alive and in distress, made her forget about the scent.

Kevin and the doctors gawked while she attempted to establish communication with the man. When he uttered a raggedly whispered name that sounded like "Julio," everyone in the room leaned closer and became aware that this man was lucid while clinging to the last strains of his life.

Dr. Hughes prepared a needle, opened the glass, and injected the man, which settled him.

"I gave him morphine to ease his suffering," he said, tossing the needle aside.

Dr. Pendergast reached down and took the man's hand while Yala whispered, "We will find out who did this to you. You'll find peace, harmony, and joy. I'm sure of it."

She believed he nodded. His frantic eyes found Yala and lingered before they darted in every direction, taking in all their faces. His free hand clenched so tightly, his knuckles strained against his skin. The peachy tint of his skin faded with every passing second. Recognition flashed in his gaze, and an unmistakable smile rested in his wide eyes but didn't make it to his lips. He knew he was dying, and Yala believed he'd made peace with the revelation.

However, when she glanced at Kevin's clenched teeth and stressed body, she realized that he was absorbing the remaining pain the man may have been experiencing.

The crew stood, helpless to save the man but determined to comfort him. Yala watched him struggle to take his last breaths. She concealed her true expression behind one she prayed reflected reassurance.

Had this man been suffering the entire time he'd been in the box? Had he experienced hunger or thirst? Endured aches and pains?

She noticed pain and biting fear in the man's eyes earlier, which made this murder more horrific than the first. Seeing this stranger like this made him real, no longer a subject nor a John Doe, but a real man with a mind and feelings.

The man's weak gaze found and locked with Kevin's, who appeared to be willing the poor soul's fears away.

His eyes fluttered a few times before they fell and remained half-mass. He was gone.

CHAPTER SIXTEEN

Kevin

"Okay, call me if you find anything I can use," Kevin said into the phone. He clicked off and considered everything he just learned. He glanced at Yala sitting behind the laptop, monitoring the camera he'd planted inside Elizabeth Paul's house.

Elizabeth hadn't returned yet, nor had she scanned her credit cards. Was she missing or hiding?

Yala had also learned how to hack into the traffic cameras and the DMV, and witnessing how proud she was of her accomplishment made Kevin smile. She was such an easy woman to like, but he'd also seen glimpses of that tough-as-nails side of her that drew him in just as much.

He redirected his train of thought when Yala caught him staring. "Doctor Nolan's phone was tracked to a hotel in downtown Atlanta. The agent in that area found the room he was renting empty, the bed still made, and no phone. Now, there was no phone ping at all, as though he knew they were coming and ran." Kevin took a seat next to Yala.

"Is it safe to say that Doctor Nolan is our number one suspect?" Yala questioned.

He nodded. "Yes. Either he is our box murderer, or someone is clever enough to make him the fall guy."

He fired up the second laptop and, within seconds, had the keyboard smoking.

"I've got something," Kevin said, as his eyes moved rapidly from left to right but remained glued to his monitor.

"What is it?" Yala asked, sliding her chair closer and leaning over to get a better look at the screen.

"I checked the background of the two guards we're keeping an eye on and found an interesting connection."

A smile flashed in Yala's eyes when Kevin pointed out the information that connected Elizabeth Paul, Doctor Nolan's mistress with Mark Jenkins, the shifty security guard.

"What's our next move?" she asked.

"Black site," he said. "We need to find them for questioning and possibly holding. If they're not the ringleaders of this circus, we may inadvertently put them in jeopardy if a part of their body is being leveraged to keep them in line."

Every aspect of this case was a tightrope walk. You couldn't do one thing without jeopardizing another.

"I'll see if I can find Mark's whereabouts," Kevin said, his fingers already moving rapidly over the laptop's keys.

***

An hour later.

"Kevin," Yala called, her tone hushed, while staring wide-eyed and aiming a stiff finger at the monitor. "Look who finally went home. Doesn't it look like she's sneaking into her own house?"

He nodded. "Yes. Let's go. I'll transfer the feed to our phones so we can keep an eye on her."

Yala and Kevin jetted out of the ME's office after sharing a quick update with the doctors. They were leaning over one of their tables, their white coats making them look like mad scientists conducting experiments.

They broke traffic laws and received the middle finger a record number of times, but they made it to Elizabeth's house in fourteen minutes. She'd disappeared upstairs and thankfully hadn't come down by the time Kevin pulled Yala's rental into a parking spot.

Getting into Elizabeth's house was a breeze. Yala waited in the bedroom until the woman finished her shower. She sat in a chair behind the area where the bathroom door remained open. The area provided the perfect hiding place.

Elizabeth exited the bathroom unaware of what waited for her. A large robe kept her hidden while she rummaged through her drawer for clothes.

Yala stood from the chair, her movement caught by Elizabeth in the mirror attached to her dresser.

"Aww!" She yelled out and scrambled to get out of the room. Yala lifted her gun.

"Hold it right there," she ordered. The woman froze, her hands lifted high in the air, her back to Yala. The big white robe she wore made her look taller than the demographics in her file suggested.

"I'm not here to hurt you. But we do need you to answer some questions. Get dressed."

She turned with her hands in the air. At the sight of Yala, the heavy coat of tension she wore grew lighter.

"You're not going to kill me?"

"No. We just need to ask you some questions."

Yala eased her weapon down before shoving it down the back of her pants. The subtle change in Elizabeth's expression and the twitch in her eyes made Yala shake her head.

"Don't try me, Elizabeth. You will not win. Now, get dressed."

"What is this…"

"Get dressed," Yala said in one of the deepest male voices she could call up. Elizabeth's lips parted and shut several times before she returned to the dresser and got dressed.

Yala wasn't intending to be a voyeur, but based on the flashes of Elizabeth the robe didn't cover, it appeared that all of her body parts were intact. It meant she could be taken in for questioning.

"Where are you taking me," Elizabeth worked up the courage to ask Yala after she was dress and walking down the stairs. Unfortunately, she kept asking despite Yala's lack of a reply.

"I didn't do anything wrong," she said. "My work with my clients is all legal and consensual. Their contracts were all written up by a legal professional and notarized."

Yala didn't reply but took her arm once they were outside her front door. If the nosey neighbors peeked, she hoped they assumed she was just a friend of Elizabeth's.

***

Kevin

Elizabeth's neighbor, Mrs. Cromwell, was forthcoming in telling him about Elizabeth's habits when he'd knocked on her door. Kevin pretended to be interested in moving into the vacant condo that was currently being renovated across from hers.

After he caught a glimpse of Yala moving toward their car with Elizabeth, he faked a headache and leg cramps and finally lied about leaving his child in the car to get away from Mrs. Cromwell.

When he climbed into the car, Yala was sitting in the back with a pissed-off Elizabeth. Chest heaving and eyes sharp enough to cut through metal, her hands were behind her back, cuffed.

"I can't wait to see the thousands rolling in from the big fat lawsuit I'm going to slap on you," Elizabeth spit out, her eyes meeting Kevin's through the rearview. "You can't take me without telling me why. You haven't even read me my rights."

"You have no rights unless we tell you what they are," Yala told her. "All we need is for you to talk when we need you to and answer our questions so you can get back to your life."

She huffed. "If it's that simple, why didn't you knock on my door like a normal cop and question me while sitting comfortably in my living room?"

Neither Yala nor Kevin answered. The *swish* of other cars and the beat of the city filled the gaping silence that filled the cab of the car.

Kevin watched from the rearview at the way Elizabeth kept assessing Yala, itching to say something. She allowed a teasing smile to flash across her lips before leaning closer to Yala in the back seat.

"Why didn't you say you wanted my services from the start," Elizabeth stated seductively.

"My clients are usually men, but you're hot," she continued, poking a hornet's nest. Yala was petite, beautiful, and appeared harmless, but Kevin knew better. Her appearance even fooled him until he remembered she was TOP. The training alone made her more than your average woman.

"Sorry, Ms. Paul, but you're not my type. You're not...enough. You see, I like to have something to grab when I knock a woman's world out of orbit."

Damn!

Kevin didn't drop his gaze, sensing Elizabeth's embarrassment from barking up the wrong tree. Even in the shadows bouncing across her face, he noticed the tent of color on her cheeks. Despite her embarrassment, he sensed how the sharp comment had also hyped up her libido.

Fifteen minutes later, they went through the same routine of being lowered into the sub-level before parking and walking up to the facility.

"Let's go, Ms. Paul."

She looked around frantically, her breathing rushed, her eyes wide and searching. "Where the hell are you taking me? You're not regular detectives, are you?"

"Nope," was all Yala said before the shiny glass doors opened for them. She gripped Elizabeth's arm to keep her moving.

The spike of uneasy tension Elizabeth was experiencing kicked up a level when she was shoved into the mirrored elevator. They were taking her down to a lower level to an area heavily warded by symbols against any magic.

The damage could go either way. Walking into the warded room could sever the magical connection, if there was one, or simply obstruct the one wielding the magic from using it against the victim.

They climbed aboard the elevator, and Yala punched in a ten-digit sequence to get them moving. The lights on the elevator dimmed when the doors closed, making Elizabeth's breaths accelerate and her body sway from side to side in an effort to control her building anxiety.

When the elevator began its descent, Elizabeth turned to Yala.

"We're going way deeper than a basement. Where the hell are we?"

"You'll know when you get there."

"Are you going to kill me?" she asked, her fear spiking.

"Depends. Have you done anything that warrants your death?" Yala asked. There was no signs of deception in the low hum of energy that radiated off Yala. She wanted this woman scared. A tactic that may eventually get her to talk.

Elizabeth bit into her bottom lip and shook her head rapidly. "No."

"Then you have nothing to worry about where it concerns your life ending. Unless—"

The space grew silent, the tension thick and suffocating until the doors sprang open to an empty white hall with lights so bright that Elizabeth blinked rapidly before turning her head down as if shielding her eyes from the sun.

"This way." Yala gripped her arm and led her closer to the warded room at the end of the hall. You couldn't see any of the warding as it was all painted on the walls with special paint that only illuminated the symbol when activated by the specific magic in which it was meant to neutralize.

Yala stopped Elizabeth at the door. Nothing happened. When they inched farther inside, Elizabeth didn't double over in pain or cry out from any power spike meant to do her harm. Instead, she kept glancing between Kevin and Yala, attempting to figure out why they stepped into the room like they didn't want to wake a sleeping monster.

Yala escorted her to the chair before she walked around the table and took one of the two chairs facing the suspect. Elizabeth glanced around the empty space, unaware that they were in a room painted with enough symbols that visibly seeing them would likely blind you.

Elizabeth sighed when she determined her life wasn't in any immediate danger.

"Ms. Paul," Kevin greeted with a nod in her direction before taking his seat. "I'm Kevin."

Her smile spread and grew wide as she took Kevin in fully for the first time.

"When was the last time you saw Doctor Nolan?" he asked, wiping the smile right off her face.

Before she could answer the first question, he hit her with a few more.

"Do any of your other clients besides Doctor Nolan work in the medical field? Why were you at the hospital searching for him on multiple occasions?"

Elizabeth released a few breathless utterances. A hard swallow made her throat jump before she cleared it.

"What is this about? Is Doctor Nolan okay?" she asked, her tone expressing concern.

"The sooner you answer our questions, the sooner you can return to your life."

She squinted, and a flash of fear peeked from the depths of her gaze. "The Doctor is currently at a convention. He's one of my most loyal customers. Therefore, I wanted to protect my investment and check up on his whereabouts since I don't know when he is supposed to return," she finally said.

Now that she knew Kevin wasn't there to flirt with her, she slouched in her seat, and the radiance that flashed in her eyes at the first sight of him dwindled down to a dull gleam. When neither Kevin nor Yala uttered a word, Elizabeth assessed them. Her eyes searched, and numerous questions danced in her gaze. A quick glance around the small room they were locked in reminded her that she couldn't run from her current situation.

"None of my other clients are in the medical field. Not that I'm aware of, at least," she finally replied.

Her gaze bounced between Kevin and Yala, dropping and rising quickly. It was a telltale sign that she was hiding something.

"We're aware that you are attending medical school. Are you involved in any unlawful practices that we should know about?"

Her head shook rapidly like a child afraid of an impending punishment.

"Does Dr. Nolan participate in any medical activities outside the hospital that you've witnessed or assisted him with?"

"No," she answered right away.

"We had a little chat with your Aunt, Lucy Jenkins. Remember her?"

"How do you know my aunt?"

Yala could see her thinking, possibly connecting the dots.

"What are the odds that your records and Mark's would list the same next of kin with the same address? When we spoke to Aunt Lucy, she insisted that you and Mark Jenkins, who work for the same hospital as Doctor Nolan, are first cousins."

Her eyes closed, and she kept them that way for a few seconds while releasing a sigh.

When she glanced up, it was into Kevin's eyes, in which she became transfixed, watching him like she was waiting for a command.

Yala glanced back and forth between them a few times. There was no energy exchange, but Kevin had to have been using his ability on Elizabeth. How? This wing was dedicated to suppressing magic.

"Tell me, Elizabeth, did you deliver a box to the medical examiner's office in the early hours of January 12th?"

She nodded.

The woman hadn't blinked once. Her admission had Yala on high alert, waiting to see what else she would admit to.

"Did you deliver the box for Doctor Nolan?"

She shook her head.

"What was inside the box?" Kevin asked.

She shrugged, her movements sluggish like she was impaired by drugs.

"I never knew what was in the box. My life was threatened if I attempted to look inside and not drop it off as instructed," she replied.

"Who were you dropping the box off for? Did you have help dropping it off?"

She shrugged. "I don't know who. I never saw the person. I was given an address on where to pick it up and where to drop it off. The box was heavy, so Mark helped me take it from my SUV?"

Yala side-eyed Kevin before studying Elizabeth. Was she under hypnosis?

"You said you had to drop off the box like you didn't have a choice. Why did you have to drop it off?" he asked.

She nodded before a tear slipped down her cheek. Her body had a slight tremble to it. Was she fighting the hypnosis, or was the hypnosis affecting her?

"Elizabeth, tell me why you had to drop the box off. Did someone threaten you if you refused?"

She nodded but didn't elaborate.

"Do they have dirt on you? Did they take something from you?"

Her facial expression tightened around her eyes and forehead.

"If I didn't deliver what they wanted, I wouldn't...wouldn't..."

It took everything within Yala not to ask the obvious question and spur Elizabeth on to spit out her answers faster. However, Yala feared any vocal interruption from her would disrupt the compelling connection Kevin had established with Elizabeth.

"They wouldn't, what?" Kevin asked.

"They wouldn't give me my body back."

Yala and Kevin's foreheads tightened.

"You're sitting in front of me. What do you mean by them not giving you your body back?"

Yala leaned over the table slightly, desperate to know what she meant. Elizabeth glanced down at herself.

"You wouldn't believe me if I told you."

"Try me," Kevin replied.

She stood and began lifting the wide loose fitting skirt she wore before she snatched down a pair of boxer briefs.

Yala didn't know what to expect and obviously hadn't paid enough attention to Elizabeth when she was wrapped in that robe at her house earlier. The hairy legs, the big calf muscles. Yala recoiled at the view before her now. She most certainly hadn't seen a dick, a big flaccid one.

"They. He. She. It. I never saw who did this to me, but I was given this lower body that belongs to my cousin, who has my lower half. They said it wouldn't be reversed until the mission was finished. I'm stuck like this. Do you know how fucking weird and terrifying it is to have to use the bathroom but go there, and nothing happens because my bodily fluids and waste are coming from the part of me that I no longer possess? Me and my cousin have to text each other each time we need to go to the bathroom. I had to touch his junk, keep it clean, and tuck it. I'll need therapy for the rest of my life. It's why I was desperately looking for Dr. Nolan. I was hoping he could help me or at least knew someone who could help us. I can't go around telling people that I woke up like this."

She glanced down at her cousin's parts. "Do you know how traumatizing it is to live like this, to look at my cousin's junk attached to my body? Every time he goes out and sees an attractive woman, I have to deal with this thing getting hard. The saving grace is that I can't feel it. I feel my own parts like they are still here. Therefore, every time I call my cousin and tell him I need to use the bathroom, I have to endure him wiping me. And let's not get started on me starting my period yesterday. Can you imagine what it's like to coach my male cousin on how to put in a tampon? Jesus."

Elizabeth bent and snatched the boxer briefs back up her cousin's legs before dropping the skirt.

Yala had never been so speechless in her life. The complexity of this situation kept getting deeper.

"We believe we can help you. But you have to *help* us help you," Kevin said.

"How? How can you possibly fix this when I've never seen the person's face that did this to us? Neither has my cousin. We woke up in a cheap motel room like this. The last thing I remember is walking to my car after a date with one of my clients outside the Lucky Stars restaurant. They must have gotten to me before I could get to my car. My cousin was taken when he was getting off work one morning."

Her admission on how she and her cousin worked together through this was impressive.

"This room you're in guards against them taking any further action on you. We need to track down your cousin and bring him here. If something happens to him out there, it will eventually affect you once you leave this room. Do you understand?"

She nodded, although her facial expression said she didn't have a clue. As far as the science in this went, there were no explanations. This was all magic.

"Give me the address to where you picked up the box. Do you know where your cousin is right now?"

"I picked up the box at 1125 Millscrest Drive. Mark is probably outside my condo. I called him when I decided to make a quick stop at my place, but you two got to me before he arrived. I've been staying with him at his apartment. He's convinced that the person doing this has been watching the both of us to make sure we don't reach out for help. Occasionally, he'll stake out my condo to see if he spots anyone. Yesterday, I believed it was you two he saw entering my side gate."

"Black Honda Accord," Kevin said.

She nodded.

"Today, I had an accident and didn't have a choice but to enter my place for a shower."

Yala didn't even want to know the details of that unimaginable situation.

"What else can you tell me about how you were brought into this? Give me every detail, even if you don't think it matters. We need anything that will help us track down who did this to you."

Elizabeth went through the story again of how she and her cousin were taken while going to their cars. They woke up with each other's lower half and a note on the bedside table with a phone number written.

The first call they made gave them instructions for the pickup and drop off of the box. Along with a second number to call. The second number was another set of instructions. Each call they made ended with another number and a time when they needed to call it. They never interacted with a person, it was always an automated voice, and she and her cousin were determined to follow the instructions in order to be made whole again.

Unfortunately, Elizabeth's story didn't provide much in the way of clues as to the mastermind pulling the strings, but Yala and Kevin had at least put another piece of the puzzle together.

"You're going to have to stay here until we track your cousin down," Kevin said. "You two have handled this situation well, and we will do everything in our power to help you get back to normal."

She nodded, and the first signs of tears appeared, clouding her eyes but not falling.

"Are you sure the person doing this to us can't hurt me or Mark in here?" She glanced around the room.

"I'm sure of it, but the key is making sure you two stay together."

He aimed a finger at the panel on the wall behind Elizabeth.

"If you hit that button, it opens a door to a small apartment. Food, clothing, cable, and books are already in there."

When they finally walked back to the car, Yala asked. "How were you able to use your ability to hypnotize her?"

He chuckled. "I wasn't using a gift. You can hypnotize anyone susceptible to falling under. I was taking her through the process of going under from the moment I climbed into the car: linking eyes with her in the rearview mirror, me tapping out a pattern on the steering wheel, and repeating certain words. When I sat in front of her at the table, I repeated the process. Tapping on the table, slowing the rhythm of the sound, repeating the words she needed to hear to open her mind to allow me access."

"That's impressive. You're turning me into a hacker. Is hypnosis another trick you can teach me?"

He nodded. "Gladly. I'll teach you anything you want to know."

***

It took them less than an hour to track down and bring in Mark once he was patched into a short chat with his cousin. Yala and Kevin questioned him extensively about what he recalled of his ordeal.

Mark, like Elizabeth, hadn't seen Doctor Nolan or the individual that manipulated them. Although, he did recall seeing a vehicle, the same one that chased Yala and Kevin, hanging out around his and Elizabeth's house.

Although Yala and Kevin found the watchman yesterday, they didn't reveal to Mark that the one who was keeping watch was also a victim of the monster who rearranged them.

CHAPTER SEVENTEEN

Yala

The suite was a haven after a day that never wanted to end for Yala and Kevin. Now that they'd found out their suspects were actually victims of this sadistic madman, they needed to strategize their next move.

Instead of relaxing, they suffocated under the weight of the multiple mysteries surrounding this assignment. They were back at a dead end. The doctors hadn't discovered any secrets hidden within the second box or the victim they took from it.

"Did you read the code in the news anchor's message?" Kevin asked while on the phone.

Yala had to use a pen and pad to decode the same message Kevin was currently mentioning over the phone. The national news anchor's message to TOP was about the rash of assassinations around the country. The anchor was an ally to TOP and was married to an agent.

Although Yala had decoded the message calling for available agents, she hadn't given any in-depth information to it because she was already on assignment. However, Kevin had received a call indicating that TOP might be pulling him as her partner to assist with what they considered a priority case.

"Yes. I arrived only…" he stopped abruptly. "I understand." He paused for another long moment. "Yes, thank you," he said before hanging up.

Yala could tell by the disappointment in his gaze that the call was bad news. Any case that made the national news threatened the delicate fabric keeping this world from going into chaos and panic. Kevin hung up and glanced at her, his eyes heavy with dread.

"They're pulling you," Yala said. It was a statement.

He nodded. "Too many dead civilians at the hands of what has to be a supernatural event or a new threat out there. They want me to sniff around, see what I can find out, provide a lead, anything to point the team of TOP agents already assigned in the right direction. It shouldn't take more than a week at the most."

She nodded. "Okay. Are they…" A hard knock sounded, stopping her question.

Kevin marched over and opened the door. The agents assigned to brief Kevin on the new case entered and introduced themselves with the sequence of numbers and letters that was as good as their agent fingerprint.

Yala knew the routine. Kevin was about to be briefed into the new case.

***

Thirty minutes later.

"When do you ship out?"

"Tomorrow," he answered, his droopy eyes likely reflecting her own.

"Big name political officials have been assassinated under circumstances that can't be explained, making it a matter of national security for multiple reasons. Another was shot twice, survived and told agents he believed the man was replicating himself. He was probably telling the truth but civilians heard him and had social media buzzing about his *mental breakdown*. However, they believe he may have witnessed the murderer using an ability we've never encountered."

She knew the routine. Knew that in cases of natural security, especially if they suspected paranormal activity or a paranormal phenomenon, all other cases took a back seat until the national threat was taken care of. In the case of Yala and Kevin, they pulled him and left her.

"The attacks occurred simultaneously in four different states and no suspects were apprehended even after TOP got involved. Unfortunately, they weren't able to stop the early media attention. Therefore, it's being labeled a planned terrorist attack."

***

Kevin

Less than an hour later, Kevin dreaded the notion of their impending separation. How had they gone from finally making headway to now being split up? This wasn't an unlikely event in their line of work, as the number of hard-to-explain events had ramped up over the past few years.

However, this was one of those times when he'd welcome a different outcome. The ache happening in the center of his chest matched Yala's droopy-eyed expression. He would be sent to Texas, and she would remain in DC with a murderer who had the ability to take people apart, exchange their parts with others, and scatter them to different locations while keeping them alive.

This methodical box killer didn't leave clues and used victims to cover his tracks.

"I'm not prepared to say goodbye to you so soon after gaining our footing in this case," Kevin said. How had he developed such an acute affinity attraction to her so quickly? This case wasn't all he would miss—he enjoyed being around Yala even if they weren't involved in a romantic relationship.

They operated in a world that often floated outside the realm of reality. Did that commonality help feed their connection? He didn't know, but she made him smile from just being near her.

Hours were all that remained before his early morning departure. He aimed a finger over his shoulder, although his body wanted to slide closer to Yala. He sensed her distress, but there was also a pleasant buzz, the kind that could make him high if he took in too much at a time.

"I'll pack up and do some last-minute troubleshooting, see if I can connect a few more dots before I leave," he said.

She nodded, and he sensed her eyes on him when he got up and walked the short distance to his laptop sitting in the small section of the living room carved out to be the office area.

Yala could have gone to bed, but her roaring curiosity kept her awake. She had to know if she'd imagined the strength of his attraction to her.

When he finished, he sat next to her on the couch, so close their legs and shoulders touched. The radiating warmth from her closed his eyes, and he inhaled her scent.

"Yala," his tone was low, but her name sounded like a question. He turned and looked into her eyes.

"Yes."

"Tell me it's not just me."

"It's not just you. But I'll be the first to admit that I don't know what to do, and even if I did, I'm not sure seeking out more would be a good idea."

He released a long-winded sigh before reaching down and taking her hand, his touch soothing. "How about we enjoy each other's company right now and not think about tomorrow, an hour from now, or even ten minutes from now."

She nodded.

"It sounds like a good idea. How about we play the age-old game of twenty questions? I'd like to know more about you."

He chuckled while nodding. "Let's order food and a few drinks, and you've got yourself a date."

And so they did. They filled the evening with food. Drinks. Laughter. And some of the best and worst highlights of each other's lives kept them going until sleep crept in and demanded they answer its call.

***

Yala

The next morning.

Yala sat on the couch pretending to watch television, but her eyes kept straying to Kevin's bag, already packed and sitting by the front door. He hovered at her back, the constant tap of his fingers moving across the keyboard signaling his efforts to help her despite being thrust into another case at the last minute.

How was she going to say goodbye without her emotions spilling out all over the place? She turned and watched him stare at the computer screen as if trying to absorb the words versus reading them.

If he sensed half of what currently raced through her concerning her feelings towards him, the entrenching stare was warranted. However, their world didn't leave much in the way of choices. Turmoil was always on the horizon, which didn't allow room for romance or whatever it was that had developed between them. Yala stood from the couch to approach Kevin.

He glanced up, and his poignant gaze gripped her attention. She stumbled, and her quick reflexes kept her from falling over her own feet. She smiled away her embarrassment, her cheeks flaming hot.

Kevin stood. "It's time for me to get out of here," he said. He forced a smile while they locked with hers.

They were a foot away from each other now. Yala didn't know what to do or her legs. She'd never had to deal with emotions when it came to the opposite sex—this ebbing and pulling and edgy tingling that made you all gooey and stupid. Finally, she planted her legs to firm up her posture and encircled herself in a hug.

"This was a short-lived partnership," she said.

"I won't be gone long. I'll be seeing you again soon," he said, his eyes roaming her from head to toe. Of course, he couldn't predict how long he would be gone, yet he made the declaration sound like a promise.

She turned toward the kitchen, failing at calming her fidgety movement and the biting edge of her hyped-up breathing.

"I need some water," she said before taking off. She needed something to dissolve the huge lump that formed in her throat. Until Kevin, she was content with fake hookups and pseudo-relationships for the sake of the job.

What was it going to take to lift the sack of bricks that had suddenly landed on her chest? Where were these emotions being created, and where was the leakage that allowed them to race through her bloodstream?

Surely, Kevin was using his gift on her. Was he experiencing the same effects as her?

Yala faced the sink and didn't have to glance back to sense Kevin's silent approach. He stood behind her now, his warm breath sweeping against her neck.

She turned to face him and to face the silent fear she lied to herself about for years. Although she often disguised herself as a man and pretended to be one, she didn't know how to be with one in a real relationship. Trapped in his gaze now, she became his captive.

The small kitchen didn't give her much room to get away from the intensity Kevin brought with him. He took a careful step closer, likely sensing her revved-up nerves.

"I'm not ready to say goodbye to you, Yala."

She maintained her stance on unsteady legs, her gaze pinned to his, although she lost her train of thought. Kevin leaned closer and took her hand.

"I'll miss you, but not for long. I want to see you again, Yala, and I'm not talking about seeing you again as *just* your partner for this case."

She couldn't decipher what he said. Kevin's closeness stole her breath and made her mental focus seep from her skull.

He assured her that he wouldn't, but the question crossed her mind again: was he using his special ability to drain her mind of its ability to think? Where had these feelings come from? More importantly, why had they grown so intense?

***

Kevin

Yala's stiff posture and charged emotions heightened his concern. One moment he sensed happiness, followed by sadness, and finally, fear. Where did the fear come from?

She turned, drinking water with her back to him. He was emerging into a world built on emotions. Like walking through a minefield, Kevin treaded lightly into Yala's personal space, testing for the emotional bombs she might have planted to ward him off.

The energy was an edgy tingle of palpable sparks. The knowledge that he made her experience this was a compliment as well.

His hand slid around her waist, the caress making her suck in a sharp breath and her shoulders shooting up to her ears. Despite her reaction, he didn't drop his hand, sensing the ease that followed. He pulled her closer, turning her body into his.

Her tension evaporated like mist, and she relaxed and leaned into his delicate hold. She closed her eyes and inhaled, using more of her senses to accept him. He allowed her to flow into him before he folded her into a delicate caress, their bodies mingling, arms encircling, faces in necks, breathing each other.

They remained in the exhilarating hold for no more than five, maybe ten seconds, but it felt like forever, yet it wasn't enough. She backed out of his embrace and focused on his chest, avoiding his eyes.

At the moment, he was thankful she didn't meet his gaze because he knew what she would find. Raw desire flowed through him like it owned his body. He bent in search of her eyes, but she wouldn't give them.

"Why won't you look at me?" The words floated softly from his lips. He knew the answer but remained compelled to hear her say it. He needed every scrap of reassurance that it wasn't just him caught in the storm of passion they produced together.

She lifted her gaze, proving her bravery. Anyone willing to take a gang beating to gain leverage on their case had balls the size of basketballs.

Their gazes locked, and some controlling force slammed into place, cementing their connection. Worlds didn't just collide, they merged, anchoring him to her in a way that he'd never experienced, never could have imagined.

Kevin adjusted his stance when his hand inadvertently slipped down her body from the potency of the piercing ache cocooning them together. Her body moved in tandem with his hands, their shared tether a flowing entity with rhythmic synchronicity.

Kevin sank deeper, losing his identity in Yala's eyes. The energy exchange flowed outside their bodies, an interdimensional linking that rendered them speechless.

Kevin's hands moved of their own accord, encircling her, pulling her in closer, tighter, while she mimicked his movement with her own hands inching up until they met at the nape of his neck. Her fingertips flirted with his warm skin, leaving a trail of tingles wherever she touched.

Her body, warm and soft against his, was an intoxication, a pool of the best drugs he wanted nothing more than to drown in.

Kevin didn't have the willpower to say a quick goodbye and let Yala go. His legs refused to work when he attempted to step away from the intoxicating woman.

"Can I ask you something?" he whispered, his words a rush of sound while his lips hovered above her ear before he lowered them to her lips.

Yala took a lingering moment to respond. Her glossy-eyed gaze let him know she remained under the effect of their intense connection.

"Yes," she answered, her voice a delicate sound he believed created for him.

He kept her close with a palm cradling her lower back. His finger twirled around a lock of her hair he'd noticed never stayed in place.

"What's your real name?"

She couldn't form a single word while his hand slid firmly up her spine. The other brushed along the side of her neck. He knew the question was one she would have trouble answering, despite his distractions. He had it on good authority that she guarded her identity like a well-kept secret.

No longer able to fight the urge, Kevin closed the distance that separated them, leaned in, and teased her lips with a delicate stroke, his lips the brush, before he deepened the pressure.

Yala stood, suspended before him, paralyzed in the same wave of sensation that spread through him like wildfire. He stroked her arms, her back, and her waist. He wanted to explore all of her all at once.

Unable to control the instant addiction claiming him, he breathed against her lips before lavishing them with more kisses. Their lips mingled like two parts of a musical instrument creating an exotic tune that couldn't be decoded.

He relished the flavor and lushness of her mouth. A sound between a sigh and a moan escaped her, a sensual response that drew him in deeper.

When Yala parted her lips and released a passionate, heavy moan, parts of him came apart and poured into her. All else in life was forgotten. This kiss became their world now. He needed to find a way to stop, or they would end up taking things to the next level. He'd sensed it in her lingering stares and bashful smiles that she wasn't ready to go there with him yet. He would wait however long it took.

He shook off the passion fog and recalled his question. He wanted to know Yala's real name. If she revealed her name, he would know that she genuinely trusted him, despite the short time they'd known each other.

She raised her head, inched up on her toes to reach his ear, and whispered, "Yancy Langston."

Realizing what she confessed, Yala closed her eyes and appeared to be praying that she'd done the right thing. The moment she revealed her true self, he accepted that he didn't mind being ensnared in the beautiful, emotional web she spun for him.

He whispered her name, "Yancy Langston," while keeping his gaze firmly locked on hers. The big grin on her face was a pleasant sight among all of the emotions fanning around them.

"Yancy Langston. So, Yala is another of your clever disguises? First two letters of the first and last name you never give anyone," he said.

He swept his lips across her cheek before lowering it to brush the corner of her mouth and finally covering her lips once more. She broke the kiss and backed away, gasping for air after a lifetime of the pleasant push and pull of them tasting each other.

He slid his hand along the contours of her stomach and inched it higher until he reached her chest. Her lips fell apart at his bold move, their gazes searching, their breaths blowing out faster. His hand rested against her heaving chest while he leaned in to graze her ear.

"This is mine. I'm taking this with me because you took mine on our first night together."

When he spread his fingers over her chest and pressed his palm into the center of it, understanding flashed in her gaze.

Was it too soon to be this possessive of her heart? It probably was, but Kevin wanted her to know where he stood before he left.

Having been frozen in place by his declaration, Yala's brows lifted. Her lips opened and closed several times, but she was unable to respond verbally.

She staggered back until the counter smacked her butt. She lifted a shaky hand and placed it over the center of her chest.

For a few seconds, her bewildered expression would have made you believe he actually uprooted her heart and snatched it from its sturdy seat inside her chest. She took deep breaths attempting to stabilize her breathing.

Kevin considered apologizing for his behavior, but he wasn't sorry for kissing her or for speaking such possessive words. She'd taken his heart, and it was only fair he took possession of hers to keep him going.

Yala remained against the counter with her hand over her chest, staring at him like he was a witch doctor.

A small smile danced across her face and zipped up to her eyes. The sight enticed his smile. She'd given him her full name. It was a priceless sentiment and why he believed he could be this open with her.

"See you later," she voiced, in that carefree way he was becoming familiar with.

He leaned in, unable to resist one last kiss. "See you later, Yancy," he whispered.

When he attempted to turn and walk away, his body grew heavy and his limbs sluggish like walking through mud. How could he have this much difficulty walking away from a woman he hardly knew?

The idea of seeing her again strengthened his resolve and gave him the courage he needed to keep walking.

CHAPTER EIGHTEEN

Kevin

The mission, if you could call it that, was over within ten days. Unfortunately, it had taken another of the nation's leaders' life for Kevin to get the initial scent of the suspect from a fresh crime scene.

The Governor of Virginia was killed. The winding trail had led Kevin through a maze of suspicious people, rats, wrongfully accused, and conspiracy theorists until he eventually found his suspect.

However, the suspect, a forty-year-old bus driver, didn't go down easily. He was considered a *hindered* in the paranormal community, which meant he'd recently discovered his ability. Unfortunately, he chose to use it for evil and had landed on TOP's radar.

He had lured the local cops and later the SWAT team into a thirteen-hour shootout. They were faced with killing the same man repeatedly, as he harbored the ability to make at least a dozen copies of himself.

Fortunately, regular bullets were lethal to him. Law enforcement killed seven copies of him before they found the original. Taking out the original proved to be the key to killing the rest. Unfortunately, the motive for his murderous rampage died with him.

Now, Kevin's mission was to reunite with Yala and to relieve his anxiety about solving the mystery of the box and finding the killer.

***

Yala

The small cozy town of Truth, Kansas welcomed her with warmth as strangers waved at her rolling by like they knew her. The easygoing vibe of the people. The quiet mountainous views. The ability to drive without honking your horn, slamming on the brakes, or getting the bird flipped at you is what drew her to the small town.

Yala bit into a smile at the sight of her home. The tension of the case was already melting away like warm butter. Dark-gray bricks nestled between large study logs made up her two story cottage-style home. Two years of searching had finally landed her the home she'd envisioned in her dreams.

She purchased the place to stay grounded and away from what she so often chased down and came in contact with in her job. Now, her home was her sanctuary, a place she could run to when she believed she needed a breather. A break. Something normal.

DC had turned into an exhausting pursuit of a killer attempting to pass himself off as a magician who wasn't leaving much in the line of clues to track him down. The suspects in TOP's custody, Elizabeth Paul and Mark Jenkins, were safe, but Yala hadn't revealed to them yet that they were only safe under the protection of TOP and the warded space in which they currently lived.

Kevin's daily text messages had gotten her through more dead-end leads, stakeouts, and chasing a ghost probably hidden in plain sight. There were no details in his pursuit of the terrorist or terrorist group he was attempting to track down.

After seven days of chasing her tail and running down useless leads, Yala decided to visit the home she paid for and rarely lived in because of how busy TOP kept her.

There hadn't been any boxed victims that showed up at the medical examiner's office or anywhere else that they were aware of. Despite it being the worst thing that could happen to someone, receiving another box may be the only way to finding out who was doing this and their motive behind the mysterious box collection.

There had to be a clue that she or the doctors overlooked, which could lead her to at least unravel a few of the demented threads holding the killer's secrets in place.

She periodically checked in with Dr. Hughes, while he continued his nonstop quest of trying to discover a scientific explanation. The doctors also had her on speed dial if more progressed in the case.

Kevin crept into her mind. Why was she so drawn to him? Maybe both of them possessing secret abilities was a part of it, but something else lingered between them that she didn't yet understand.

Ten days had passed since she first laid eyes on that devilishly handsome man. Thankfully, work kept her busy enough to lessen the time she spent thinking about him.

Hours later, fresh from a shower and relaxed, she headed toward the comfort of her living room couch with dinner—a bag of Twizzlers. Although dusk had fallen, a steady flow of energy continued to run through her, so going to bed wasn't an option. There was nothing worse than lying there staring at a dark ceiling while thinking about every negative incident that came to mind.

She picked up a book she'd read three times already, *Topaz*, by one of her favorite authors, Beverly Jenkins. She was reading the description of the sexy-sounding Dixon Wildhorse when a weird vibe struck her senses and made her shoulders tense.

She shook the sensation off. She was home now. She could relax. There were no supernatural monsters she needed to chase down, catch, or put down.

No less than ten minutes later, she jerked up, her neck cracking from her head's fight with gravity. The strawberry Twizzler she'd been snacking on was still pressed between her lips, a portion continuing to spread flavor over her tongue.

The chime of her doorbell called her attention, making her adrenaline shoot through the roof. Eyes glued to the door, she threw her legs over the edge of the couch.

Who was at her door at ten at night? She lived in a discreet location, away from the small town, out in the sticks, and not found unless a nosey sightseer accidentally stumbled upon her residence.

She jammed the nine-millimeter she kept under her couch cushion into the back of her pajama pants and crept toward the entrance. A tall, dark shadow silhouetted the glass portion of the door. She'd had the original glass replaced with bulletproof glass and most of her house reinforced with other protective measures—in case her work world ever came knocking at her door.

Her hand rested at her back as she gripped her pistol. She sprang the door open and lost her breath at the sight of *him*. She couldn't move. All parts of her were stuck in time like one of the ominous time-frozen crime scenes she'd witnessed a year prior.

"Kevin," his name blew out barely above a whisper, her voice trapped in her throat.

He smiled, perfectly content to stand there ogling her. When he showed the hand he'd had behind his back, out came a single red rose.

Her gaze remained glued to his face while accepting the gift. Finally, her gaze dropped to the flower in her hand, and she imagined she looked crazy. She'd never received any gifts from a man before.

"Thank you. Come in," she said, reeling over him being there. Was she on the couch sleeping and having an out-of-body experience? Anything was possible now that paranormal activities were becoming the new norm.

She stepped aside to allow him to enter and instinctively peeked outside to scan her surroundings. Satisfied with the swaying dark trees blanketed by a bright moonlit sky, she closed the door.

The second deadbolt clanked noisily into place before she took a few memorized steps toward her lamp to bring more light into her living room and this unexpected situation.

"I'm sorry. You can have a seat if you'd like," she offered, lifting the rose.

"Thank you. This is beautiful. I need to find something to put it in." She stepped away and headed toward the kitchen, glancing over her shoulder. *What now?*

"Would you like something to drink?" she called back from the kitchen.

Her nerves were hot-wired into an engine of chaos. Deep breaths did nothing to calm her. She wasn't this girl—dainty, feminine, shy, and unsure.

Kevin was the first man she'd invited into her home, and she chose to believe his presence had nothing to do with her amped-up nerves. At least, that is what she was attempting to make herself believe.

Who was she kidding? He had everything to do with her nerves. He was a first for her. The first man she'd taken an interest in. The first she'd trusted so easily.

Him being here meant he'd survived whatever monster he'd had to chase down, and now he'd chased *her* down.

Kevin's light steps drew him closer, his presence tightening the space in her kitchen and heightening the wattage of her nerves. She was trained and certified by one of the best agencies in the country. Surely, she could handle this personal situation, one that many would find relatively easy to manage.

She rummaged through her kitchen more so for something she already knew she didn't have, a vase. She picked up a pitcher that she half filled with water. She turned toward Kevin, who hadn't said a word yet.

"As you can see, I don't get flowers often."

His tongue slid across his bottom lip, an enticing action that drew her gaze to his mouth.

"I guess that means I'll have to start giving you more," he replied, his smile growing wide while his gaze remained pinned on hers.

He took a cautious step closer like he expected her to stop him before he reached out and took her hands and lifted, pressing kisses to the back of each. He transferred his hands to her waist, drawing her closer.

"Come here," he said, his words barely audible.

Her fingers traced up his arms. Instead of shying away like she assumed she would, she drew closer. She'd missed him. Was it possible to miss someone she hardly knew?

She swallowed her quick breath, but it didn't calm her racing heart. Roaring heat rose to the surface and added strength to their reacquaintance.

Neither spoke. Their emotional exchange expressed more than their words could.

Kevin tightened his embrace, squeezing her like they were an established couple that hadn't seen each other in months. The hug was too tight, but she didn't care. He'd taken possession of her mind for days, and finally, having contact with him soothed her busy mind.

Did he have any idea how worried she'd been for his well-being? Had he been worried about her too?

He eased his hold as if to let her go but reclaimed it, deciding they needed to add more depth to their reunion with a kiss.

He leaned in, and she met him halfway, their lips a light brush of warm, soft mingling flesh before he deepened the kiss. He captured her lips, pressing with a firmer intensity that she graciously accepted. A moan of appreciation escaped when his tongue traced her bottom lip and licked up her tongue.

Breathless, Yala broke the kiss to breathe and think. Why was she thinking? This wasn't the time. The warm wisps of her breaths enticed her to seek out more. She tilted her head to give him better access while he cupped her jaw to recapture her lips.

"What are we doing?" she managed to ask between the most sensual kisses she'd enjoyed yet. He took one last pull of her lips.

"I don't know, but I can't get you out of my head, no matter how much time passes."

After another peck, she took his hand and led him to the living room. They needed to talk, specifically about how he'd found her.

"I need to be seated if you intend to keep taking my breath away," she admitted, glancing back at him.

The comment was meant to stay in her head, but with her mental focus stolen, it made Kevin lift a brow before a sneaky smile spread over his sexy lips.

She waited until he sat before she took her seat. He patted the area right beside him when she tried to put too much space between them.

"Will you please sit closer? I promise I won't make you lose your breath again."

So he had jokes now? She tapped him playfully on the arm and lost her breath once more when he lured her clean across his lap with a hard pull.

This was new territory. Intimacy. The many times she'd shifted into a male and had to pretend didn't count because she knew she was acting. She and Kevin were not make-believe.

The ideas in her head scattered when his lips raked her neck and sent her body into a heat-filled frenzy. He drew her against his chest before enveloping her in his arms. This intimate exchange should have induced more uncertainty, but she found a different kind of rush filling her senses.

"I'd like to know about you, Yala," Kevin whispered. "I want to know everything about you if you're willing to share it."

She acknowledged that she trusted Kevin, but she needed to figure out what made her trust him so easily.

CHAPTER NINETEEN

Yala

Yala didn't want him to know everything, but she couldn't say no to him, even when her brain screamed for it. Her actions with Kevin scared her to death but, at the same time, gave her the type of quiet satisfaction she'd never known.

Kevin didn't say a word while she sat in the eerie stillness of her living room atop his lap and considered his request.

"I must warn you about something before I start this story," she said. Her long pause after the comment put a crinkle at the corners of his eyes.

"I have done things that I'm not proud of. Some horrible things that I sometimes have trouble believing I'm capable of doing. But, however horrible my actions were, I'm not sorry for them."

He took her hand before readjusting their seating arrangement so she could sit beside him and maintain eye contact. With his empathic ability, he sensed her need for encouragement.

"We catch killers, and sometimes we have to kill bad people to do our jobs effectively; therefore, I don't think there's anything you can tell me to make me think less of you," he assured, squeezing her hand.

She snuggled onto his side when he wrapped an arm around her back, laying her head against his strong shoulder.

She breathed, long and deep, and released it gradually, relieving her last bit of tension.

"When I was a girl, I lived with my mother, Nikki, in one of the worst areas in Miami, Liberty City. Nikki was crack-addicted my entire life, possibly while I was inside her. She was one of those serious cases of an unfit parent. If it hadn't been for our elderly neighbor, Mrs. Bertha, I'm sure starvation would have been added to the list of neglect my mother bestowed on me.

"I managed to scrape through my first five years, thanks to Mrs. Bertha and her prayers. The older woman was afraid I'd end up raped or killed as a result of my mother's lifestyle. Mrs. Bertha was the one who registered me in school and, for years, ensured I ate at least one extra meal besides what I received from school."

Yala swallowed a knot of reluctance and continued. She dreaded telling this story because it dredged up the worst part of her life. However, she'd endure the tortured memories for Kevin.

"Unfortunately, Mrs. Bertha died when I was eleven, leaving me to find a way to take care of myself. I loved school. I found comfort in learning and dreaded going home every day because my mother entertained a different man every night. Loud drinking and drug parties greeted me most nights. Multiple times, I'd walk into the kitchen or the bathroom and find her having sex with a strange man or taking drugs. Nikki was usually too drunk and drugged to care about being on display.

"At eleven, I possessed more worldly knowledge than the average child since I'd spent most of my life watching my mother's mistakes. I was teased and taunted at school about my scraggly appearance, but I didn't care about being teased. Life at school was ten times better than what I endured at home. When Nikki disciplined me, it was with her fists, sometimes with no reasoning behind her actions. The beatings were always brutal, like she was taking out her failures in life on me. She'd go through long spells of total detachment that left me wondering if the verbal and physical abuse would have been better than the neglect she dispensed. The school, students, and faculty knew my mother as a well-known crackhead, and their knowledge of us was an added punishment as far as I was concerned."

Yala shook her head in an attempt to ward off her childhood memories because they dredged up feelings of loneliness and helplessness.

"I was way too young to work, but I got lucky when the owner of our neighborhood store, Mr. Lee, allowed me to bag groceries for tips in the evenings. The job couldn't have come at a better time because it was a few weeks after Mrs. Bertha passed away. Massive heart attack. With the little money I earned, I purchased food and clothes."

Although Kevin remained quiet, Yala sensed his tension growing with each sentence she added.

"I spent the next couple of years much the same, working for tips and taking care of myself, all while my mother's habit worsened. Instead of leaving for days at a time, she began leaving for weeks and occasionally forgot to pay the rent and electricity bills. It was difficult to sleep in a hot apartment teeming with rats and roaches. I often used what little money I made to keep the power on. My mother was ignorant of the fact that I even had a job. If she'd known, she would have taken my money for drugs."

Yala clinched her eyes tightly against the jarring memories flooding her brain like a swarm of biting insects.

Kevin squeezed her hand while rubbing a caring hand up and down her back. She was dragged so deeply into her memories that she'd forgotten where she was and who she was currently curled up to until he shifted next to her. The gentleness Kevin lavished on her gave her the encouragement she needed to continue.

"I hated the word Section 8 until it came to mean that rent was fifty dollars a month, and I wouldn't have to sleep on the streets when my mother left for long periods.

"About a month after my thirteenth birthday, I suspected Nikki was in trouble, but I didn't know to what extent. She'd been gone for three weeks this time."

Kevin's breathing sped up, and the muscles in his arms twitched against Yala's back. He sensed the worst of her story was yet to be told.

"I knew every nook and cranny of our neighborhood. After two days of searching, I found Nikki. The hateful stench assaulted me first. I found her in a dumpster covered by a dirty blanket which was a representation of how she lived, surrounded by vile filth of every kind. Seeing a dead body in our neighborhood wasn't a big deal, but seeing someone you knew made death a reality. I stared into my mother's dead, glossed-over eyes while rats scurried away from nesting and eating what was left of her body. Even now, it was one of the most haunting things I've seen. Her face was forever frozen in sorrow, it was like she was laying there begging me for forgiveness."

A shiver shook Yala to the core and caused Kevin to pull her more firmly against him. Yala pried the words loose from the lucid memories that continued to plague her dreams.

"Nikki's mushy flesh and the stench suggested she'd been there for days. Her eyes had changed from light brown to a grayish blue, wide open and empty. Her skin, normally light beige, had turned a dark ashy gray.

"I didn't know what to do. I rewrapped her rotting body with the blanket I'd found her in and stood there for what must have been an hour in an attempt to figure out my next move. I had to find a way to get her into a grave."

The delicate kiss Kevin placed against her forehead when he felt her shiver from the memory gave her a spark of strength.

"Take your time or finish later. You don't have to keep going if you don't want to," he said.

Yala shook her head. "I want to finish. I need to finish." She sucked in another shivering breath. "After discovering Nikki, I walked home. Numb, I couldn't feel anything mentally or physically. No hurt. No sorrow. No heartaches. Only a sense of relief. I went to work and called the cops from the phone inside Mr. Lee's stockroom.

"I reported a dead body and the location without giving my name. Since everyone knew my mother, I assumed people would figure out who she was. However, no one came forth and identified her or even mentioned that she was missing. The cops never came searching for me, either. Nikki to them, was just another dead body."

Kevin's frown deepened.

"I followed Nikki's case based on what the streets whispered. I don't think the cops bothered investigating and simply labeled her death an overdose and her a Jane Doe. I don't believe they even bothered to identify the body before they ordered it cremated.

"At thirteen, I was alone but with enough experience to survive. There were so many horror stories about foster care, I believed I was better off on my own. I avoided opening the front door for fear it would be child protective service coming to take me into custody. I knew how to feed myself, how to cover the rent and the electricity bill, and how to purchase the few personal items I needed. No one but me and the person who dumped Nikki in the alley knew she was dead. She was already known for her disappearing acts, so when someone stopped by the apartment, I told them she was away, getting high."

Yala adjusted , burrowing deeper onto Kevin's side.

"Guys who used to ignore me started to whistle at me and heckle me on the way to my apartment. I worked late for Mr. Lee, because I desperately needed the extra money."

"My mother's behavior with men and the way they treated her gave me a warped view of how I should interact with them. I was naïve and believed that not showing any interest at all in men would deter their interest in me. Many of the women and girls in my neighborhood were easygoing with men. They accepted disrespect and, in some cases, abuse. My luck ran out the night of my four-teenth birthday."

Kevin slammed his eyes shut. His shoulders dropped, and he stilled, having an idea of where her story would lead.

"That night, a group caught me before I could enter my apartment. They dragged me through the window of a boarded-up apartment building. One of the saddest parts of the incident was that there were people sitting outside, talking and drinking. None of them saw fit to help a young girl, kicking and screaming against the will of four guys. I was ignored, even laughed at by a few."

Kevin placed his forehead against the side of her head, likely sensing the ache of her past radiating through her. If she stopped now, she feared she'd never restart, so she was set to tell him the rest.

"Two were teenagers, and the others were at least in their early twenties. I was their temporary entertainment. My screams and thrashing around didn't deter them from taking my virginity. The pain—there was so much. It got to the point that I slipped in and out of consciousness and was unable to hear and see them half the time. I did hear enough to know that they bragged about doing the same thing to my mother in exchange for the coke they gave her laced with fentanyl. They were the monsters who killed her. They'd likely had eyes on me the entire time. After the third guy began, I'd found a way to block out the pain."

Yala's voice cracked partly because of Kevin's reac-tion, his head shaking against hers. It had taken her a long time to accept that the events of that night had shaped her entire adult life.

"I stopped fighting. Stopped screaming. Stopped moving. I believe my mind separated from my body to endure what was being done. Help never came. I was trapped in a nightmare and laid there helplessly enduring the torture."

Although she promised herself she'd never spill another tear over her torturous past, one slipped from Yala's eye. She sniffed a few times and steadied her voice.

"I filed those four faces away in my brain. Assaulting me hadn't meant a thing to them. They left me lying on an old dirty mattress like a piece of trash. They'd ravished me. Ate my soul and threw away what was left until I blacked out. I believed I died. I woke up alone and folded into a tight casket of pain."

Yala paused when Kevin's shoulders quaked as if he was crying. She eased back from him enough to notice water glistening in the corner of his eyes. Touched by his sentiment, she fought tears of her own and used her thumb to wipe away his wet empathy.

"It's okay. I'm okay now. It's not the most conventional way to gain strength, but I found a way because I survived it. I believe that young girl died that night. Yancy died in that apartment on that old dirty mattress."

Kevin had listened, absorbed her sorrow, and shared her pain. It was there on his face, in the way he gazed at her and in the way he comforted her. He placed her hand up to his cheek before he kissed the inside of her palm.

She continued where she'd left off.

"I stumbled out of there, crying and with blurred vision, to the nearest bus stop. Making it to the hospital was more of a blur than an actual memory. The nurse at the desk took one look at me and immediately knew what had happened. The hospital called the cops, but I knew the cops couldn't help me, so I pretended I hadn't seen any of my attacker's faces.

"I explained my mother's absence by blaming it on her drug abuse. I couldn't tell anyone my mother had been dead for nearly a year at that point, and I'd been on my own the entire time. The doctor and nurse did their best to explain that because of the brutality I suffered, some of my reproductive parts were damaged and I'd never be able to bear children. I spent a few weeks in the hospital before I was discharged.

"Reluctantly, I returned to my neighborhood. I didn't see the guys who'd raped me for nearly four months. I began carrying the gun, and the switchblade my mother kept in the shoebox at the top of her closet.

"I believe that tragic event is what sparked the energy I didn't know I possessed to start my disguises. I began dressing like a boy, and people treated me differently. They respected me more and treated me nicer. I hadn't glanced in a mirror since the rape. Therefore, I was unaware that I wasn't only dressing like a boy but also shifting into one. It was people's reactions that forced me to finally take a look at myself."

Yala tilted her head, her thoughts running rampant.

"The thing that blew my mind was Mr. Lee. He knew who I was the entire time. Yet, he never asked or commented on my appearance even though I was showing up to work as a different person."

Yala paused to smile at the sentiment, the acceptance.

"After another month went by, I spotted one of my attackers. Since I could become a guy now, it was easy to lure him, with drugs, into the same abandoned apartment he'd raped me in. I intended to shoot him and get the deed done fast, but I didn't. I wanted him in pain. I wanted him to suffer as much as I had. I stabbed him repeatedly. I was small with no upper body strength, so it took longer for my stabs and slashes to seriously impact him. I stabbed him until my hands went numb, and it still wasn't enough to make up for what he'd done to me."

Yala snuck a quick glance at Kevin. She suspected that he schooled his expression so as not to let her see what he truly thought of her.

"He begged for help and pleaded for me to stop. I revealed my true face, which added fuel to his horror. I let him see the monster he'd helped to create. Like me, no one answered his cries. I studied his despair and observed his pain to compare it to my own. He begged for mercy. He apologized for what he'd done to me, but I didn't accept it. I enjoyed seeing my tormentor fight for his meaningless life. Time. Consequences. Nothing mattered until he was dead."

Kevin hadn't released his caressing hold of her yet, so Yala kept going.

"I didn't call the cops to get his body. I wanted to feed the rats. People say killing someone that wronged you won't make you feel better, but they are wrong. Killing my rapist did make me feel better. It also meant he couldn't hurt anyone else."

Her words should have led Kevin straight out of her front door, but other than a raised eyebrow, he didn't appear disgusted in the least by what she'd done or what she was capable of doing.

"It took less than a month to find the other three, and I got rid of them all in the same manner. They all begged for their lives. They all apologized, but I wasn't remorseful about any of their deaths. I was relieved. Minutes after my last tormentor took his final breath, two men in black suits entered the abandoned apartment. Knife in my hand, a bloody body at my feet, and three other dead bodies half-eaten by rats. No explanation could help me. The men in the black suits were there to take me to jail. I was sure all they saw was a soulless monster. I didn't protest their approach but found it odd that they were not aiming guns at me. I sat my knife on the floor and raised my hands in surrender without them prompting me to do so."

Kevin's breathing slowed, and his tight caress loosened now that the worst of my story was over.

"TOP," he said.

Yala nodded.

"They hadn't come to take me to jail. I'd proven to them, at a young age, that I was capable of killing with no remorse. Not only that, they'd been spying on me long enough to know that I was shifting."

Yala paused to glance into Kevin's eyes.

"There was never much good in my life, so I gave you the bad and the ugly."

His smile shined through his gaze.

"I appreciate you sharing that part of your life with me. I sensed how hard it was for you to tell me."

She squeezed his hand. She wanted to know how he felt about her now that he knew what she was capable of doing.

He drew her tighter into his arms.

"I accept every part of you," he whispered against her hair.

He placed his forehead against hers before pressing a tender kiss to her cheek.

"I don't blame you for what you did either. As it stands, I'm not a woman and I'll never know the true level of your suffering, but I can say that if I happened to stumble upon something like that, the one committing the act would no longer exist. I also know that I won't do anything to cross you because despite you looking about as innocent as a baby lamb, I now know you won't hesitate to put a knife in my chest."

The statement made her giggle.

Aiming to take the spotlight off her, Yala set her gaze on Kevin.

"Okay, your turn. Now that we've gotten my horrid past out in the open, what's your story, Kevin? You never say anything about yourself."

***

Kevin

Kevin had never shed tears for any woman except his mother. The knowledge that he couldn't do anything to take those painful memories from Yala wrapped itself around his brain.

He sensed there was more she wasn't telling him, but he hoped patience and earning her full trust over time would allow her to open up more. Physically, Yala appeared to be fine, but he didn't have to be a doctor to know how badly the horror she'd suffered had affected her mentally. Her story helped him understand her comments from that day at the restaurant about sex being overrated and her choice not to date often.

As far as telling his story, he didn't know where to begin. He schooled his expressions in an attempt to hide his discontent about having to relay his past to Yala. In telling her story, she bared a part of her soul, and despite his feelings on the matter, she did need to know more about him, especially about the demons that had camped out in his head.

His voice squeezed past his vocal cords, a low rumble of sound.

"When I was fifteen, my mother died. Her death deeply affected me and made me hate everyone, myself, the most. My aunt and uncle took me in, and I gave them pure hell. Always in trouble. Picking fights. I didn't understand my actions or why I couldn't avoid trouble. I know now that I acted out because I'd seen my mother's death."

He shook away the troubling memory.

"I couldn't deal with the guilt of not being able to prevent it because I'd seen the person who committed the brutal act—my own father."

At those words, Yala's eyes grew wide.

"He would have killed me, too, but he was interrupted by the chime of the doorbell before he got the chance. It took me years to overcome the gruesome act and just as long to learn to trust people again. My mother…"

Kevin shook his head, his voice falling into the depths of his sorrows.

"My mother…"

Yala rubbed his shoulder, her gaze reflecting her empathy level.

"You don't have to tell me until you're ready."

"The devastation and abuse at the hands of my father was our hidden secret from the rest of the world. We became experts at figuring out ways to hide our bruises, the scrapes, and cuts. The mental effects, not so much. But, like all secrets, they eventually get revealed. My father went on the run after he killed my mother. He was never found, not that the authorities put a lot of effort into finding him. After I became an agent with TOP, finding him became an obsession. I didn't even know what I'd say to him if I ever saw him again. Let's just say that after the three years of time and energy it took to hunt him down with the lifetime of abuse still fresh in my mind after he killed my mother, I didn't do much talking when I finally confronted him. He's in hell. He'll never be found, not even his ashes."

The expression on Yala's face was unreadable. She was processing what he'd just shared and likely realizing that he was as much a monster as she assumed she was. No hints of judgment were in her eyes. If anyone understood his need for revenge, he believed it was Yala.

She stepped through his wall of silence and brushed away enough of his pain to reach into his heart. Her story had cemented her place there. Her admission revealed that they were similar in the way they spoke for the silent. For her, it was the little girl within her that had been snuffed out by brutal violence and for me, it was my mother's tragic death.

His arms and chest became her new blanket. She relaxed against him as they talked about the rollercoaster ride he'd been on, tracking her down. He'd begun the process with her rental, but the fake address they'd given him had thrown him off, along with the rental's license plate. However, he'd combed through months of traffic camera photos to find out where the car had been and where it had come from.

Dawn broke through the window, and Kevin needed to choose between breaking their connection or being selfish. He was wrapped up in her tender embrace as she was his. It was the remedy he didn't know he needed to help heal his tortured soul.

"We should get some sleep," he suggested.

Yala made a move to get up, but he kept her in place, folding her deeper into his chest. With his head next to hers, he savored the way she filled his arms. He wanted to tell her that he wasn't like those men, the ones who'd taken a part of her soul. He wanted to restore what had been so savagely ripped from her, but he wasn't sure he knew how.

"Kevin, I don't know anything about being in a relationship. I'm not one of those girly girls who knows her way around sensitivity and romance."

He nudged her neck with his nose. "I happen to like you just the way you are. We have scars that may never heal, but maybe we can help each other patch up what we can and see if the bleeding stops."

Her lips brushed his cheek.

"Poetic. I believe it describes us perfectly."

Reluctantly, Kevin let Yala escort him to the guest bedroom. He wanted to protest, but after inviting himself to her home and listening to her history, he'd need to tread lightly where it concerned moving to the next level.

CHAPTER TWENTY

Kevin

Kevin woke in a warm, soft bed, with fresh, crisp sheets, and walls painted with splashes of colorful designs. It took a moment to remember that he was in Yala's home. The refreshing rays of the sun streamed through the sheer curtains and the large windows and lured him towards the source.

He tossed his legs over the side of the bed and sat there, acknowledging that he felt rested. Standing, he took a few steps and drew the curtains open. Instead of finding a large window, it was a large glass door that presented a side view of what lay outside Yala's house.

Sliding the door open, Kevin stepped onto the small patio and welcomed the beautiful, wooded hillsides and small stretches of water off in the distance. At first, the quiet greeted him until he stopped thinking and listened.

A choir of roving animals sang, their voices mingling with the billowing breeze that flirted with the trees. The swaying sigh of wind-tossed grass and the energetic rippling of free-flowing water greeted him. Nature was speaking its own language—one he didn't understand but respected.

He was falling as much for nature as he was for his partner. The fresh air and beautiful scenery added to the peace he was finding being here.

The position of the sun suggested it was closing in on noon. He'd slept longer than he anticipated.

Images of Yala marched through his mind. Sweet, beautiful, and tortured. Though, for as sweet and as beautiful as she was, she was capable of being as deadly. She didn't want pity, but her story had ripped his heart to shreds.

Was she his girlfriend now?

They definitely weren't lovers, and after her story, he pinned his romantic intentions to the wall. It was a line he would not cross unless she clearly invited him to.

He bounded down the steps and didn't stop until he stood at her slightly ajar bedroom door. He peeked in and smiled at her sleeping form among a heap of covers. The folds and wrinkles of powder-blue cotton swallowed her. He didn't wake her. Instead, he headed toward the kitchen.

He found eggs, fruit, and frozen veggies but not much else. Silently, he thanked his lucky stars that there was coffee. He also sent a silent thanks that the Box case had stalled, despite his intentions to give it his maximum attention. For now, he would take the gift of time with Yala for what it was and for as long as it lasted. Every minute was a gift and who knew how long before they'd receive a call informing them of another box arriving at the ME's office.

While the coffee brewed, he made two cheese omelets and toast. Yala hadn't lied about not being a girly girl. His search for a food tray was futile. She owned items of necessity only.

He was held captive by her presence alone the night before and therefore hadn't taken the time to check out her home.

The living room was sparsely furnished with earth tones, giving the place a comfortable and welcoming glow. No pictures hung from the walls. A large mural with splashes of colors and angled designs decorated the one full wall in the space. The mural gave the room a unique look that reminded him of the simplistic depth of Yala. Her flower posed uncharacteristically from a water pitcher.

She clearly wanted her place to be simple and uncomplicated—a direct contrast to how she lived daily as a TOP agent. This place was her refuge from the drama, and he invited himself by tracking her down and showing up unannounced. He wouldn't have blamed her if she'd slammed the door in his face.

One corner of his mouth hiked up. He would definitely have to go shopping, at least for food—if she invited him to stay past today.

He knocked before he entered her room, but it hadn't roused her sleeping form. He placed her coffee and food on her bedside table and watched her sleep before he shook her shoulder.

Sleep released her slowly. When her gaze settled on him, a smile brightened her face.

"Good morning."

The sound of her voice ignited an instant spark in his heart. She stretched and covered her mouth when a yawn escaped.

"I brought you breakfast," he pointed out.

She glanced at the plate on her bedside table.

"You did? I don't know how you managed to get breakfast from my kitchen, but it's a miracle that I'm grateful for because I'm starving."

Her grin spread wider, highlighting the sparkle in her eyes. She took the plate.

"What about you? We can share."

She was already cutting the omelet in half to share with him.

"I've already eaten, but I'll drink coffee with you if you don't mind?"

Her hand hovered before her mouth as her words edged out between each chew. "Yes, of course. This is great, by the way."

The one chair in her room, a wicker-style chair with a plush pink cushion, sat next to her bedside table. Kevin dragged the chair closer to the bed. He took a sip from his second cup of coffee while she ate.

"I'll go shopping. You don't have any food in this house. I saw microwave dinners, noodles, and lots of Twizzlers. How do you live on that stuff?"

She dropped her head. "It's no secret. I can't cook. How do you know how to cook so well?" she asked.

"I had to cook for my mother when she couldn't."

Yala nodded. He changed the subject.

"Thanks for letting me stay. It's peaceful here…beautiful."

He stared around her bedroom until his eyes landed back on her.

"So, I guess I should ask rather than assume since I showed up unannounced." A small wrinkle lined the center of her forehead, and the smile on her lips also shimmered in her eyes.

"Would you mind if I stayed for a while?"

She lifted her eyes to the ceiling. "Um, let me think about it and get back to you," she replied.

Another bite and she closed her eyes to the flavor of the food, shaking her fork in celebration of what remained on the plate. "You can definitely stay."

CHAPTER TWENTY-ONE

Killer

My search for a new subject has been tough. The one I truly crave to get my hands on won't be easy to catch, but I am patient. My thoughts drift, and I remember how I arrived at this point.

In my early teen years, my curiosity increased, and I went from taking insects apart and putting them back together to small animals. It was a hobby well hidden from the well-to-do members of my family. They wanted perfection, and I acted the part, showing them what they wanted to see. What they didn't know was that I was striving to create my own perfection.

My curiosity grew into a full-blown fascination at seventeen, and I progressed to larger animals. This interest might be considered a sick act in normal society, but it's necessary if we are ever to progress. This gift wasn't bestowed on me to sit dormant and not be used for the greater good.

My ultimate goal is to take a person apart and reconnect them to their fully functional self. Once that is accomplished, I'll be able to formulate the perfect specimen of my choosing.

Currently, and unfortunately, I have hit a snag. I have been unable to accomplish my goal.

The decision to pursue a career in medicine was my way of learning the key aspects of human anatomy as well as proper medical procedures to prolong life. It was a good decision that provided access to many bodies, dead and alive.

In college, love took an unsuspecting hold of me and I was sidetracked. Her name was Lori Hendrix. Lori was perfect in every way: beautiful, smart, and from a good family.

Self-consciousness ate my confidence, which was a little elusive at the time, but Lori, as beautiful as she was, took an interest in me.

I approached her with reluctance. My being just cute enough to catch her eye helped, and Lori began to pay more attention to me. My first date with Lori was lunch at the college dining facility. I would have preferred a more traditional setting like a movie or restaurant, but I wasn't picky. Lori was a beautiful girl. I would have done anything to win her affection.

I found happiness with Lori, but my joy was short-lived. Catching the woman I loved having sex with the star football player, tore my heart out and inspired me to perfect my gift and release it to this world. If I couldn't have the love I wanted, I'd make myself one.

How could she sleep with Matt? He and I were total opposites, and I would have never pegged him for Lori's type.

The guys on the football team worshiped Matt for his sexual prowess, and his confidence had led him to drill a peek-hole into his dorm room wall. Matt had drilled the hole so his teammates could preview his sexual adventures with different girls.

The dorm wall was adorned with many faded pictures of past professors and educators that hung, tilted, inside weathered frames. Matt had drilled the hole behind one of the pictures, so all one had to do was tilt the edge, and Matt's bed would be on display.

I knew about the hole behind the picture because a friend of Matt's, Rusty, was also a friend of mine. We'd attended the same high school, and I'd always taken advantage of him because I knew he had a crush on me.

One night, Rusty approached me in the lobby of my dorm, breathless, informing me that he'd spotted Lori going into Matt's room. He was concerned; he knew Lori and I were friends and didn't want her to become the latest victim in Matt's little game.

Five minutes later, I found myself at the hole in the wall after sneaking into Matt's dorm. What I observed excited me in the most disturbing way. I discovered that night that I liked being a voyeur, but it was who participated in the act that made my blood boil.

My Lori was riding Matt like a porn queen. He was positioned so the top of his head was pointed in the direction of the hole, which meant that Lori's body and face were on display.

Matt would occasionally glance at the hole and give a thumbs-up like it was all a game. He started lifting Lori's body, so the person or people watching could see him pumping his large, disgusting appendage in and out of her.

Her face revealed everything. Lori was not new at sex like I had assumed based on her charming personality. She was enjoying the sex so much that she never noticed the hole in the wall. I couldn't stop watching as Lori expertly did things to Matt that I couldn't imagine her doing with me.

The next day, I found the perfect spot, hidden deep within the woods, around the back of our dormitory. I pitched a tent after a thirty-minute hike into the plush thick brush and trees. I knew couples frequented the woods to drink and have sex, but they never ventured too far off. Therefore, I wasn't worried about being caught.

I set up a makeshift instrument table and a line of equipment and tools I'd need to explore my fascination. Yes, I was sick by society's standards, but someday the world would come to embrace my brilliance.

Alcohol laced with a sedative aided in enticing Matt into my web. I lured him to my tent in which I had Lori already tied up and gagged inside. Matt was a big guy, so I had to use quite a bit of drugs to keep him under control. I took him apart. I cut him into pieces as Lori screamed and fought the rope binding her hands. She threw up while fighting my effort to stick a pair of Matt's bloody gym socks into her mouth.

I loved her. She said she loved me, but all I wanted was to make her pay for her sins against me, against our love. I loved that I frightened her so badly that she wet herself. I loved seeing her be the opposite of how she'd been when she was so wet and spread wide for Matt.

Seeing the fear in her eyes gave me a wicked high. It made me feel powerful. I couldn't stop thinking back to when I caught her screwing Matt. The scene had ripped me apart, taken my mind to new depths, and made me embrace my ability.

I enjoyed the sound of cutting and sawing through human flesh and bone. The slippery tendons, the sinewy ligaments, the strong muscles, and the bone. Each sound was distinct and relaxing. I enjoyed the sensation of holding quivering warm flesh in my hand while life slipped from it.

While Lori squirmed and screamed, I sawed and hacked my way through her neck. I worked at a measured pace to ensure I didn't leave any jagged or rough edges on the parts I severed. I wanted her to look as perfect in death as she did in life.

The best part was neither he nor Lori died while I created my ultimate masterpiece. On the contrary, my ability kept them going while I explored my fascination, even after I had dissected them into parts.

The fragrance of fresh death enticed my senses and made me feel liberated. My joy would later be shattered when bacteria started to eat away at the flesh and bring about those not-so-pleasant gasses that I learned to tolerate. I never stuck around for the insects; I couldn't bear to see them destroy my work.

It wasn't until I'd hacked through Lori's neck that I realized I still wanted her. I still loved her. A mind-blowing epiphany made me sorry I'd killed her. I forced her head back onto her body, mushing it against her tender, open flesh and protruding bone.

After a while, she began to twitch. Before long, I embraced this untapped power, more than I'd ever *experienced before. I poured my energy and sheer will into putting Lori back together again. I made her breathe again. I enjoyed the deliciously terrifying look on her face.*

Intrigued by what I discovered, I tested it over time. First, taking apart portions of Lori's body that wouldn't kill her. I detached her legs and reattached them and found their motor functions fully restored. I did the same to her arms and her lower body.

My love for Lori was strong, but I couldn't control my impulse to master my newfound ability. I would put Lori back together, and by the time she was mended, I'd be ready to dismantle her again. I was obsessed. Although I hadn't perfected my craft, I gained a good amount of insight during my experiments.

It wasn't until I was in medical school that I understood the human body best. It was when I began cutting bodies into halves and eventually thirds. I discovered I could take them apart and keep them apart for long periods of time before death came looking for them. They were never people to me but subjects. Lori was the only one who I considered a person.

There was one small problem I faced when I put my subjects back together. I discovered there was a short time period in which they would actually live before succumbing and dying altogether. They would survive for four days, at best, despite how long I'd kept them apart and despite my strong attempts at nursing them back to health. As long as I poured my energy into them, they'd live even if I cut them into cube size pieces. Without my energy, their life force would seep out like a tire losing its pressure.

I never understood what was so special about Lori that allowed her to survive so long after I'd repeatedly taken her apart. Was there something special in her blood—something reacting to the power I poured into her?

My need to perfect my craft has me obsessed. I need answers. I need someone as gifted as me to help find out why my subjects continue to die after they've been put back together.

So, here we were, years later. I created the boxes and sent my subjects to the medical examiner's office.

I knew Dr. Hughes. I'd fought to win an internship to be his student and witnessed him solve problems and fix people when other specialists had written them off. Actually, I'd killed the person who was initially picked for the internship so that I could take his place and learn from Dr. Hughes. I'd also studied the doctor's background extensively.

The way I see it, even if Dr. Hughes can't figure out how the bodies were taken apart, he might find a way to keep them from dying after being put back together.

I hated to enlist the help of another. It's a risky move, but with multiple backup plans in place, I'm certain it will keep me from the path of the law. I refuse to allow years of work and research to go to waste. If Dr. Hughes can help me work through my problem, then—and only then— will I know I have achieved true perfection in my ability. And I'll finally be free to unleash my gifts to this world.

CHAPTER TWENTY-TWO

Yala

Two days after Kevin's arrival.

After trekking through the woods and enjoying the intimate communing with nature, Yala dreaded nightfall. Night was the time when her mental capacity to resist Kevin was tested.

Like now, he was massaging her neck and shoulders after their hiking adventure. She enjoyed his smooth caress, her body limp and relaxed under his touch. If his goal was to wear her down, it was working.

She squinted when a random idea popped into her head. "Hey, I don't even know your last name."

Chuckling, he nudged her teasingly. "My name is Arlano Kevin Nazari."

She turned and reached out a hand in greeting. "So nice to finally meet you, Mr. Nazari."

His name echoed in her head. "I like your name: Arlano. And Nazari, is it Italian?"

"No, it's actually Egyptian. My mother was Egyptian. I had my last name changed to my mother's maiden name when I was eighteen. I never liked my first name because it was the one thing I shared with my father. However, after hearing you say it, I think I'm starting to like it again."

Yala managed to speak through the pulsing exhilaration Kevin's compliments set off within her. He sat so close behind her, she couldn't help surrendering to her desires for him.

"Let's switch," she suggested.

Kevin turned down her request, but Yala was already moving. She climbed onto the arm of the couch and perched on his shoulders.

He leaned his head back and glanced at her over his shoulder. The moment their eyes connected, the radiating energy exchange that bubbled up between them silenced her. She broke the tension by cracking her knuckles in preparation for giving him a massage.

The moment she pressed her fingers into his muscular shoulders, his head dropped, and his body sank deeper into the couch.

"I didn't know how much I needed this until now," he said.

Yala had come to the realization that Kevin was the proof she needed. Proof that *they* weren't all monsters. She wanted to tell him about her concerns, but she wasn't sure how.

How do you tell someone that, at twenty-three, the one experience you've had with the opposite sex was your worst nightmare?

What she had with Kevin was the closest thing she experienced to a relationship. He knew how to make her smolder and never made her feel threatened.

"How's that?" she asked.

He turned his head in each direction, kissing her hands, before pulling her arms across his shoulders. Her legs slid down and around him as she was lured against his back.

He tugged until she kneeled behind him with her arms wrapped around his neck. Her tight nipples were snug against his back. She no longer fought to resist his pull. Her lips brushed his neck before she could stop herself.

The magnetic call of their attraction lured them closer until their lips met. Yala maneuvered around his body to deepen their kiss and became the one advancing on him. Face-to-face on her couch, they kneeled before each other.

She leaned in and initiated another kiss. The slide of his tongue over her lips drew instant heat. On the one hand, this type of play terrified her because of what led to; but on the other, her passion for Kevin trumped her fears. She couldn't stop kissing him. It was positive proof that he'd somehow carried her past a great threshold of what was stolen from her and walked her into a place of comfort.

He placed his hands on Yala's shoulders, intending to stop her, but their closeness intensified, and she drew him right back in. She swept his leg and wrapped hers around his thigh. The move made him flash her wide eyes. Had he forgotten her strength as a TOP agent?

His stiff heat pressed against the inside of Yala's thighs, the hard, unyielding flesh demanding attention. The first time she'd felt him like this, she'd been reluctant to explore him further.

Now, his hard need excited her, warmed her body, and magically drew wet heat from deep within her. She traced the outline of his erection with her fingertips, lifting a high-arching brow at his large size.

Her brazen exploration caused him to grit his teeth and shut his eyes tight. It astonished her that she could make him want her in that way. She wanted him equally as bad.

She closed their circle by wrapping her other leg around him. The move had him pressed hard and pulsing against her hot center and stomach. Her body found a rhythm on its own as she ground her pelvis into his. He was lengthy, so there was plenty of him for her to climb while her tongue slid between his lips.

She lost her will to be modest, and a heat-laced moan escaped. She needed to stop. He needed to stop. Didn't they?

How could she have been so stupid as to think that it would be any other way with him? She enjoyed the way he responded to her. Breathlessly, he called out her name.

"Yala."

He stood, but she remained locked around him, his hand cupping her ass. He assisted her down his body like a fireman would down a pole. Her lust-heavy eyes bore into his while his own gaze reflected a need that had him speechless.

The way he licked his lips like she belonged on his menu kept Yala turned on. Her words edged out husky and raw. "I'm glad our paths crossed, Kevin."

His fingers edged down either side of her body like he was sizing her up. "Me too."

His tongue slid across his lips again, relishing her flavor left there. "It's time I let you go to sleep," he said.

She flashed an, are-you-kidding-me look. "The only way I'm going to bed is if you're in it with me."

She recalled expressing a similar statement the first night they met. He stood at an angle now, struggling to maintain a small semblance of decency that was unnecessary at this point.

Yala didn't give him time to allow whatever was rolling through his head to manifest. Instead, she took his hand and tugged him toward her bedroom.

They stood at the foot of her bed, staring at each other. Yala inched closer.

"Maybe I was wrong about men having one-track minds. You look terrified."

Her statement broke the tension, making his tight shoulders inch away from his ears and his lips curve into a smile.

"I don't want to do anything to drive you away, but being this close to you in this way is very—"

"Distracting. Enticing. Tempting," she finished. She inched up on her toes and kissed him with tender pecks. She lost count of the number of times he stuck his hands in and out of the pockets of his sweats.

"Are you sure?" he asked.

After revealing the horror of her past, Yala understood Kevin's reluctance. She dotted his lips with more kisses.

"Yes. Can't you tell?"

She tugged him along, attempting to lure him into her bed before her own apprehension reared its ugly head.

"I want to be with you more than anything, but you have to tell me if I do anything you don't like or want. Promise me," he demanded.

She lifted her hand as if standing in front of a judge. "I promise."

No further words were needed. The tips of his fingers slid below the rim of her top before he lifted and removed it with ease. Her fingers glided through his hair as he mapped carefully placed kisses along the side of her neck.

"Sit and lie back," he directed.

Am I about to do this?

Sitting, she inched back before lying back, her eyes locked with his heavy-lidded ones. He leaned down, sending a smooth caress over the delicate skin of her neck and arms and down the center of her chest before he added his lips.

She sucked in a deep breath and forgot her thoughts when his warm lips skimmed the hard tips of her nipples through her bra. Her shortness of breath grew sharper when he chartered a warm path south.

Gone were her top and bra, and it was only a matter of time before she lost her shorts and panties. She missed seeing Kevin remove his shirt. Was she losing track of time?

"Beautiful," he said, admiring the tattoos running along her side. He stroked them lightly before pressing soft kisses to each of them one by one. His mouth reignited her passion.

The intoxication of her heady desire made her eyes keep fluttering shut. She flicked them back open every time so she didn't miss seeing a thing he was doing. His tongue slid across her stomach and shimmied into her belly button, making her heave for each breath she dragged in. The view was too much for her to handle.

Now, closing her eyes dragged in images of his exploration, heightening the physical contact.

Her eyes snapped open to Kevin's strong, chiseled, and naked body. She dropped her view over his chest, paused at his abs, and kept moving down.

Well-endowed.

The sound of her harsh breathing accompanied her shameless staring. The sight of him made her question if she was ready, but at the same time, it increased her arousal.

He let her look until her gaze rose to meet his. She didn't know what her facial expression showed him, but she wanted him.

"We don't have to do this if you don't want to," he said.

Her warm cheeks rose into a deep smile.

"Yes, we do. I want to. Now, more than before."

Her words prompted him to continue the journey and put a smile on his face. His warm lips skimmed her thighs and traveled over her belly button before he left hot pecks on her stomach.

When he inched up again and his warm lips closed around her nipple, she moaned and let her head fall back onto the comforter.

"Oh. That. Feels good," she whispered as hot wetness flowed between her fidgety legs.

She had always equated sex with pain, but so far she was finding that she couldn't have been more wrong.

If he knew how to use his well-endowed prize the way he used his mouth, she would delete her preconceived notions about the act.

He sucked tender pockets of her hot quivering flesh until he reached her inner thighs. Her gasps became more frequent, her moans more urgent. She bordered on the threshold between passion and control-shattering madness.

He used his teeth to drag her panties down. Her participation in the process, as she lifted her hips and used her fingers to shove the thin material down, made the task exquisite—hot. Once her purple panties fell from his lips, he made his tongue snake up her leg, skim over her knee, and tickle her thigh.

Yala caught the mischievous glint Kevin flashed right before his hands slid down the inside of her thighs and spread her legs further apart. It only took a moment for him to put action to his unspoken words as his tongue sank into her hot, wet folds. The magical flicks across the jewel that stood guard at her entrance sent her over the edge.

It was too much, too fast, and she couldn't control the heady rush that took her by force. He kept his tongue dancing softly against her jewel, making the sensations last for a blissful lifetime.

He lay next to her and stroked the warm trembling flesh of her legs and stomach until she regained her composure.

"So that's what the big fuss is about?" she whispered, her breath heavy and her mind not fully returned.

Not believing how clueless she'd been, she sought to hide her naivety with a grin; but Kevin cast no hint of judgment as he nibbled her bottom lip.

"Let's see if we can get you another one of those."

His words enticed an instant smile, but her forehead creased questioningly. The idea of him making her lose control again had her nearly drooling and licking her lips in anticipation.

His hands coursed over her hip and brushed all the areas in between until he cupped her ass and pulled her against him before he lifted and eased over her with the smooth moves of a ballet dancer.

The crinkles along his forehead and tightness between his eyes highlighted his stress. She leaned up and gifted him with a kiss, gripping his bottom lip with her teeth before sucking on it. It was too late to turn back now. He pressed hard and hot against her drenched sex. He wanted her as badly as she wanted him.

"Keep your eyes on mine, okay," he said, his expression reassuring.

The sweetness of his gesture warmed her heart. Cupping his neck, she drew him in and kissed his concerns away.

"It's okay. You've made me so wet and ready."

Her actions and words lit a blaze in his eyes. His first attempt to enter her, however, was about as difficult as punching through a brick wall, but Yala refused to let him stop.

"There may be some pain, but I promise you I'll stop if it doesn't turn into pleasure," he warned.

Her hard, quick breaths bounced off his neck. "It's okay. I trust you, no matter what."

His slick head licked at her opening until he entered her inch by inch, determined not to force it. Her tongue sliced across his earlobe while his hot fingers traced the outline of her body and the hard tips of her nipples.

"My pain tolerance is high, so all you have to do is turn it into pleasure."

He turned his lips to graze her jaw and neck. "Okay, baby."

Did he just call me baby?

"I feel everything," he gritted out, jaw clenched and his muscles pulled taunt enough to snap. With every easy stroke, he coaxed more wet heat from her. Her juices coated him, making their erotic interaction slick as he eased in and out of her quivering resistance.

He clenched his teeth so tightly she was afraid he would crack a few. Her mental reflection moment disappeared with his promise to bring pleasure. The idea dragged her further into the intoxicating world they created together. Each time he sank too deep, pain sparked, and he'd kiss her to make up for it, unaware that she didn't mind the sweet sting.

"It's good. So, so good."

Kevin released a long breath of relief accompanied with a smile at her words. His thrusts picked up speed, his downstrokes long and lingering. Her reaction ate away the last of his unease and sparked his enthusiasm to enjoy the experience.

Her moans floated into his ear. Her breath caught with every hard thrust. She gripped his neck and pulled him tightly into her, but it didn't disrupt the flow of his movement against her body. They sang together, crooning tunes of pleasure.

Her body fell into submission, yielding to his erotic demands. His heavy-lidded eyes kept snapping back open each time he closed them like he was fighting not to miss a thing. He wanted to see her.

At first, the bulk of the pleasure lingered near her core, sending sparks through the rest of her body with every turn. The deeper he went, the more ecstasy built and spread equally throughout her body, and as he stirred deeper still, she questioned how much more she could take.

She watched his lips as his hot words bounced off hers. "I want you to tell me the way you want it."

She could hardly get a syllable out, let alone words. "Oh…" was all she could manage at that moment.

Every few minutes, he changed his rhythm and angle or tilt her in a certain way, and it all blew her mind. Her loud moans projected throughout the room. The ruffling of the sheets, the groaning of the mattress springs, and the knocking of the headboard became the backup choir to their cries of pleasure.

Kevin's taunt muscles and damp skin yielded to her nails that scraped repeatedly across his lower back. At the moment, Yala didn't have the mind to compare one pleasure to another, as each gave off distinct toxins that saturated her brain with endorphins.

Overwhelming delight flooded her system, mystifying her with maddening intensity that made her shutter. It didn't matter what he did at this point. Her pleasure outweighed all else. Her own words threatened to choke her as they tore raggedly from her throat.

"I. I like this," and "There, oh…oh, please there."

His soft lips flirted with her earlobe. "What about this?"

She responded with rushed words that slipped between pants and harsh breaths.

"Yes. Right there. Deeper. Don't stop. Faster."

She sang her explicit demands with no inhibitions. Groping and grabbing, she gripped his tight, flexing ass one moment and scratched at his back the next. Something this good could easily become a need versus a want. It should have been illegal to engage in an act that took her mind further than the most potent and addictive drugs on the market.

Kevin was right about something else; the tingling sensation resurfaced. Sharp spurts of electricity shot up her spine and left goosebumps on her overheated skin. Her body rippled with pleasure as the beat of her pulse thumped and marched up her back. It grew more extreme this time, like a timer sounding on an explosive about to blow her, and everything around her to kingdom come.

Please. Don't. Stop.

She was burning in an inferno of pleasure that ignited an aching need so strong she was sure she'd become combustible. She begged, her whispers exasperated.

"Kevin, please. Please."

One hand gripped his bicep, and the other gripped and tugged on his lower back. She relished it, absorbing the intensity of that final thrust. He was all in, so deep now, they'd become one.

Control was lost. Time had run out. She exploded into uninhibited delight.

"Kevin! Oh, God!"

She bit down on his shoulder to preserve his hearing and save her voice box. She would apologize later. She was slung in every direction. There were no words for this spell being cast. This went beyond any addiction she knew, and she enjoyed every splendid moment.

***

Kevin

Witnessing Yala's blissful frenzy sent Kevin into the land of enlightenment. He couldn't catch his breath as pleasure flung him into an abyss so deep that he'd lost all sense of self-awareness. Pleasure took possession of him and steered him into a world in which he'd never traveled.

An infinite amount of desire filled his body, consumed his psyche, and prevented him from forming a concise thought. He spit out a few choked utterances that didn't form words. Just when the wave released him, a stronger current sucked him right back under.

Control was a concept lost on him as his body involuntarily shook. He slumped, unable to do a thing to right himself. All six senses fled his body, replaced by the driver that took control.

Had he actually passed out?

God.

He rose from his haze on wobbly arms, unable to recall anything like this happening before. It took him a moment to notice it, but he wasn't inside Yala anymore. His body ceased motor functions as he lay helpless, halfway on top of her.

He ran a feathery light caress over her cheek with the back of his shaky fingers before his lips brushed her hot cheek.

"Are you okay? Your eyes are open, but I don't believe you're home."

She nodded, her eyes not fully back in focus.

Kevin attempted to conceal his chuckle but failed. He'd never taken hard drugs, but he knew their effects. The glossed-over eyes and the lazy drift you couldn't shake off. He'd experienced both.

He shook his head in an attempt to shake off the lingering effects. When Yala glanced at him with a wide smile, he mirrored her happiness.

"Thank you. That was better than great. Beyond exceptional," she said, her words easing out, her voice dragging on lazily.

"I'm glad you enjoyed yourself; otherwise, I'd be too ashamed to face you again."

She giggled, but she obviously had no idea she and only she had taken possession of his mind by overloading his body with her own brand of pleasure.

What kind of unique creature was he dealing with? She was something that wasn't supposed to exist.

First, he lost his heart to her; now, she had control of his mind and body. The idea of it frightened him. Although he'd refused to believe it before, he knew he'd loved Yala since the first night he'd spent with her.

He tugged her closer, closing her in a tight embrace. Sleep lured them under quickly and tossed them into a surreal world of peace-filled nothingness.

CHAPTER TWENTY-THREE

Yala

Yala awoke the next day with a smile but worry etched her forehead when she didn't spot Kevin beside her. Finally, the clinking of pots and silverware lured her gaze toward the kitchen and set her mind at ease.

The first thing she did was check her phone and Doctor Hughes a quick text. Three days, no word on the case, and no closer to answers. The only solid pieces of evidence were the victims who'd died and the suspects who had turned out to be victims who desperately wanted their bodies returned to normal.

Yala was out of bed and halfway to the bathroom before she noticed her nudity. Flashes of her night with Kevin made her body tingle.

She jumped in the shower and threw on shorts and a top. She didn't bother with a bra. Kevin had already seen everything, and whatever apprehension she'd clung to had disappeared. She shook her head and placed a hand over her mouth to stifle a giggle, not believing she'd been so brazen with him.

When she stepped back into her bedroom, Kevin sat on her bed, his eyes sparkling with a charming gleam.

"Good morning. I brought you breakfast."

She was never this happy to see anyone. She stepped into his personal space and stood between his legs. After wrapping her arms around his neck and having him reciprocate the caress, she closed her eyes to savor his closeness as his head rested against her chest.

His hands made her burn with desire as they inched up the sides of her body. It was getting harder to hide the fact she was possibly falling in love with him. He glanced up at her, his eyes flowing with emotions radiant enough to feel.

"Your food will get cold," he said unenthusiastically.

His mention of food awakened her hunger, but her craving for him overrode her most basic need. However, she appreciated him and didn't want his efforts wasted. She left a quick peck on his cheek before turning to the food.

"Thank you."

"Wait a minute. Let me do that," he said.

She didn't argue. If he wanted to serve her, she wasn't going to stop him. She climbed back into bed, and he assisted by stuffing an extra pillow behind her back before he placed the tray across her lap. He poured her coffee and added cream and sugar.

He leaned over and placed a sweet kiss on her forehead. "Enjoy."

"Aren't you joining me?" she asked, not ready for him to leave.

"Not this time. I'll leave you to enjoy your breakfast while I shower."

She dropped her eyes from his lingering gaze, still not used to the rush of emotions he stirred in her. He possessed a way of making her feelings rise to the surface and demand attention. She was either falling in love with him or already there. Either scenario was a shock to the system.

***

Kevin returned a while later to retrieve the dishes, and like before, he kissed her forehead sweetly before announcing, "I'm going to take a walk."

Although she believed he was avoiding her, Yala appreciated the break. It was difficult to concentrate with a foggy brain. She'd assumed he'd be purged from her system as soon as they had sex, but she was wrong.

Everything she assumed she knew about relationships, which truthfully wasn't much, and men couldn't have been more wrong. She'd spent most of her time perfecting a man's persona, and from what she'd experienced, women didn't want them around after sex as much as they let their egos believe.

In her case, with Kevin, she found she couldn't get enough of him. This couldn't have been normal.

CHAPTER TWENTY-FOUR

Kevin

Every time he looked at Yala, Kevin couldn't help thinking about being with her. However, he gave himself a few points because he also considered how much he truly cared for her.

His gaze followed her to the sink. She palmed a ceramic bowl and spooned vanilla ice cream and pie into her mouth. They'd left the counter and sink a mess with dishes after they'd made one of her favorite desserts—cherry pie.

She did a little dance while eating, like the pie provided a beat he couldn't hear. Her carefree nature was a joy to see, and he believed it was beginning to rub off on him. No matter how small, she took the time to enjoy life's pleasures. After sitting his plate on the sink, he stood beside her.

"I was supposed to take that."

He swiped a finger through her cherry filling and licked his lips at the sight of her lips wrapping around the finger he shoved into her tempting mouth. Her soft, warm tongue cupped his finger as she sucked. The action sent sparks of desire radiating all over his body.

He backed away, determined to remain a gentleman and allow Yala the opportunity to lead their intimacy. Sparks of desire danced in her eyes, making them sparkle.

Her jittery body joined in, telling him the perfect story of want and need.

"I assumed once we did it, the hormones would go away."

He stroked her cheek, as curiosity creased his face. "What do you mean?"

He knew what she meant but wanted to hear her say it.

"I want to be with you again, but I don't want you to think I'm a needy woman who can't control her hormones."

Her words were music to his ears. "Yala, trust me on this. Knowing that you want me is the ultimate compliment."

He drew her closer and kissed her into a boiling hot fever. They overflowed together, a mixture of lust and heated passion.

"I don't think I can get enough of you. I have taken two cold showers since last night, and neither helped," he whispered against her ear.

His words brimmed with enough heat to make her grip his shirt and pull him closer. She lost her smile when he lifted her and sat her atop the counter. Plates, dishes, and cups crashed to the floor and into the sink with loud clunks.

Neither cared about the dishes, not even glancing in their direction. He slid her shorts and panties down her legs as she hastily attempted to undress him. She'd managed to unknot the string holding his sweats up. He helped by shoving his pants down his thighs.

More dishes and silverware crashed to the floor as he traced fire-hot kisses along Yala's neck. The hard tips of her breasts pressed against her top, revealing one of the many ways he turned her on.

Each button he undid on her top enticed him to move faster. With no bra to restrict access, he left her top hanging open and her tits exposed for his viewing pleasure. His eyes feasted as her perky mounds yielded to his soft squeezes. The vibrations from her erotic moans teased his senses.

Hands gripping and squeezing her thighs, he dragged her closer to what he believed she craved most. He couldn't touch enough of her fast enough. He drew her in more, making the anticipation of their impending connection more urgent and desperate. Finally, her pulsing center pressed against his taut need, causing a whimper to escape her and a groan to ease from his throat.

He handled her body, taking her clothing and stroking and caressing her without breaking their kiss. Her slippery, wet, and tight heat accepted his hard, slow stroke while he fought to overcome the fiery need to rush the enticing entry.

He deliberately thrust into her at a lingering pace, loving the way her eyes flashed appreciation, her moan sang her gratitude, and her gasp expressed her desires. Inch by agonizing inch, he moved, sending her eyes rolling to the back of her head.

One of her legs was positioned so that her calf flirted with his flexing ass muscles. He nudged apart her inner thigh and spread the other leg wider. The action made him sink deeper and hit a spot that sparked pain based on her tightly shut eyes and wrinkled nose. However, it also ignited pleasure because her leg at his waist drew him in deeper. Her teeth sank into her lower lip, further expressing her amped-up desires.

"Fuck," he yelled out, thrusting harder than he intended but unable to regain control of his runaway body.

"Are you okay?" he asked, his heart pumping fast for multiple reasons.

She smiled through the sweet torture. "Please, don't stop," was her answer.

Despite her plea, he stopped. He wanted her to control the flow, tempo, and depth.

However, she wanted him to keep going so badly that she shook her head rapidly to keep him from stopping. Her body began a slow dance against his hard penetration, picking up the pace and taking pleasure the way she wanted.

Her hands slipped and slid through the spilled pie and ice cream before she inadvertently transferred it to various parts of his body. He did the same, smearing the sweet treat over her tight nipples so he could lick and suck it off. The dessert added flavor and another level of ecstasy to their sensually charged connection.

Kevin's hands pressed firmly into her thighs, but he restricted his movement as much as possible. He wanted her to continue to control the deep depth and juicy flow and ride out her pleasure as fast or slow and as deep or shallow as she wanted.

Each wave of her body fanned his pleasure, the rhythm mesmerizing. Yala increased the intensity of her movement and spread her legs wider, sending him in so deeply he couldn't back out. A series of moans filled the air, and he couldn't tell if they were hers or his.

When he wrapped his hands around her dancing waist, melted ice cream and pieces of cherry filling made his hand slick and sticky against her warm, soft skin.

Yala gripped the faucet handle with one hand and hung onto the edge of the cabinets with the other. She couldn't stop her body as it danced an ocean-like wave against his. Each wavy thrust made her hand inadvertently flip the water on and off, on and off.

Buried deeply, Kevin stopped his in-and-out motions. The pause encouraged Yala to move, which allowed his rock-hard gem to stroke every pleasure point inside her.

Every rotating thrust forced her legs open wider as they danced at his sides. Pleasure shot from the tip of his dick and raced to his toes before it zipped up to his head. The same sparks of passion had taken possession of Yala, her body rocking, eyes shut tight, mind in another dimension.

When she increased her dancing rhythm, his eyes rolled to the back of his head, and he called on every god he knew to give him the strength to hold out until she finished.

"Yala, baby. Please," he cried, his voice a low, hot whisper.

He begged her to succumb to her release because he was determined not to let go until she did. Yala gorged on him by hungrily taking every fulfilling inch. He believed she recognized his dilemma the moment their eyes met.

The deep penetrating rhythm she maintained sent her over the edge. Kevin could hardly stand on his own two legs. He came so hard that he saw tiny pinpricks of light bouncing behind his eyelids. The realization that they were in danger of tumbling to the hardwood floor kept him on his feet.

The top of Yala's body lay halfway in the sink, and cold water flowed over the top of her shoulder, waking her from the erotic trance in which she'd fallen. The weight of his quivering body atop hers registered, his head laying atop her chest.

She ran shaky fingers through his hair, a caring action considering how they'd lost control. Leaning in, he placed a delicate kiss on her lips.

She took in the way their bodies were decorated with cherry pie and melted ice cream. A saucer was wedged against her lower back, and plates, glasses, and utensils were all over the floor. They'd had a food fight of a different kind. They were a sticky mess, but he'd never been so satisfied in his life.

Kevin handled her with care as he lifted her from the countertop. She swayed from the aftershock of their lovemaking. With a firm grip, he assisted in holding her upright until she was able to stand on her own.

"Sorry about your dishes," he whispered.

"What dishes?"

She set her gaze on him like she was clueless as to what he was talking about.

They laughed while glancing around at the mess they made.

CHAPTER TWENTY-FIVE

Kevin

They spent the following three days in much the same manner. Enjoying each other and sharing sweet, hot, sexy, and erotic moments that would live vividly inside Kevin during this lifetime and the next.

He hadn't seen the inside of the guest room since they spilled cherry pie all over the kitchen and each other. Neither could get enough of each other.

However, the party was finally over. Yala was heading back to DC to team up with the doctors and to check on Mark and Elizabeth, and Kevin was preparing to fly to Atlanta to chase down a lead he'd gotten on the whereabouts of Doctor Nolan.

While he was putting in an order to TOP for travel plans to Atlanta, his gaze tracked Yala's every move. It was useless to even attempt to hide their weakness for each other.

Fresh from the shower, she joined him on her bed later. She snuggled onto his side, and he automatically wrapped her in his waiting arms.

"I know that you've been with TOP long enough to take care of yourself, but I'd like to see you again, so please be careful," he said before placing a kiss on her forehead and giving her a delicate squeeze.

"Aren't you tired of me yet?" she asked.

His penetrating gaze locked with hers. "No. That will never happen. Honestly, I've never been this happy, and the idea of not seeing you again would probably break me."

His intentions weren't meant to be so serious, but Yala brought out a side of him he didn't even know he possessed. She tensed at his impacting words but kept her head resting against his neck and shoulder.

"So, what is this? I mean, what's going to become of us in the future? If I dare to say such a thing."

He shrugged. "I don't know, but I know I want you in it."

Yala stared, wide-eyed and searching. He knew she found nothing but genuine truth.

"I know people like us don't get involved, especially not with each other, for obvious reasons. From where I'm sitting, when it comes to us, we have crossed a line that can't be uncrossed; and I don't regret it one bit," he admitted.

Yala remained silent, no doubt turning his words over in her head. Instead of commenting, she increased her hold around his body.

Kevin caught her subtle gesture and sensed the impact of the energy and emotion she poured into it. She didn't have to say a word to express herself if she didn't want to, and although he didn't want to put her on the spot, he believed he needed to tell her how he felt.

His heart pounded, but his voice broke through his emotions.

"I know we're trained to ignore certain emotions and impulses; we're trained to endure and forget, but when it comes to you, there is no turning it off. It's impossible. I have feelings for you I can't even describe."

She stared at him, swallowing hard, her gaze projecting a thousand questions.

"Yala...I love you...I'm in love with you...and I can't...I don't want us going our separate ways again and you not knowing that."

Frozen in time, Yala's lips parted, but she couldn't speak, swallow, or breathe. The L-word. He scared the hell out of her with it.

"I accepted as a young girl that I'd never be loved. But it looks like I was wrong, and love has finally found me," she whispered, her gaze fixed on his.

The smile on her face was all the reassurance he needed to know that she was willing to accept his love.

"I love you, too," she whispered. The words formed the most beautiful sound he'd ever heard. They were the perfect combination of syllables designed to invoke a storm of emotions—their one mission—to spread explicit joy.

The kiss that followed, filled him to the brim with overpowering passions. They clung to each other until a calming peace settled and lured them into sleep.

***

Hours later, Kevin reached for Yala, and emptiness responded. She was already gone. "Damn it," he cursed, but acknowledged that she preferred sneaking away over saying goodbye just as she had the first night they met. He was relieved she left the way she did, or he may have been tempted to follow her, assignment be damned.

He reached over to the nightstand for water and found a note sitting next to the bottle. Under the note sat a key.

The note read:

Here's the key to my house. It gives you easy access to my home. It means you'll always be welcomed, and you'll always have a place here.

I'll miss you. Take care. Until I see you again.

***

Killer

Another masterpiece. Now, all I have to do is make sure those idiots get the first part of this set to Dr. Hughes without incident.

CHAPTER TWENTY-SIX

Kevin

Back in Atlanta, Kevin's attempts to track down Dr. Nolan was a bust. But the trip hadn't been for nothing. He ended up sniffing out news that had ties to the infamous Truleta Cartel.

The Cartel had been a thorn in TOP's side for a decade, and although it was slowly being demolished by TOP, there remained a large contingent of supernatural criminals continuing to operate under the authority of the cartel. However, dismantling it by any means necessary was the new rules of engagement. Hanging out in a dusty alley, he watched a cafe that was reportedly the front of one of the Cartel's underground safe houses.

Kevin moved through the streets with a sense of purpose, using his spy glasses to snap photos and record the place. The zoom on his glasses was good enough to give him a clear picture of what was taking place in the kitchen.

His phone vibrated, revealing an incoming text. It was Sori. She rarely contacted anyone. If you wanted to talk to her, you made the call. Besides, a text from her wasn't good, and receiving one made his thoughts spin out of control. He ducked into the next alley and called her.

He sensed something was wrong, tasted it in the air, and breathed in the edgy sensations that stabbed at his skin. Tension swarmed him from the inside, attacking his nerves and putting him on high alert. His pulse jumped, although he hadn't a clue as to what Sori might say.

"K," she said, her tone low with a cautious edge to it.

"Yes," he answered reluctantly.

"You were working on a case in DC." He couldn't tell if it was a question or comment. And it didn't matter because she already knew he'd been working that case with Yala.

"Yes, the strangest, most bizarre case I ever worked on—even for me. One of the reasons I'm in Atlanta now is because a lead on that case brought me here. Yala went back to DC to continue working on it."

Silence on the other end of the line lingered like spoken words.

"K, Dr. Hughes called me because he couldn't get a hold of you. He received a torso today, and I think it belongs to Yala. I think it's Yala."

Yala's name and the word torso in the same sentence stopped him in his tracks. His shoes scraped the gravelly ground. His body froze like he'd been zapped by a steady flow of electricity. His breaths became quick spurts of air that didn't allow him to get enough oxygen into his lungs. He kept the phone to his ear with one hand and used the other to prop himself against the side of a dirty brick wall.

Sori was rarely wrong. If she'd concluded that it was Yala in that death box, it probably was.

It was difficult to keep the phone to his ear because his hand trembled so badly. His voice cracked.

"What makes you think it's her?"

Sori's voice came across steadily like she should be named one-who-remains-calm-in-the-face-of-doom.

"K. I have worked with her a number of times. The few times she wasn't in disguise, I got a glimpse of the line of tattoos she has up her side."

He felt like he'd been dropped twelve stories and had landed on his head. That was how badly Sori's words wounded him. The tattoos were the only markings on Yala's body. The scars had healed just like she said they would and left no trace of the wound he'd stitched on her back the night they'd met in the alley.

The tattoos were cursively written, starting under her right arm and stopping at her right pelvic bone. 'Life. Death. Rebirth. Love'. The tattoos may have been simple words to people who didn't know Yala's story, but they represented different stages in her life.

'Life' was preceded by a tiny heart and a two-digit date, representing her birth and first heartbeat. 'Death' was preceded by a flat line and a two-digit date representing her death at fourteen years later. 'Rebirth' was listed before a pulse point symbol and a two-digit date that she'd officially become a TOP agent at twenty-one. 'Love' had a strike-through line, signifying she either didn't believe in it or that she'd never given or received love.

Yala had never explained the tattoos to Kevin. He never asked her to. However, she shared enough that he understood their meanings. It appeared Death was paying her a visit again.

The dirty alley became Kevin's private room as he huddled near a dumpster. He may as well have been a drunk regurgitating his lunch. He was sure that's what he looked like, propped against the dirty brick wall. His arm slid down the wall, scraping the skin from his forearm on the way down. His chin pressed into his chest as he crumbled to his knees.

The phone sounded like a walkie-talkie from Sori repeatedly yelling his name to get his attention. His head jerked when his current reality snapped back into place, urging him to put the phone back to his ear.

"I'm here," he said, his voice raspy and rough like his words were being raked over broken glass.

"Dr. Hughes tells me the key to this case is not to open the box, wait until all the parts are here, and there's a good chance of survival?"

"Yes! Please. Sori," he yelled louder than he intended. "Whatever you do, please don't let anyone open that box. The first two victims didn't make it because each time, the boxes were opened or broken before all the parts arrived."

He removed the phone from his ear, slipping back into a trance. He closed his eyes.

"Yala. Not you. God, please don't let it be true."

His chest rose and fell with quick and jerky movements from his erratic breathing. His splintering heart threatened to pound its way from his chest. The devastating news made it difficult to keep a mental grip on reality.

He searched, frantically scanning his surroundings for nothing in particular. He forced himself to talk, his voice cracking.

"Sori, please promise me you won't let anyone open that box. Please."

The quiet coming through the phone reiterated the seriousness of the situation.

Sori's voice finally broke the tense stillness. "K, you have my word. The box stays closed, no matter what—or who. I'll fuck somebody up before I let them open this box. I promise."

Kevin managed to hang up after several shaky swipes across the shiny surface of his phone. All that kept him from falling apart further was a promise from the one person he knew would keep it.

Kevin played doctor to his nerves during the plane ride to DC. He raced into the medical examiner's office like hell spawns chased him and were gearing up to light his ass on fire.

Doctor Pendergast was standing in the hallway waiting. The doctor walked with him, ushering him to the exam room like he didn't already know the way.

Sori stood next to the box like an armed sentinel. A shoulder holster displayed a weapon on one side and another anchored to the opposite hip. Kevin knew her well enough to know she hid more weapons on her body. About five-five and small framed like Yala, Sori had a reputation and presence that gave many, twice her size, pause.

Those who underestimated her physical strength, incredibly beautiful features, and charm were lured into her web. She reminded Kevin of one of those female comic book heroes who always had weapons in their hands. She maintained a poker face but couldn't hide what Kevin sensed—her grief.

His ability to detect intangible elements in people helped him tremendously in this field of work. He spotted lies in criminals and found evidence that was usually over-looked.

The extra spark woven into his senses was a gift he used to his advantage, but not this time. He didn't want to absorb anyone else's emotions, especially when they stirred because of someone they knew personally.

Although Sori was shielding her emotions, it didn't stop Kevin from sensing them anyway. His ability to break down an emotional wall was a new element to his gift that he'd discovered within the last year.

Sori cared deeply for Yala. Nothing he knew of or had ever witnessed scared her. He'd seen her stare Death in the face and kick him in the teeth, so for this situation to spark a certain level of fear within her, it set his nerves pouring over the edge of his sanity.

Doctor Hughes reached out and put a calming hand on Kevin's shoulder, realizing that Yala was much more to him than a partner and fellow agent. Kevin made himself look. He hadn't fully accepted what had been said and needed confirmation that it was Yala.

Quicksand legs carried him closer to the box. His eyes zoomed in on the line of tattoos along her side. Her arm rested atop her stomach, her elbow covering part of the tattoo, but Kevin recognized the words 'Rebirth' and 'Love'.

He knew the tattoo well. His lips had been intimate with that area of her body. He stared, transfixed. Yala's torso was on display—no head or lower body. She wore a bra, and he was thankful the monster had enough respectability to put her into the box with decency.

The first two victims hadn't made it out of their boxes alive. He reached out and placed a hand atop the glass.

"I can't live again until you are taken from this box in one piece," he whispered, glancing at the area where her head should have been. With haunted eyes, he glanced at Sori. "I will not rest until we have the monster that did this."

She grasped his shoulder. "I know, and neither will I. We can take turns, one of us keeping watch here and the other hunting down that asshole. We can work however you want. TOP and the doctors filled me in on the first two victims. I have questions but can work with what I have so far. I think you guys were on to something with Dr. Nolan. I believe he is the key. We find him, we find our murderer, or he leads us to the monster."

"Do you know about Elizabeth Paul and Mark Jenkins?"

Sori nodded. "I'll check out all avenues, but you know as well as I do that the murderer has the leverage that can stop us in our tracks." She glanced at Yala in the box. The asshole we needed to hunt down like a dog had the rest of Yala's body.

"We have to be careful how we talk, who we talk to, and how we pursue. Until we have all of Yala back together, we'll be walking on eggshells. The monster doing this was clever in how they laid out this situation. Having a part or part of a victim is one hell of a safety net."

The lump in Kevin's throat was as plump as a watermelon, but he managed to squeeze a few words past the obstruction.

"I'll do anything," he said, looking but not really seeing her. The overwhelming blow to his psyche made rational thinking an impossibility he was fighting to overcome.

Sori, always so intuitive, must have grasped as much. She nodded before tilting her head at the box.

"There will be someone here at all times, so whenever you want to leave or need to work, let me know. I called for extra eyes around the hospital, too."

Her sharp stare met his, followed by a little nod to ensure he understood her words.

"Expert eyes that won't get caught," she reiterated. "Dr. Hughes will be back later. He's giving me the evil eye right now because I asked him to go home and rest so he can return fresh. He and Dr. Pendergast will be on overlapping watches."

Kevin listened to Sori's words, but half weren't making it past the horrific images of Yala clouding his brain.

"Together, we'll get Yala back, and we're going to *kill...* this murderer. TOP can kiss my ass if they attempt to pull one of us off this case again."

If he weren't weighed down by despair, he would have hugged Sori. She knew some powerful people in TOP, and he believed she possessed the power to stop any further attempt to stall, stop, or pull anyone else from this case.

***

Kevin decided after an hour of sitting and staring at Yala's torso that he couldn't do it anymore. His gaze traveled toward Sori, pouring over surveillance footage in the corner of the room. Yala's box was left in the same manner as the first box—in the entranceway that led into the ME's office.

"If the box was dropped here, it could mean that the monster doing this may have another victim doing the dirty work while *it* lurks in the dark corner like a dark, nasty stain," Kevin spit the words out at Sori, shaking off the haze of his despair.

He dragged a seat next to hers. Feeling sorry for himself, and Yala for that matter, wasn't going to help solve this case.

CHAPTER TWENTY-SEVEN

Yala

The dark, cascading walls of despair were closing in on Yala, but she fought the wrathful beast tooth and nail, searching for any speck of light. Where was she?

Was she experiencing an emotional or physical reaction to pain? It was everywhere. Seeping from her pores, stabbing her in her stomach, the bottom of her feet, her head. She couldn't understand what she was experiencing. Something was off.

She believed she was talking out loud, but the sound didn't carry like it normally did within this blackness she waddled through. Each time pain engulfed her body, she became a slave to despair. She couldn't move or hear her own voice, even when she called out and yelled. Even when she opened her eyes, all she saw was darkness.

Was she stuck in a nightmare?

No. There was too much stabbing, ripping at her skin, and burning of her soul to be asleep. She screamed inside her head because her outside voice wasn't working. The relentless pain was sobering yet so forceful that it prevented her from thinking too far beyond it. It was a continuous fight to purge the pain enough to ease her suffering.

Memories of Kevin helped her find focus until the pain fought its ugly way to the surface and won the battle of control again and again. All she wanted was to be put out of her misery as extreme bouts of roaring aches shot through her system and punctured her senses. Paralyzed in a cocoon of agony, Yala forced herself to think.

Where am I?

Remember!

A desperate call while she was on her way to Doctor Nolan's house to talk to his wife. Doctor Hughes had found a note. Someone claimed to have information about the case and had left their number on the note. Yala called the number but remained skeptical. It could have been a prank or a trick.

During the call, she calmed the frantic woman on the line. The woman claimed that someone had taken a portion of her body and that she'd been instructed to deliver a box in order to get it back.

The call from the prospective victim had gotten Yala's immediate attention. She considered she could have been flying blind into a trap, so she instructed the victim to meet her in a public place, the local supermarket.

The woman lifted her shirt while they were surrounded by produce, proving to Yala that the torso section of her body was being kept as leverage until she delivered the box to the address scribbled on a yellow sticky note. The address explained why the woman knew who to contact for help.

When Yala dragged the woman into the bathroom for some privacy, all hell broke loose, and now, this darkness had become her reality.

"Aww!" She yelled like a woman gone mad but sensed that again, her voice wasn't being projected beyond her own scope of knowledge.

The agony alone was enough to keep derailing her train of thought. The sharp aches knifed through her tendons, her bones, her skin. Someone had to have soaked her brain in gasoline and tossed it inside an incinerator, leaving her mind to slowly cook.

It hurts!

She'd been the unlucky victim of a devastating rape as a teen. The pain, long and lasting, made her find a way to separate her mind and body to cheat it. How had she done it? At what point had she been broken so severely that she'd reached beyond the pain and embraced Death?

That's it!

Only when she'd reached out for Death's cold hand had the pain stopped. She'd courted pain by embracing Death. That day, she'd sensed Death. It lingered over her like a deadly protector, but Death hadn't been there to take her soul, at least not that day. It had been there to collect a piece of her. It had taken the part that should have stopped her from retaliating and brutally killing the men who'd raped her.

Although she'd been ready to die and believed in her heart she had passed away, Death didn't want her. It wasn't until she'd become an agent that she truly understood Death's trade-off. She'd become one of his best laborers, delivering people and creatures to its door like the mailman delivered packages. Death had given her a pinch of his madness, allowing her to kill with no regrets.

Since she'd become an agent two years ago, she'd executed twenty-seven people and hadn't felt an ounce of guilt about any of them.

Where was Death now that she needed him to take the pain again? Maybe this time was different because she didn't have anyone readily in her mind that she could kill in exchange for Death's help.

It hurts so bad!

Blackness had teamed up with a thick silence that formed a heavy blanket of endless ways to induce suffering. Yala screamed, her inner voice thundering inside her head. She was now turning over a pit of burning hot coals, the heat searing her from every angle.

Why can't I see? Move? Yell?

This dark endless purgatory she was trapped in must have been her hell.

Am I dead?

Had Death returned this time to retrieve her?

Kevin. Think of Kevin.

Handsome, sweet, and sexy, Kevin. The first man who'd shed a tear on her behalf. She'd relived the nightmare of her rape for nearly a decade, and he'd lassoed those horrific images from her head and replaced them with new ones.

He made her smile and laugh, and for the first time in her life, she anticipated seeing someone—him. She needed Kevin now. Needed him to pull her from the deep dark hole in which she'd fallen.

Aww!

A tidal wave of sharp jabs started beating against her back before they morphed into a dozen blades that took turns stabbing her in the stomach.

Help!

CHAPTER TWENTY-EIGHT

Kevin

Sori and Kevin drove to interview a colleague of Doctor Nolan, a fellow doctor who believed Nolan was missing and not hiding. He claimed the doctor had never previously taken off without notifying someone. The friend had nothing but good things to say about the doctor, just as the nurses had. They received the same story from other doctors in the field that knew him.

They stopped at Doctor Nolan's house to talk to his wife. They found the nanny taking care of his four-year-old daughter and eighteen-month-old son while the wife was out running errands.

"Hello," Sori called into the phone while they drove to check in on Mark and Elizabeth at the black site. "Okay. We'll be right over," she said while glancing in his direction. She didn't have to tell him. He could tell by the distressed look in her eyes that the doctors had received the second box.

Kevin decided then and there that he would continue the search and drop Sori off at the medical examiner's office. The idea of seeing Yala in pieces affected his ability to think, weakened his body, and squeezed the life right from his soul. His heart was invested, so much so he believed staying busy was his saving grace.

***
Sori

Dr. Hughes sat the second box containing Yala's legs atop the table next to her boxed torso.

Helplessness was an emotion Sori didn't like to acknowledge and was often able to shrug off. In this case, the irritating feeling kept her company as she stared at her detached friend.

She hit the record button on the camera before the doctors slid Yala's boxes together. Like magic, her parts reconnected. The spontaneous reaction happened too fast for their eyes to break the action down.

Never having seen anything like it, Sori was caught like a moth drawn to a flame. Her mind formulated a hundred different scenarios, but none explained the miraculous reconnection of the boxes or, more importantly, Yala's body.

How can a person, even a person with abilities, be alive in three different boxes and, at a certain point, in three different locations?

The doctors checked Yala's vital signs and confirmed that although sedated, her headless body remained fully functional. Like Yala's first box, the murderer had the decency to leave her in her underwear.

Hours later, Kevin entered the room. His usual handsome face drooped. His bloodshot eyes allowed a glimpse into his tortured soul. He stood, slumped in swaying silence, observing the doctors run their tests. He alternated between standing and pacing as his teeth tore off what was left of his nails.

The space in the room grew tight with four people. Therefore, Kevin's pacing was a distraction. If he got his hands on the killer, Sori was sure she'd have to find a way to keep him from ripping the person apart.

"I'll be outside," he announced to no one in particular before stepping off.

He'd hit an emotional rock bottom when Sori caught him outside the building, smoking. She jerked the cigarette from his jittery hand and stomped it out.

"We need your nose to find this asshole. Don't mess that up. One more box and Yala will be fine. She is strong, and if she has any consciousness about what's happening to her, I guarantee you, she is lying there fighting to figure this shit out."

Kevin nodded, his head motioning like a bobblehead.

"You're right. Dammit. She's a prisoner in that box, trapped in her own body, and I can't get her out because I can't find the answers."

Sori folded her arms over her chest and projected a hard stare.

"You have known me for years. It's difficult for me to befriend people, much less form an attachment to them."

Yala became like an adopted little sister who'd scooted her way into Sori's life for reasons she still couldn't figure out.

"Most people are afraid of me. They treat me like I'm the people-eating lion they have to beware of. Not her. She treated me like I was something special since the day we met and somehow got me to like her. I can't figure out how she did it, but I'm glad she did. She was the first female to see past my frosty nature and find something likable within me." Her forehead wrinkled in frustration. "I need you on this, K. I need you to focus. To be strong for her. You have a set of skills that can find this asshole after we receive that third box. If we don't put a stop to this, that fucking bastard is going to keep doing this. You are one of the only people I know who can track him despite the tightrope we have to walk while receiving these boxes."

Kevin looked at her like he'd never seen her before. She wasn't the kind of person that asked for help. However, in this case, he nodded, understanding they needed to do whatever it took to get Yala back in one piece and track down this madman.

***

Kevin

Sori's words gave Kevin hope. If fighting Death was the key to getting Yala back, he was ready to face the entity with confidence. She was the one good thing in his life—a life he once dedicated to work while ignoring his personal life.

Shrouded in death and mayhem for years as a TOP agent, he embraced the darkness as easily as he rejected happiness. Yala had changed his outlook on his personal life. She'd taken his heart, filled his chest with her love, and filled his soul with her own brand of happiness—a happiness he couldn't reject. She was the irrefutable force that made him long for things he assumed he would never have. He was in that box with Yala, whether she knew it or not.

Kevin and Sori spent the remainder of the day interviewing doctors and nurses and tracking leads as shaky as a fat woman's thighs. Their strongest lead had the potential to guide them to Doctor Nolan's whereabouts. Unfortunately, it hadn't borne fruit. More and more it looked like the doctor who'd built a reputation of being the good guy, may, in fact, be the monster they were searching for.

Half of the staff claimed he was still at a medical convention, and half believed he was on vacation. Some claimed they had spoken with him recently. The strangest thing how none of them worried about how long he'd been away.

A phone conversation with his wife, who was living her best life at the spa, was more of the same. Mrs. Nolan wasn't worried about how long her husband had been away. She believed he was at a medical convention and stated she'd spoken with him the day before.

Since suspicion was Kevin's and Sori's anchor, they wasted no time confirming and tracking the phone number the wife had given them to track down the doctor's whereabouts. The doctor wasn't where his wife presumed he would be, which was a medical conference in Chicago. The conference center representative confirmed that they didn't have a Doctor Charles Nolan registered.

Staking out the Nolan's home, Sori and Kevin decided to pay the wife a visit as soon as the babysitter drove off. When Mrs. Nolan answered the door, Kevin had to fight to keep his eyes from going wide. The youthful and slender brunette staring at them wasn't someone he pictured with a cheating older husband.

He stuck out his hand. "Mrs. Nolan?"

She inclined her head. "Yes?" Before she took his hand. Sori wasn't so kind. She was already glancing inside the living room over the woman's shoulder.

He and Sori flashed FBI badges.

"Would you mind if we talked to you briefly on a matter concerning your husband?"

She shook her head and waved them into her home.

Before their butts were comfortably placed on the furniture, Kevin began.

"You mentioned your husband was in Chicago at a medical convention, but a representative confirmed that your husband was not there. And the one medical convention they've had so far this year happened about a month ago."

Mrs. Nolan schooled her face into a frown, but he sensed her lack of an emotional attachment to her husband. She didn't love him. Did she relish that he wasn't around? She noticed the way Sori and Kevin stared at her.

"I'm not naïve to the fact that my husband is cheating. My children and I live a nice, pampered life. He doesn't bother me about what I do with my time, and I don't nag him about his."

Her telling words had their eyebrows lifting. They hadn't suggested that her husband was cheating because he wasn't where he was supposed to be, but Kevin was now aware that Mrs. Nolan likely knew about Elizabeth.

He tasted the bitterness she harbored for her husband flowing off of her like smokestacks.

"I understand you attended medical school, Mrs. No-lan? Why didn't you resume your studies?"

She cast a guarded look at Kevin before she answered. Sori eyed the woman with a probing glare.

"I dropped out to help tend to my mother, who had breast cancer at the time. By the time I was ready to return to school, I was married and pregnant with my daughter. I believed it was best to devote my time to raising her."

Mrs. Nolan was hiding something. She was just as disconnected when she mentioned her mother and daughter as when she mentioned her husband. Kevin was fishing for information and prayed she'd volunteer more.

Her lack of emotional attachment to her family had him questioning whether she resented them for her not finishing medical school. Did she have deeper issues? Was her husband abusive? Did she feel neglected?

When she finally expressed concern about her husband's safety, Kevin knew it was forced because her face and tone didn't match. He didn't pick up an evil vibe or malicious intent, but a neutral front like a cool breeze versus a cold one.

"Do you mind if I use the bathroom?" he asked.

She nodded before pointing him in the direction. Kevin took the long way around the Nolan's home and did a quick search of the couple's bedroom. A note was all that was worth finding.

However, it wasn't what was written on the note that got his attention; it was what the note was written on that made him do a double take. It was written on stationery from the Oakwood Apartment complex—the same complex in which the first boxed victim lived. After being gone for far longer than he intended, Kevin walked back into the living room and found Sori had moved closer to the woman, and questions flew around like lit bullets.

Kevin sat and passed the note to Sori before pointing at where the stationary had come from. Sori squinted, eyeballing the woman with enough venom in her gaze to take out a city block.

"We're going to need the phone number your husband called you from?"

She provided it without hesitation. If Mrs. Nolan knew what they were up to, she didn't comment. She remained calm about the entire ordeal.

After the team left the Nolan residence, they used the doctor's cell number to triangulate his phone's signal to pick up his location. The doctor wasn't in another state at all. According to the number, he was somewhere in or near DC.

It took thirty minutes to pinpoint his location. He was at the last place they expected him to be: The Oakwood Apartments. The doctor had likely been hiding right under their noses the entire time.

***

The worst part of this situation, neither Kevin nor Sori could approach or interact with Doctor Nolan until they received Yala's head. He and Sori flashed badges and proceeded to obtain information from the front office assistant at the Oakwood Apartments.

They discovered that Dr. Nolan was a long-time tenant who rented an apartment in the complex. The assistant also revealed that a woman had stopped by days ago and inquired about the same apartment.

Was the apartment Dr. Nolan's sin-den for the escorts he hired? Was it his demented workshop? Could the woman who'd inquired about the apartment have been Yala chasing down this lead before ending up in one of his boxes?

Kevin and Sori set out to spy and see if they could spot the doctor inside the apartment, but Doctor Hughes called, informing them that they'd received the third part of Yala's box.

The box had arrived earlier than the usual timeline. Was it because the mastermind behind this believed the agents were closing in on him? The agents they'd left keeping watch of the medical examiner's office called a few minutes after Dr. Hughes to report that they had a suspect in custody. It was a man claiming he'd been paid to deliver the box.

Kevin and Sori left two agents on duty at the Oakwood Apartments while they raced back to the medical examiner's office.

**

Doctor Hughes stood at the head of Yala's body. Sori stood at her side. Doctor Pendergast stood next to the box containing her head that sat at her feet.

Kevin slumped near the camera, taking in the mind-jarring sight. Everyone pretended like seeing Yala's head sitting at her feet wasn't the most insane thing they'd witnessed.

Doctor Pendergast swiftly moved the box, aligning it above Yala's torso box. Kevin closed his eyes and bowed his head in prayer. It had been a long time since he'd prayed for anyone since his mother. He'd been angry at God ever since that day and hadn't put much stock in communicating with the deity on his worst day. Now, he prayed again, asking for Yala's life to be spared.

The head box was moved into place, and as soon as the box hit home, Yala became whole again.

Why isn't she moving?

The room became as silent as Yala's motionless body. They drew deep breaths and may as well have been marble statues. The thump of the blood vessel in Kevin's head indicated that he may be on the verge of a brain aneurysm.

He radiated his power, pouring it into her to convince Yala to move. She needed to express any sign of life before he passed out.

A gasp sounded that bowed her back and lifted her chest before she took in a deep breath of air. For a split second, sheer joy entered his bloodstream and raced through his veins. Her body began to convulse after that one breath.

The doctors snatched the box open. They rolled Yala from the box with such speed and precision that you would think they practiced the move. They hooked her up to machines, and jabbed needles into her arms and hands as they worked swiftly to restore her life. They managed a weak heartbeat, but another series of seizures sent her body into shock.

Kevin seized along with Yala. His body shook violently, but his eyes never left her. His first nervous breakdown was in progress.

CHAPTER TWENTY-NINE

Sori

Sori kept one eye on Kevin and the other eye on the doctors and Yala. At any moment, Kevin would likely keel over. Not eating, not sleeping, stressing over Yala mingled with stress of him overworking for the last five days. He was down at least ten pounds and looked like life was seeping from his body.

His ability made it worse because he carried his own sorrow and bore the burden of taking on everyone else's too. His sharp breaths mingled among the doctors' scrambling bodies and shuffling feet.

When it appeared the doctors had it all under control, an ominous sound filled the room. The sustained beep of the heart machine filled their ears. The tone signified death, a finality no one was ready or willing to accept. The screeching beep mirrored one of the tattoos Yala had etched into her side.

Kevin staggered. He fell against the table, unaware of his own despair. He was broken, destroyed by the sound of the machine, the constant beep that signified Yala's heart had stopped.

Beeeeeeeee…

The doctors didn't give in to the beep; they continued to pump Yala's chest and inject her with medicines meant to revive her as they prepared equipment that would send jolts of electricity into her body.

When Doctor Hughes plunged a large needle into Yala's chest, Kevin lost the use of his legs, and his knees buckled. His hand slapped hard against the floor to keep the rest of him from following.

He forced his legs to straighten, not realizing how weak he'd been. His arms shook under the weight of his body as he struggled to lift himself from the floor. He made it back to his feet and stood bent with his hands resting against his wobbly legs.

"Why is this happening to me?"

Sori didn't have to have his ability, but sense that was one of the questions swimming around in his head. He was losing the person he'd undoubtedly fallen in love with.

Sori didn't immediately run to Kevin's side. She gave him a chance to recover on his own. She inched closer after viewing him slouched over the table, attempting to stand upright.

The doctors initiated manual CPR on Yala, one at her head and the other at her chest.

Sori closed the remaining space between her and Kevin. She placed an arm under his shoulder to help him stay upright without taking her gaze off Yala and the doctors.

She shoved Kevin against the wall and held him with her hip as she watched the doctors continue fighting to save Yala. She tuned out the horrible beeping sound because she didn't sense the one thing that would solidify Yala's end…Death. The dark entity had a presence, and she'd been on this job long enough to know what Death felt like when it arrived.

Kevin shook, his body hunched, his eyes begging and pleading and saying what his mouth wouldn't. Sori couldn't stand seeing him this way. He was one of the best agents she knew, but at this moment, she wasn't sure he was in the right frame of mind anymore.

He sensed things in people. That he may be experiencing what Yala was feeling could be his undoing.

Sori took in the tortured expression that poured from his face. It was the look of a thousand blades stabbing him in the heart. Love was the most powerful mystery in the world. Nothing else she knew of that could weaken Kevin's resolve. She'd worked with him many times before and had witnessed him stare Death in the face and challenge it.

Now, in this exam room, he reached toward the table for Yala, unconcerned about his own well-being as the horrible sound continued to wreak havoc.

Beeeeeeeee...

Like a scene straight from the television show, *Dexter,* Sori reached into the pocket of her cargo pants and removed a syringe. She bit the cap off with her teeth and plunged the needle into Kevin's arm. He was too distraught to even flinch at the prick. The doctors were too busy to voice their concerns over her actions, if they had any.

Sori dragged Kevin to the couch in the small break area three doors down. He was out. The sedative had dragged him into the underworld, where dreams and nightmares ruled.

By the time Sori made it back to the exam room, Yala was gone. The machine screamed, and the doctors stood frozen in place.

Dr. Hughes glanced at his watch, prepared to call Yala's time of death.

Sori yelled, "Nooo! Don't do it. Don't say it. Sometimes death is not the end. I'm sure you've seen people come back, even after you think they're dead. I have. How many people have come through this office presumed dead and have ended up walking away from here or returned to the hospital?"

Dr. Hughes didn't have to think about the answer. "Eleven," he said, his eyes never leaving Yala's.

He considered Sori's point and dropped his arm, unwilling to destroy her hope by placing a timestamp on Yala's death. As far as Sori was concerned, she wasn't dead. Doctor Hughes did, however, cover her lifeless body with a thin white sheet before he cast a grief-stricken glance at Sori and Doctor Pendergast.

The doctors' wild-eyed expressions suggested she was crazy, but Sori didn't care. Yala was strong enough to fight whatever force had a hold on her. Besides, Sori still didn't feel the familiar tingle, the creeping ache that warned her when death was near.

If Kevin's frame of mind was sound, he'd have sensed it too. The calmness. The silence. The lingering residue of her life and the whisper it made alerted you to her lingering spirit.

The doctors exited the exam room with their heads hung low, beaten by a case that had a life all its own. Sori didn't care what the doctors believed about Death. She'd had a few dates with the entity and knew from experience that death didn't always represent the end. If it were the end, she would have been dead three or four times over.

Maybe if the doctors had the privilege of knowing Yala longer, they would be more optimistic. Yala was small and pretty, which usually meant that she was under-estimated and counted out when it came to anything physical. They had no idea she'd breezed through her training at Top with such strength that she continued to be talked about by her trainers. She may not have looked it, but she was tough as nails.

Sori flipped the sheet back from over Yala's face and stared at her lifeless body. She had not silently slipped away.

"He hasn't come for you. If you're somewhere lost, you need to find your way back, and fast. Kevin loves you. I can spot it a mile away. If you don't want to come back for yourself, please come back for him," she said, sensing that Yala received her words.

Sori joined the doctors in the break room. She glanced at Kevin, still out. He'd admitted to his feelings for Yala. Given what she knew of his personality, him admitting his feelings was an eye-opening admission that had left her mouth hanging wide open on the other end of that phone line.

Moments ago, she felt Kevin's grief over Yala when she grabbed him. His grief bounced off him in aggressive ripples that hurt like physical pain. It clung so strongly that she believed it was a monster that chilled her to the bone. This was the first time she'd experienced anything like that all-consuming heartache that was hell-bent on keeping possession of his body. Kevin had somehow transferred a part of what he felt to her, and it made her want to throw up.

She couldn't shake the notion that loving someone could send one into such debilitating despair. By observing Kevin, she'd learned that love could reach down into a person's essence and rip out their soul.

CHAPTER THIRTY

Yala

Yala reminded herself, "*Don't Panic!*"

Where am I? When am I? All she knew at this moment was who she was, even though that notion was foggy and sloshing around in her brain like mud.

Time and reality escaped her. How had she ended up here, plunged into an endless pit of darkness she couldn't escape? Wherever she was, she was in deep, the darkness thick and vast, like she would be lost in it forever.

Yala suffocated as something deviant, dirty, and devilish took her mind and controlled her body with stabbing aches and mind-numbing pain. Its dark boney fingers pressed into her skin and sank down to the bone.

Don't panic!

She repeated the words in her head. If she was where she assumed she might be, the last thing she needed to do was to panic.

Was her body cut into three parts like the others? Was she at the mercy of a warped lunatic who would send her to Dr. Hughes for reassembly?

"*Aww!*" she yelled out when an explosion of twisting and sharp aches erupted all over her body.

The aches continued to course through her. It was a sign that she was alive, wasn't it? She shivered without movement. She screamed without sound. She breathed without oxygen. The longer she remained in the dark, the more she was convinced that she was inside the box.

How long had she been in it? Would Dr. Hughes receive all of her parts before she became another dead body on his table? Would she be the recipient of Dr. Hughes's next y-shaped incision in preparation for an autopsy that would reveal the cause of her death was something impossible?

She prayed that the old saying, 'third times a charm,' was true. If a part of her were with Dr. Hughes right now, this would be the third box to grace his table. Nausea hit hard, and her sense of understanding began to fade. She was about to black out again.

She needed to remember where she was. She needed to remain calm.

What was the woman she'd met wearing? Could the woman have been in on the ruse to get her alone and into the box?

Dammit! As soon as she believed she was linking a clue together, it fractured like a broken mirror, breaking apart the reflections of her memories. How could she think her way out of this?

Wait.

The pain had lessened considerably. Was she dying? Was her body being rebuilt as the doctors reconnected her parts?

Her mind fog had cleared enough to string together more logical patterns of ideas.

Did Kevin know she'd been snatched into this deadly game? Could anyone identify her in the box?

If they received her head first, they would know. Kevin would know her by the tattoos on her side, but only if they were exposed. She had too many questions and no answers.

She drifted, eyes heavy and body demanding sleep, but she refused to let go of the little bit of awareness her mind clung to desperately.

A sudden jolt shook her and yanked her away from what was assuredly dragging her under. Her determination to fight was much stronger now.

She had embraced the cold hand of death the first time because she was fourteen and naïve. There was someone to fight for now. Kevin was her wonderful someone, and she couldn't bear to let go.

Another surge of energy pulsed through her body like she was the car hooked up to jumper cables, and her mind and body sputtered with every spark. Was it life? Was it her body fighting to function?

She couldn't tell. A sense of reality peeked into her mind and put her in the right headspace and time.

Yes. That was it.

She'd located and pieced together her scattered ideas. She was inside that horrendous box, fighting Death to find her way back to life—to Kevin.

Blood danced through her veins, pulsing against the coldness of her skin. The sensation made her quit her mental rant and enjoy the moment as warm pulses of energy coursed through her and eased the pain.

A sound called, urging her to move.

Beep. Beep. Beep.

The repetitive *beep* drew her attention. It resounded low, off in the distance, but it was easily distinguished. She wanted to say something but she had yet to regain control of her mouth.

My eyes.

They fluttered, anxious to see beyond the darkness. She poured all of her strength into opening her eyes, the safest things to move to avoid the risk of opening the box.

After what felt like an hour, her eyes flickered furiously before they popped open. A blinding light filled her view, but she fought it, searching for anything familiar. Something covered her mouth and the breaths she released made it billow and slink across her cheek. She turned her head until the cloth fell from her mouth.

Where am I?

Dingy walls. The sterile taste in the air. The looming presence of death peeking from every corner.

Panic hit her in the chest at the realization, and she wheezed to get air into her lungs. The sudden intake made her cough and set off a detonation of sharp explosions that ripped through her chest. The view from where she lay put her in the last place she wanted to be, on the exam room table. The cloth that had covered her mouth was a sheet. She sensed it now, covering the rest of her body.

Is there a rest of me, all here, in one place?

A tremble of anxiety threatened to attack her. Her shaky fingers inched up, searching to confirm whether or not she was in parts. Not yet ready to glance down, she feared she might be a head. One that was missing her middle or lower parts. It didn't matter much what part was missing. The sight would be traumatic.

Her gaze crept down. She lifted her head inch by inch until the view of the rise and fall of her chest registered. The view of the points of her toes under the sheet peaked. She sighed, exhaling a long breath. Relief swept through her at the knowledge that she was in one piece and gave her the spark of strength she needed to move other parts.

She wiggled her toes first. Her fingers flexed, and her shaky hands lifted on command. Finally, she turned her aching body. She scanned the room, her eyes moving wildly in her sockets.

She jumped. The box she'd somehow escaped was there like it had a life. The thing stood in the corner of the room like a goon straight from hell. As soon as she found matches, she would burn it.

How had she survived it? Why was she alone?

"Am I dreaming? Dead?"

The tone of her cracked voice registered and confirmed that she was alive. The air flowing into her lungs and the aches shooting through her like fireworks were a few other reminders.

Muffled voices seeped through the cracked exam room door. The distant sounds drew her attention and urged her to keep moving. She rolled, inching carefully over the edge of the table, the slightest movement making her wince and moan.

She paused halfway into the turn to swallow a gripping spike of sharp pain, allowing it to subside. Her gaze landed on the cracked tile on the floor. Grunts and groans accompanied her movement as she inched over the side. Squealing and making animalistic noises helped during the process. She needed to let someone know she was alive.

CHAPTER THIRTY-ONE

Sori

Sori glanced at Kevin, who was still out cold. A few more hours and the sedative would wear off.

Death hadn't come to collect Yala's soul, but another issue remained. Would she recover from the shock and trauma she had gone through?

Although she didn't understand everything about this case, Sori still didn't bombard the doctors with a bunch of questions. She'd been around the bizarre, the strange, and the unexplained for years; herself included on the list. As much as she knew she shouldn't admit it, compared to the doctors, she wasn't that interested in finding out what made the boxes work.

The thing that plagued her most was the person responsible for it. Taking a person apart was personal. It was intimate in a way that required a tremendous amount of time and devotion. It took a dedicated mind to perform that level of painstakingly complex work.

Why would someone do it?

Sori's job was to think like and sometimes be like the monsters to catch them. Was this mastermind testing his victims to see who would survive being taken apart and put back together? Were they doing this simply because they could or were they fulfilling a sick fantasy that could lead to more evil deeds?

After Kevin's breakdown, Sori wanted to shut her mind off from this harsh reality, but now was not the time. She needed to help the two people she considered friends—Yala, fighting for her life, and Kevin, fighting for his sanity.

Handling circumstances where emotions were front and center proved difficult for Sori. A situation she would have mind handling at the moment was placing her hands around the box murderer's neck and choking him until he French-kissed Death.

***

Sori and the doctors jumped to their feet at the loud groan and hobbling steps that broke through their silence. The sound reminded Sori of a zombie shuffling across the doorway, releasing a creepy death moan.

When Yala stumbled into the room, Sori was at her side in seconds, supporting her twitchy body. Yala blew out sharp breaths as Sori assisted her into a chair.

She swiped sweat from her brow with a quick swipe of the backside of her hand. She strained to keep her body upright and her eyes open. Her lazy gaze strayed toward Kevin, and she lifted a shaky hand in his direction.

"Don't worry. He's fine. I had to give him a sedative."

Yala shook her head before her brows pinched. She didn't understand, but she didn't have the strength to ask for an explanation. She slouched in the chair, her body tilting to the side. The doctors appeared, asking her questions that she was too slow to answer.

"How do you feel? Does your head hurt? Your back? Your neck? Does your stomach hurt? Can you feel this? What's your name?"

She didn't answer but looked at them, her eyes attempting to convey what she couldn't spit out. She wore a heavy coat of fatigue that kept pulling her down. She may as well have been a piece of clay molded to the chair in which she sat. Her skin glistened with sweat from the exertion of dragging her tortured body from the exam room.

"I'll get you a wheelchair. We need to get you into recovery," Dr. Pendergast announced.

"Will she be okay?" Sori asked. Doctor Hughes nodded without pulling his gaze away from her while Doctor Pendergast attempted to get her to follow his fingers.

Sori didn't care what the doctors said about her recovery. She wasn't leaving Yala's side until she was stabilized. She was hooked up to intravenous drips and a few other machines, but her color was returning. Sori sat while Yala slept, the sight enticing her first sincere smile since she'd arrived.

When she finally returned to the break room, she waited until Kevin awoke. He tossed and turned and mumbled words she couldn't understand before he jumped up with a start.

"Yala! Yala!"

Sori placed a hand on his shoulders to keep him seated. The lingering effects of the sedative would be with him for a while.

"K. Yala is okay. Sleeping. Recovering. Please, don't stand."

She explained all that had occurred during his time out before taking him to Yala's room, where the doctors monitored her closely.

Sori sat Kevin in a chair near Yala's bed and stood in the corner, observing him with her.

"I believe it's time I go and find Dr. Nolan and, hopefully, a way to keep myself from killing the monster," Sori declared once she believed Yala would be all right.

***

Kevin

A wave of relief swept through Kevin upon learning and seeing that Yala would be okay. He leaned closer to her and let her warmth comfort him.

Sori's words resonated, finally soaking into his brain. She was about to go and track down the killer. They made eye contact before she stepped away.

Kevin had worked with Sori on several occasions and knew the look well. She got this chilling look when she was about to kill someone. Death danced behind her eyes.

If Dr. Nolan was the box killer, Sori would kill him, and nothing or no one was stopping her. The man would suffer, his death wouldn't be quick, and it definitely wouldn't be painless.

"Sori, wait up," Kevin called after her.

Although Kevin wanted the man dead, he also had questions he wanted answers to before he had the honor of killing the monster.

Kevin remained at Yala's side until the doctors practically shoved him out the door for asking so many questions concerning her recovery. Once he was satisfied with their answers, he placed a kiss on Yala's forehead and found Sori waiting at the exit.

He and Sori drove to Doctor Nolan's secret hideaway after confirming with the lookouts that hadn't left the apartment. Sori was speeding like they were on the last lap and Dale Earnhardt Jr. was on their tail.

Although he knew she was capable, Kevin couldn't stomach the idea of letting Sori go at it alone with a monster that butchered people and put them on display in boxes. And he'd be lying if he said he didn't want revenge for what Yala had gone through.

They approached the apartment, ready to start a war, but kept a calm and professional demeanor. They used their professionally acquired burglary skills to enter the place. The stench of death burned through the air like a wicked curse and immediately overwhelmed Kevin.

He placed the back of his hand up to his nose. His face schooled into a deep frown. Sori swallowed hard, wrinkled her nose, and aimed her weapon higher.

The two traversed the distance from the foyer to who they assumed was Doctor Nolan sitting in the living room. The scene began to match the vile odor the closer they stepped to the doctor, who was seated on the couch, facing the television.

A gun rested on the floor near his feet. A large chunk of his skull had fallen over the back of the couch and landed on the carpet. Clumps of brain matter and blood was blown about the area and clung to the carpet, couch, and nearest wall.

The air conditioning was turned to its coldest setting to prevent his body from being discovered right away. However, he was in the beginning stages of decomp, which meant he'd not been dead for more than a day or two.

Sori shook her head. "Damn!"

They went about the business of processing the doctor's suicide. A crease lined Sori's forehead, and Kevin gave her a sidelong look. There wasn't a suicide note, and something was off.

"Why would he commit suicide?" Kevin asked. "It doesn't make sense. If we were closing in on him, why not just run? He has the means. And is it just me or is something about this timeline with taking Yala and sending her to Doctor Hughes and then killing himself not making any logical sense?"

"No, it's not making any sense. He either has a partner or he's the scapegoat," Sori added while her sharp gaze traveled around the room.

For someone so dedicated to his murderous project, taking his life wouldn't have been the next logical step. If he was the fall guy, this wasn't over. They still had a lot of work to do.

They poured over Doctor Nolan's cold, stiff body before stepping away to thoroughly check the rest of the apartment. When Kevin entered the master bedroom, he inhaled the familiar sweet and spicy scent that matched the smell on the boxes.

The faint odor of decomposition drifted into this area from the living room. A glass coffin lay atop the bed's wooden frame. The mattress from the bed stood at the window, obstructing the view into and out of the room.

An arsenal of cutting and surgical tools sat atop a slender metal table next to one of the infamous boxes. A tall standing light stood over the bed, waiting to illuminate the path of madness.

A check of the smaller bedroom didn't reveal anything but cleaning and medical supplies. Other than the bed, metal table, and tall lamp, there was no other furniture in either of the bedrooms.

When Sori entered the master bedroom, she took in the box before her gaze locked with Kevin's. He stood in the middle of the room, wiping his nose.

"What is it?" she asked.

"The scent. I didn't smell it on the doctor, but this room is filled with it."

The team had their ground zero, but Kevin wasn't sure they had found their killer. The bathroom attached to the master bedroom was converted into a washroom. Tools and other equipment lay soaking in the tub and the sink.

Based on the amount of medical equipment in the apartment, the doctor had been conducting illegal experiments on people for years, and his operation was sanitary enough to keep the eyes of suspicion at bay.

Sori shook her head. "Motherfucker's one sick fuck. He probably thinks this chop shop he's been running is somehow for the greater good of humanity. People who are *that* sick in the head always dream up justifiable reasoning."

Kevin pulled open the wooden door to the walk-in closet. Behind the wooden door sat a sturdy half-metal door supported by the bricked-in wall of the closet. A thick metal lock adorned the half door, and three thumb-size air holes were drilled into the smaller door. A sinister vibe crawled over Kevin's skin and clung to his senses. He glanced at Sori.

"My senses are tingling," Kevin stated before he shook off a chill.

"Mine too," Sori announced, her gaze locked on the mysterious half door.

They drew their weapons and prepared to meet what lingered behind that door. The door was borrowed from a horror film, the kind that creaked open right before the monsters attacked.

Kevin slid the lock from its housing. The screech of metal scraping against metal cast a sound like a woman screaming a tortured cry of pain, a deep hurtful hair-raising kind of pain.

They waited, weapons at the ready, for a disfigured soul-snatcher to spring from the dark after the door was half opened. Kevin continued to toe the door open. A gust of wind flew from the darkness.

Kevin hunkered down before dropping to his knees. He followed his gun into the tight dark opening, inching further cautiously. The light that illuminated the dark came from a ghost-white figure huddled in the corner of the bricked-in tomb.

Kevin shivered as goose bumps beaded up his arms. Terror leaped off the figure in waves. He projected a low, calm voice that pushed through the darkness and met the figure.

"I'm not here to hurt you. I'm here to help you. We found the one who's been hurting you. He can't hurt you anymore."

Kevin holstered his weapon, and although he could have stood, he remained low. His eyes adjusted to the dark and allowed him to make out the figure huddled atop a small mattress.

He drew closer and reached out to what he sensed was a female. Her body trembled with fright. She pushed into the bend of the wall for protection, desperate to get away.

He called back to Sori, "I may need you to do that neck grab thing."

Kevin had gotten a lesson from Sori on how to apply a neck grab, like the Vulcans on Star Trek, but he hadn't perfected it yet.

Sori was either stronger than she appeared or knew the human body better than most because the move required pressure to be applied to specific areas of the neck to render it effective. He'd witnessed her pull off the nonlethal move several times.

They switched places, and it took Sori less than thirty seconds to subdue the woman. Kevin carried her to the loveseat while Sori called their TOP contacts. They needed to get the victim to one of their hidden facilities for medical attention and questioning and to enable them to collect evidence and clear the scene.

The emaciated female reminded him of a helpless and starved dog left tied to a tree. Depending on what the death doctor had done to her, she would need a lot of nourishment and care.

After the victim was taken, Sori and Kevin stayed at the apartment to continue processing the scene. They found a journal the doctor kept that detailed a decade of him taking people and animals apart.

The last few entries in his journal explained why he created the boxes. He needed help keeping his subjects alive longer after reassembly. He'd handpicked Doctor Hughes for the task.

The last journal entry caused an uproar in Kevin's head. Was Yala's life still in jeopardy?

CHAPTER THIRTY-TWO

Kevin

Kevin and Sori had the unpleasant task of informing Doctor Nolan's wife of his death. Samantha Nolan answered the door with a cheerful smile.

"Please, come in."

They entered, and Kevin got straight to the point.

"Mrs. Nolan, we are here too..." he stopped and sniffed several times.

Sori's back stiffened. She eyed him and scooted to the edge of the chair she'd sat on. She hadn't wanted the task of telling Mrs. Nolan the bad news, and Kevin knew from working with her that she wasn't the most compassionate person. However, when he took too long to continue his speech, Sori decided to finish it.

"Mrs. Nolan, we're sorry to inform you that we found your husband. He committed suicide. Please, let us know if there's anything we can do for you and your family," she blurted. Her words sounded rehearsed and mechanical.

At first, Mrs. Nolan's face remained devoid of sadness; but then tears began to fall like she had to turn them on. Kevin placed a tender hand on the woman's shoulder in an effort to comfort her, but his face remained fixed, tight with what he sensed.

"Ma'am, you're not sorry about your husband's death, are you?"

The lines of her face tightened into a question, and she backed away from him.

Sori sat higher in her seat, likely noticing his words weren't a question. She placed her hand on her weapon as she stared between him and Mrs. Nolan.

Kevin backed away, putting more distance between him and the woman.

"Ma'am, your fragrance. What is it?"

She swiped away a few lazy tears.

"It's a fragrance I have enjoyed since college. It's called Spicy Lady."

Sori must have pieced together his body language and line of questioning. She stood, but Mrs. Nolan's baby boy crawled into the living room. He went straight for Sori, latched onto her pant leg, and pulled himself up.

The little guy begged Sori in baby talk to pick him up. His chubby little fingers gripped her pants while he flashed her an undeniably cute, red-cheeked smile.

Sori plastered a fake smile on her face and stared at Mrs. Nolan to retrieve her child. The little guy clung to Sori's leg, smiling at her with four top teeth, one bottom tooth, and a mouth full of drool.

Kevin would venture to say that Sori had never held a baby a day in her life. She revealed to him once that kids were weirdly drawn to her, the one person who knew the least about them. Mrs. Nolan scooped the baby up and turned to Kevin.

"That's the scent. It's a combination of baby lotion and your perfume."

Mrs. Nolan gave the expression of a deer caught in the headlights, but Sori knew what Kevin was getting at. She took a step closer to the woman who now stared between him and Sori like they were a pair of attack dogs.

Due to the presence of the baby and the other child in the next room watching cartoons, they didn't draw their weapons. Sori reached out and placed her hands over the baby's ears, making the little fellow fight to leave his mother's arms to climb into hers. The baby laughed, a jolly little toddler laugh, while Sori kept his ears sheltered from the harsh words Kevin knew she was set to release.

"You're going to call someone to pick up your children and come with us. You set your husband up, staged his suicide, kept a hostage, and cut my friend into pieces. Your mind is pure darkness. You fucking monstrous bitch. I should bust your fucking—"

The easy smile and innocent eyes of Mrs. Nolan's baby boy stopped Sori's rampage of violent words that were sharp enough to slice the woman into pieces.

Kevin didn't utter a word. He was proud of the way Sori was handling this situation. Luck was on Mrs. Nolan's side, that's for sure. Not much kept Sori's temper in check except expelling her anger on its intended target.

Instead of fear, or protest, Mrs. Nolan smiled. She accepted that she'd been caught.

"Did the beautiful detective survive?" she asked, as a smug smile danced across her face.

The tight pull of Sori's expression, and her clenched fist, revealed the amount of willpower she used to remain calm. Of all the things Mrs. Nolan could have asked, she wanted to know if Yala had survived her monstrous science project.

Kevin clenched his fists so tightly that his knuckles cracked. He'd never laid a hand on a woman a day in his life, but this one made him question his morals.

As badly as he ached to put a bullet in Samantha Nolan's head, he refrained when Yala entered his mind. She was alive, and he no longer needed to execute revenge because he didn't want to take that opportunity away from Yala if she wanted it. For now, they needed this monster alive to reverse what she'd done to Mark and Elizabeth and find out if she had more victims.

Sori's face went cold, the sight making Kevin shiver. Having seen this look before, he knew dead bodies usually accompanied it. She glared into the woman's eyes after covering the baby's ears once more. Her voice projected low, but the jagged edge to the tone of her words cut deep.

"Wouldn't you like to know? If you didn't have this baby in your arms, I'd kill you slowly with my bare hands. You better pray no one in law enforcement is crazy enough to leave you alone with me."

Mrs. Nolan was smart enough to be afraid this time. Her chin trembled as she adjusted the baby on her hip and took out her cell phone. She called her mother to come and take care of the kids.

***

The team had found the true box murderer, a woman willing to use everyone in her life to perfect her twisted fantasy.

When they finally interrogated her at one of TOP's black sites, they uncovered an arsenal of secrets Samantha had hidden. At the Nolan home, they'd found a hidden flash drive containing a scan of the original lease Samantha Nolan signed for the Oakwood apartment along with files of research she conducted on the fifty-one people she documented. There were no names. All of the files were labeled as 'subject' and preceded by a number. Bank statements from her private account revealed payments for the apartment and large medical equipment purchases.

As a stay-at-home mother of two, Samantha Nolan had evaded suspicion. No one had questioned that she dropped her kids off at daycare daily and often left them with a sitter when they weren't at daycare.

Her time was being spent at the apartment she'd turned into a lab. She hadn't quit medical school for the sake of her children. She just believed she'd acquired the knowledge she needed to become a full-time body dismantler.

It was frightening to think her plan would have worked if not for Kevin's sharp senses and Doctor Nolan's death.

"You knew your husband was cheating because you sought out Ms. Paul on his behalf?"

306 · KETA KENDRIC

She nodded nonchalantly. They found evidence of her making the initial payment to the high-end escort service Elizabeth worked for.

"You wanted him to cheat so you would have an excuse to keep doing your dirty deeds on the side," Kevin stated, squinting at the woman with no emotional attachment to her family. Nothing stirred within her concerning her husband's death.

"You wanted him to cheat so you could kill him with more ease if the time came," Sori said, spitting out another accusation the woman took in stride. She harbored no shame about anything she did to manipulate her husband and fool all of her friends.

Instead of sitting across the table from the monster of a woman, Sori paced to control her urge to kill her. Kevin possessed the same urge, but he also wanted answers.

"The woman in the closet, who is she?" he asked.

Samantha smiled while eyeballing Kevin under her lashes. She didn't reply, but he sensed the sparks of emotions rolling off her at the mention of the woman in the closet. Samantha Nolan had a personal attachment to the woman. The sensation was warm with a brutal edge to it, like she loved and hated the woman at the same time.

Sori spun on her heels, causing Kevin and Samantha to snap their heads up. She leaned over the table, getting into Samantha's face.

"Why the fuck would you do this type of sick, fucked up shit?"

Samantha shrugged. By now, she believed that she was under the protection of the law and that she couldn't be hurt. She was unaware of how TOP operated when it came to paranormal criminals who murdered the innocent.

"You think you're safe because you're in this government facility," Sori stated before a creepy smile breezed across her lips.

"You signed your death certificate when you tortured and killed innocent civilians. We don't fall under the regular criminal justice system. You don't get a phone call. You don't get read rights because they no longer exist. Therefore, you don't have a right to an attorney. This agency will do whatever they want with you, and you can trust and believe it will not be pretty. This is preliminary, you may not talk now, but I can guarantee you, you will be singing like a fucking canary someday."

The word, *someday*, made the woman flinch. It was a trigger word that forced her to accept that she was no longer free or could no longer practice her evil science projects. Not being able to mix and match people's parts was the true punishment for this lady. Pure unadulterated evil poured off her the moment she realized she couldn't perform her medical experiments anymore.

"Would you have taken your kids apart too?" Kevin blurted the question.

She frowned. "I wouldn't have touched my kids. What kind of sick monster do you think I am?"

Sori leaned back over the table, practically snarling in the woman's face.

"The kind that takes people apart, knowing they'll linger around and die because you didn't have the brain power to figure out how to keep them alive."

Samantha blinked rapidly and swallowed hard. The comment got under her skin. Kevin let her sit in the jab for a while, hoping it repeatedly stabbed her in the heart.

"Your husband was your scapegoat all along. You planted his phone. First in Chicago, so we would buy into him being at that medical convention. Then, when we went to the Oakwood apartments that first time, you must have panicked and assumed it was because we were closing in on you. It prompted you to hide your husband's phone in Atlanta to make it appear that he'd run. I get that, but I don't understand why you killed him when you could have kept using him as your fall guy?" Kevin asked.

She pursed her lips, looking down her nose at nothing in particular before she rolled her eyes and released a long sigh.

"I took him to the apartment and confessed my vision and what I was doing. Being a doctor, I'd hoped he'd understand. He didn't and threatened to call the cops. He called me crazy and said he'd take the kids. I couldn't let any of it happen."

"Those kids were as much your cover as your husband was," Sori mouthed. She stood at the far end of the room with her arms folded over her chest, eyeing the woman like she wanted to play target practice with her.

Samantha contemplated Sori's words or whatever memory of her confrontation with her husband was playing out in her head.

"I brought him back. Afterward."

"After you *butchered* him you mean. You only brought him back so that you could stage his suicide,

THE BOX · 309

aware that he may not survive your iffy resurrections," Sori corrected, interrupting her and ensuring Samantha didn't sugarcoat what she'd done to her husband and a slew of others.

She didn't reply to Sori's statement, nor was there an emotional reaction from her concerning the man she'd been married to for years.

"But, like the others, Charles didn't live past four days afterward. If I could have kept him alive…" she said, allowing her words to trail off. He was her long-term backup plan.

"Why one of us? Why did you choose to box an agent of the law?" Kevin asked. Sori glanced down at his shaking hand, positioned like he was choking Samantha already. He closed his hands into tight fists.

"I spotted her at the hospital when I went to my husband's office to pick up a few things. She…"

Samantha let a smile slip and glanced up to see if they noticed. The smile wasn't a demented one. It was one of admiration. She liked Yala, and he believed it may have been motivated by a sick attraction the woman may have towards her.

"You sick bitch," Sori blurted. "You saw her the same way as you did the woman in the closet. You wanted to make her your replacement for the one you had locked up like an animal. But, first, you had to see if she'd make the cut."

She didn't respond, but she didn't have to. The answers were written in the telling sparkle shining in her eyes.

Kevin had heard enough for one day. Samantha was at their disposal for questioning whenever they wanted, and based on her rap sheet, *however,* they wanted.

***

Kevin sat at her side when Yala opened her eyes. She reached for his outstretched hand and mirrored his smile. He whispered, his words carried by emotions.

"You came back to me."

Her smile deepened, and too weak to squeeze his, she tried shakingly.

"Of course I did."

"The doctors are sure you'll make a full recovery. I can sense how strong your energy is flowing," he said, reassuring her as well as himself.

He gave her a brief rundown of Samantha Nolan and her plot to perfect an ability that he wasn't sure was a gift or a curse.

"Do you have a picture of her?" Yala asked him. "Samantha Nolan."

He nodded before stepping out and returning with one of the cameras he and Sori had used to document the scenes.

Yala shook her head and shut her eyes at the picture.

"She was the one who lured me to that bathroom. After she revealed that her torso was missing, I automatically assumed she was a victim."

Piece by piece, they were gluing this mystery together. Holding Yala's hand, he closed his eyes to the life-given warmth of it. When he opened his eyes, she was staring at him, her smile alight with life and relief.

"I love you." he said.

"I love you, too," she whispered.

CHAPTER THIRTY-THREE

Yala

Two weeks later.

Yala was finally back on her feet. Based on the diary notes discovered, Samantha Nolan had lost all except two subjects. Yala was one of them.

It had taken aggressive persuasion tactics on Yala's part, but Samantha had admitted that Mark and Elizabeth would probably die if she reconnected them to the way they were originally. Now, they would have to tell the two they were stuck with the wrong parts, and if they left the safety of the black site's warded apartment they lived in, they would probably die.

Since Yala survived the boxes, TOP suggested she interview the woman from the closet. Neither the doctors nor therapists had succeeded at persuading the woman to speak a word. They surmised she was detached from reality due to the traumatic events she suffered. She was mute, and her mental state remained in question.

Sori and Kevin briefed Yala on the conditions in which they had found the woman, and she studied what the doctors had compiled on the woman's current state. They were unable to tell how long she was imprisoned. It was evident that Samantha Nolan had tortured the woman. Nearly fifty percent of her body was covered in

scar tissue where she'd been cut, dissected, and reattached. The poor woman was Samantha Nolan's version
of a lab rat.

Yala sat and stared at the woman whose shoulder-
length hair had turned snow white, the kind of white that
didn't come from a box of dye. Although the woman's
features suggested someone much younger, the light
bounced off her skin like bleached teeth and appeared as
brittle as wet paper due to lack of sunlight.

They labeled her mute, but after observing her, Yala
wasn't so sure. Her tormented soul lurked behind her
haunting gaze. The light in the woman's eyes hadn't
been fully extinguished. A small glimmer remained. She
survived a living nightmare, which alone suggested she
possessed a level of strength that she herself wasn't
aware of.

Yala had long ago accepted her special ability to
shift. Was her ability a part of the reason she'd survived
the Box?

If so, it meant that this woman possibly possessed an
ability that kept her from succumbing to death at Samantha Nolan's hands.

If they couldn't get any information from the woman,
she would eventually be transferred to The Center,
TOP's version of a mental hospital. Yala didn't agree
that the woman belonged in a mental hospital.

They stared at each other for three minutes before
Yala placed a pad and a pen on the table and slid them
across to her.

"Can you tell me your name and how long you were
held prisoner?"

The woman's body language didn't change, nor did she pick up the pen.

"Can you write your name? Please."

Nothing.

"Can you write where you're from?"

Nothing.

Maybe she needed to speak a language the woman would understand, a language the woman may respect. Yala placed her elbows atop the table and leaned closer to the woman across the table. She waited until their gazes locked.

"We have your tormentor imprisoned. She can't hurt you, or anyone else, anymore. She took me apart too. She left me in pieces for my friends to put back together. I barely survived."

Yala eyed the woman with a hard stare.

"I know what she did to you. I understand what she did to you. I experienced the kind of pain she put you through. However, I don't know who you are or how long she tortured you."

Yala edged further across the table, making her chair creek under her movement.

"If I had time alone with her, I'd make her beg for death. I'd hurt her as badly as she hurt everyone she's taken apart and take my time doing it."

The glimmer within the depths of the woman's gaze revealed itself to Yala. This victim wanted revenge. She wanted Samantha Nolan punished or dead for what she'd done.

Yala asked again, "What's your name?"

The lady lifted the pen and slid the paper closer before she scribbled in shaky letters: *Lori Hendrix.*

***

Two weeks later.

"So you cast yourself as the jaded lover. Used your husband as your get-out-of-jail-free card and ransomed people's body parts to get them to do your dirty work," Yala spat the statements at Samantha while looking through the glass at her, securely tucked away in her prison home.

Top kept her imprisoned on the bottom level, twelve stories underground, inside a glass prison cell. The collar welded around her neck prevented her from using her ability to hurt others. She was finally where she belonged, caged like the animal she was.

"I was given those gifts for a reason. You can't blame me for fulfilling my purpose," she had the nerve to finally reply.

Yala's face squinted to contain her anger. "Are you listening to yourself?"

The woman was delusional, and Yala didn't believe any amount of questions or talking would convince her that she did anything wrong.

"Why me?" Yala asked.

She fidgeted with her fingers and avoided Yala's eye contact before she glanced up. She was hiding something.

"I saw you at the hospital, knew you were helping the doctor, and searching for my husband. Figured I'd take you out to get you off my trail."

Yala shook her head. "That makes no sense. In your warped memoirs, you wrote that your whole point of enlisting help was for Doctor Hughes to help keep your patients alive permanently. The one way you could have been certain that I would stop coming after you was to kill me immediately, not box me. You wanted to see if I'd make it."

She didn't offer a comment but paused in contemplation, stalling so she didn't have to answer the question.

"You know what. I don't need to know your reasoning. But I do want you to know that I have something special for you," Yala said.

"What?" Samantha asked. Her eyes widened and brightened like she expected Yala to give her a special gift.

"I have a promise that I would like to make to you."

Her expression went blank. She wasn't as excited as she was a moment ago.

"Aren't you going to ask me what promise I want to make to you?"

No response. Yala smiled, that innocent one that made people trust her easily.

"I promise you, Samantha Lily Nolan, I'm either going to kill you or permanently put you in the same pain and anguish you put me and countless others in."

Yala let her smile grow wide, and her eyes filled with the dark energy she reserved for people like Samantha. The woman picked up on the vibe, her body stiffening and her brows lifting. The little spark that shined in her eyes before had been extinguished. Yala held the woman's stare before she turned and left her with the idea of her exacting revenge in her head.

EPILOGUE

A month later.

Samantha turned at the sound of Yala's approach. Yala wore one of her bulletproof leather outfits, which she usually wore on her typical action-packed cases. In this case, she wore the suit to deliver her promise to the creature who had taken her apart and had her delivered like pieces of mail to be put back together.

The ten-by-ten glass prison cell Samantha was enclosed inside was fitting. She wasn't allowed any privacy, and it resembled a larger version of the kind of box she'd enclosed her victims in.

At the sight of Yala, Samantha squinted, her face pulling tight. The woman reminded Yala of a pale-faced wicked witch.

Yala stood at the portion of the glass cage that housed a thick door that blended into the rest of the glass. She pressed the button on the glass, much like a doorbell, that turned on the microphone.

"Hello, Samantha. You look...boxed."

The comment turned her already severe expression into an evil grimace that came alive on her face. Yala pressed the button again, holding it down.

"I saw Lori earlier today. She's recovering. Turns out she didn't die from what you did to her because her ability involves absorbing energy from the sun, which heals her. Keeping her away from the sun weakened her, but once she was able to draw enough energy, all of the scars, the graying hair, and the badly mended bones began to heal. She looks like her old self again. Here, let me show you a picture."

Yala lifted the phone, and the sight of Lori encouraged Samantha to move closer. She stood less than a few feet away, her eyes glued to Lori's picture on Yala's phone."

Lori wasn't speaking complete sentences yet, but she communicated through writing and had told the story of how she met Samantha in college seven years ago and discovered too late that Samantha was obsessed with her.

"What you did to her was inhumane? Cruel. All so that you could hang on to your first girlfriend and torment her because you believed she betrayed you with the football player. You do understand that you had no claim over her—that you didn't make it clear to her that you were in love while she believed she was in a friendship with you?"

Samantha didn't answer, but her sharp eyes finally lifted to meet Yala's. There was no telling what was swirling around in that head of hers.

"I made you a promise the last time I saw you," Yala said.

The statement put a little arch in Samantha's brow before she cast a glance around her surroundings. Yala lowered her voice, the tone scraping across her vocal cords.

"You think I can't make good on my promise because I'm outside your box?"

Samantha's lips twitched along with the smile in her eyes. The sight ticked Yala off so badly that she closed her eyes and breathed before she lost her temper and dragged the woman through the bars by her eyelids.

Yala inhaled deeply and held the breath, thinking of what she wanted the air in her lungs to become and where she wanted it to go. She placed her lips against the microphone and released the breath.

Eyes pinned on Samantha, Yala took in the way her head began to twitch as if to shake something off her face. Her forehead creased into a tight knot before her mouth gaped open, and she placed her hands on either side of her head.

"Wh...wh...what are you doing to me?" she asked Yala. "What the fuck are...?" She released a strangled cry before she started slapping her head.

The breath Yala released was meant for Samantha. She and Kevin had been exploring how far they could take their abilities, and she found that she could manipulate matter as minute as the air itself, replacing it with her restructured DNA.

When she blew her breath into the microphone, it held supercharged copies of every image Yala had ever duplicated compiled into microscopic air particles. However, the moment Samantha breathed Yala's air, the particles were free to expand and would be trapped inside her forever.

Samantha dropped to her knees, her cries now yells of shrieking pain that brought the medical team of four charging into the area.

Yala stepped aside, sure they wouldn't discover what was wrong with Samantha because they couldn't see what was inside her. To add insult to the millions of injuries Samantha had ahead of her, her body would keep healing itself even while the particles would continue stabbing, cutting, sawing, and destroying her insides. She would be stuck in the endless cycle until a miracle doctor found a way to kill her since, technically, her ability prevented death according to the tests TOP had conducted so far.

The collar around Samantha's neck was as much a cage as the one she was in. It prevented Samantha from projecting her energy outside her body, but internally, it raged on like storm-swept winds, healing her in time for her to sustain more injuries.

Despite her shrieking yells, her wide eyes found their way to Yala, whose lips turned into a devious smirk.

"Welcome to hell," Yala mouthed. Samantha's already wide eyes filled with terror, and her skin grew paler with every passing second. While the medical team wasted their time attempting to figure out the source of Samantha's pain and distress, Yala walked away.

TOP wanted to study the woman to find out the secrets to her power. Yala believed she would eventually find a way to escape and get back to her obsession with taking people apart. Now she couldn't.

A part of Yala would always be inside that monster, but it was a tiny part of herself she could live without. Samantha would be stuck suffering the same pain she inflicted on the people and animals she tortured for years.

Yala would continue her reign as the innocent little TOP agent who, in her natural state, others wanted to protect, unaware that she could be as vicious as the people they hunted. It was the reason TOP had recruited her in the first place.

This assignment had taught her a wealth of knowledge in a short span of time. However, the most important thing she found was waiting when she stepped into the hallway. *Love.*

Kevin's smile greeted her like a warm hug, and he didn't wait for her to approach. He met her halfway and drew her into a heavenly embrace.

End of The Box

Author's Note

Readers. My sincere thank you for reading The Box. Please leave a review or star rating, letting me and others know what you thought of Yala and Kevin's story. If you enjoyed it or any of my other books, please pass them along to friends or anyone you think would enjoy them.

Other Titles by Keta Kendric

The Twisted Minds Series:

The Chaos Series:

Stand Alones:

Novellas:

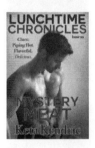

Paranormals:

Kindle Vella:

Audiobooks:

Connect on Social Media

Subscribe to my <u>Newsletter</u> for exclusive updates on new releases, sneak peeks, deleted scenes, and much more. Join my <u>Facebook Readers' Group</u>, where you can live-chat about my books, enjoy contests, raffles, and giveaways.

Paranormal Newsletter Sign up: https://mailchi.mp/38b87cb6232d/keta-kendric-paranormal-newsletter
Newsletter Sign up: https://mailchi.mp/c5ed185fd868/httpsmailchimp
Instagram: https://instagram.com/ketakendric
Facebook Readers' Group: https://www.facebook.com/groups/380642765697205/
BookBub: https://www.bookbub.com/authors/keta-kendric
Twitter: https://twitter.com/AuthorKetaK
Goodreads: https://www.goodreads.com/user/show/73387641-keta-kendric
TikTok: https://www.tiktok.com/@ketakendric?
Pinterest: https://www.pinterest.com/authorslist/